VERTIGO

LOVE

AND

VERTIGO

HSU-MING TEO

ALLEN&UNWIN

First published in 2000

This project has been assisted by the Commonwealth Government
through the Australia Council, its arts funding and advisory body.

Allen & Unwin
83 Alexander Street,
Crows Nest NSW 2065
Australia
Phone: (61 2) 8425 0100
Fax: (61 2) 9906 2218
E-mail: info@allenandunwin.com
Web: www.allenandunwin.com

National Library of Australia
Cataloguing-in-Publication entry:

Teo Hsu-Ming
  Love and vertigo.

  ISBN 1 86508 278 3.

  I. Title.

A823.4

Set in 11.5/14pt Adobe Garamond by DOCUPRO, Sydney
Printed by Australian Print Group, Maryborough, Victoria

10 9 8 7 6 5

For my late aunt, Siew-Choo Lai,
who succumbed to vertigo in 1978

ACKNOWLEDGEMENTS

I would like to thank Annette Barlow and Christa Munns from Allen & Unwin, who made the publishing experience such an interesting and enjoyable one.

I would also like to thank my editors, Meredith Rose and Jo Jarrah, for their enthusiastic engagement with *Love and Vertigo*. Through their efforts, they taught me much about the craft of writing.

Finally, I would like to thank my parents for their support over the years.

'. . . vertigo is something other than the fear of falling. It is the voice of the emptiness below us which tempts and lures us, it is the desire to fall, against which, terrified, we defend ourselves . . . vertigo, the insuperable longing to fall.'

Milan Kundera, *The Unbearable Lightness of Being*

PRELUDE

These are the myths I tell about my family and, like all myths, they are both truths and lies, simultaneous buffers of love and betrayals of trust.

I begin on the eve of my mother's wake, four days after she jumped. I cross a continent and two time zones to land in Changi Airport, Singapore. I dump my bag in a hotel room, take a quick lukewarm shower and step out into the sweating night. I catch the MRT train to Raffles Place, walk to Collyer Quay and wander along the waterside, glancing into the nightclubs, restaurants, bars and karaoke clubs in the restored colonial shophouses that line the waterfront.

I enter a pulsating karaoke bar where, on gigantic video screens, pouting Hong Kong singers with full fringes of red-streaked hair and huge kohl-lined eyes toss their heads and wail out slow, sentimental Cantopop ballads about love and loss. Men in striped short-sleeved shirts or brightly coloured polo shirts and black trousers croon into hand-held microphones, eyes squeezed shut, sweat running down the bridges of their noses and pooling at the lower metal rim of their spectacles, fogging up the glass in the soupy humidity. Lost in sentiment, lost in the sound of their own voices. Women decked in heavy gold chains and garishly patterned dresses hold tumblers of whisky or flutes of champagne, their diamond-flashing watches snuggled close to elegant wristbones. Mobile phones ring and people reach automatically for their pockets. The microphones do the rounds from person to person. Everyone has come in impregnable groups.

This is not the Singapore my mother told me about. Her stories are a world apart from this; no longer reality but history. Just like my mother herself.

I think of the one and only time, when I was fourteen, Sonny and I had been forced to come to Singapore with Mum. To pay our respects to the relatives, she said. She brought us to visit the relatives and they took us to the Rasa Singapura hawker centre so that we could have satay, Hainanese chicken rice, Singaporean Hokkien noodles, *tah mee*, *laksa*, *gado gado*, *rojak*. This was my mother's comfort food. She wanted to share it with me, but I complained about the noise, the smells, the disgusting charnel-house of the table where the previous diners had spat out pork ribs and spewed chewed chicken bones all over the surface.

'Come, Grace. Eat,' Uncle Winston ordered as he belched and dropped prawn shells onto the table top, adding to the carnage. 'Don't be shy.'

I was baffled that my mother could belong to these people. For the first time in my life I saw my mother in relation to her family and I did not recognise her anymore. Her carefully maintained English disintegrated and she lapsed into the local Singlish patois, her vocabulary a melange of English, Malay and Chinese; her syntax abbreviated, chopped and wrenched into disconcerting unfamiliarity. These Singaporean roots of hers, this side of her—and possibly of me too—were unacceptable. I looked for difference and sought superior disgust as an automatic response. I realise now that I had gone to Singapore with the attitude of a nineteenth-century memsahib. I was determined not to belong, not to fit in, because I was Australian, and Mum ought to be Australian too. The tug of her roots, the blurring of her role from wife and mother to sister and aunt, angered and frightened me. Years later, Sonny and I returned to visit the relatives by ourselves, to pay our respects to grandmothers and grandfathers and great aunts and uncles before they died. But Mum never returned to Singapore after that one visit. Not until she went back to die.

When she returned, did she gaze uncomprehendingly around her and realise that this was no longer her home?

I walk out of the club, back into the muggy night. I walk as if I have a purpose. In and out of neon-signed pubs, bars, restaurants, jazz nightclubs, milling night markets clustered under red and white striped awnings. I don't even know what or who I'm looking for. It's the eve of my mother's wake and I feel no pain, no grief, no guilt. Nothing.

I just want to live without ghosts, sleep without dreams. I want to blur the boundaries of my body in a mechanical and mindless fuck. Instead, I walk back to the hotel, strip, shower, then dry myself off and climb into bed. Alone in the dark, with the motor of the air conditioning humming away, I hug myself for comfort, turn my face into the pillow and begin to masturbate.

My mother's wake begins the following morning. It is being held in the concourse under Uncle Winston's apartment block. It should have been at Donald Duck's house since he is Mum's eldest brother and the head of the Lim family. But Mum had died at Uncle Winston's, and there was more room in the void deck—the concrete-pillared open space under the apartment block—than there would have been at Donald Duck's house along Upper Thomson Road. Permission to hold the wake had been sought from and granted by the Housing Development Board. This is quite a common practice in Singapore. Someone from Singapore Telecom had even come to drop a line down from the apartment to the concourse below so that the phone could be taken downstairs.

The closed coffin hulks on a table, a garden of funeral wreaths growing around the base and rearing up over it, green tendrils strangling the polished wood. Auntie Percy-phone sits alone beside the coffin. A plaid-patterned plastic thermos of tea nestles comfortably among snarling orchids. The other relatives are up in Uncle Winston's apartment, admiring his latest acquisitions before the wake starts. A self-made million-aire, Uncle Winston can easily afford to move into a newer, more luxurious apartment or even a house. Instead, he tunes out the constant reproaches of Auntie Shufen and spends his money ripping up the floor tiles to replace them with marble, furnishing his home in the grandest old Chinese style, equipped with the latest new Japanese entertainment toys.

I go in search of my father and find him in the kitchen washing dishes left over from the previous night's dinner. Resolutely he ignores his wife's relatives, blocking them out with a fierce concentration as he stands at the kitchen sink, preoccupied with cups. 'Jonah, leave them, *lah*,' one of the women had called out half-heartedly. 'The maid will do them when she comes.' But he prefers silent activity to the strain of making conversation. Already, on the two-tiered aluminium drying rack, plates and saucers of all sizes are ranged precisely. He is such a neat man, my father. His lips are pursed into a familiar, prissy grimace of disapproval directed towards the world as his square, capable dentist's hands deftly pluck up cups, tumblers and mugs from the black granite benchtop and plunge them into steaming water. A brisk hospital scrub with the scouring sponge to remove the dun-coloured rings of tea and coffee stains, a quick whisk under the running tap, and the cups squat in orderly rows on the drying rack. There is a beautiful economy and a certain sort of poetry to his practised motions. He is inhuman in his smooth efficiency.

I join him and Sonny in the kitchen. They are not speaking to each other. My brother and I take it in turns to reach as unobtrusively as possible around him to grab a cup. Eventually, instinctively, we work out an intricate cotillion whereby we step, shuffle and sidle past each other, damp tea towels dangling like delicate eighteenth-century reticules from one hand, the other hand outstretched to grasp the slippery surfaces of wet cups.

'You're late. There are so many cups,' he complains. The Patriarch has had a closed cupboard policy on cups for as long as anyone can remember. Now he counts them off accusingly, peering into glass and ceramic depths to discover their erstwhile contents. 'A mug for coffee and another for tea. A shot glass for whisky and a tumbler for orange juice and another tall glass for Coke.'

'Why don't you leave this, Dad?' I say. 'Sonny and I will finish it. Go inside and sit down.'

But his martyr complex has floated to the surface and hardened into a crisp crust. He has loudly sacrificed for us all his life and sees no reason to stop now. It's a habit he enjoys immensely. He ignores me and only scrubs the cups more vigorously.

'Nothing would ever get done if I didn't do it myself. Grace, you're so late this morning. And Sonny, I saw you using one cup for Chinese tea last night, and then another glass for Coke!'

Convicted, condemned, Sonny dries in silence.

The Patriarch continues to wash cups to the accompaniment of his own low grumbling. There is no doubt that he is dismayed by his wife's relatives' prodigal use of drinking vessels. He had previously considered such extravagances limited to the circle of his own insufficiently disciplined and uneconomical family. Now he is alarmed at the thought that it might be a genetically inherited trait, passed down through his passed-away wife's errant chromosomes.

Mum had been the real cup culprit of our family. Her unstinting and incorrigible use of cups, tumblers and mugs knew no bounds. She used a new one every time she wanted a drink, and she wanted many drinks during the course of a day. This resulted in her attachment to the toilet and accounted for her many anxious visits there before stepping out of the house—whether she was just going to the corner store to buy a carton of low-fat milk, or leaving for a weekend trip to the Blue Mountains. Having relieved herself, she would then imagine herself dehydrated or feel the need to flush her kidneys with fluid to remove toxins from her body, hence the next glass of water. Her incontinence with cups was directly proportional to her incontinence of the bladder. And with each vessel, she left behind her telltale signature: reddish-brown lipstick marks on the rim.

'It's a *filthy* habit,' the Patriarch used to say. He would pull out the upper tray of the dishwasher and be unbearably irritated to find it crammed and creaking with cups.

Her improvidence with cups bothered him greatly, for it was symbolic of her wasteful extravagance in all other aspects of life. His wife loved expensive things. She shopped for clothes in Double Bay, haunted the designer halls of David Jones, hunted down Hermès handbags with the zeal of a big game hunter, and regularly popped into pricey boutiques all over Sydney, where she was on a first-name basis with most of the salespeople. The use of first names in expensive stores thrilled her; she felt that she belonged in Sydney. Her credit card paid for small talk, service with a smile, acceptance.

Her extravagance was not confined to her wardrobe. Furnishing the house had been a contest of wills between her and the Patriarch; a contest that had ended in an unsatisfactory compromise for all concerned. She wanted reproduction Provençal country furniture in walnut and mahogany. He agreed grudgingly, then went off to order some chunky mid-priced Keith Lord furniture and the requisite Asian leather sofa in peach tones to appease her because she was female and had pastel-loving DNA in her genetic makeup. She nagged the Patriarch into buying genuine Persian carpets, which he then hung on the walls because, at nearly eight thousand dollars each, they were too expensive to bear the sweaty footprints of family and friends. Instead, he got the whole house carpeted, wall to wall, in synthetic beige pile. Beige was a good neutral colour; it didn't show the ordinary day-to-day stains, and it formed a bland and soothing background to the emotional turbulence of his life.

She had also tried to buy elegant new crockery from the fourth floor of David Jones' city store, but the Patriarch stored it in the fluorescent-lit Parker display cabinet, together with the EIIR soup bowls he had purchased in London, and the Charles and Diana teaspoons he had collected in 1981. We used ugly gilt-edged floral plates that he had picked up at a garage sale. He did not permit the use of saucers in his household. Saucers were an unnecessary item in the kitchen and took up space in the dishwasher or the drying rack. Instead, he brought home free mugs from dental supply companies such as Oral-B, Regional or Kavo: white mugs screenprinted with heavy sans-serif typeface slogans announcing the names of the proud makers of drill bits, fluoride products, toothbrushes, toothpastes, dental floss and mouth rinses.

'Each person at the wake will be allowed only one cup,' the Patriarch now announces, turning off the tap and shaking dry his hands before patting them fastidiously on a hand towel. He opens the cupboard and, with a smug air of triumph, brings out several plastic-wrapped columns of white styrofoam cups. 'I have a list of the people who are definitely attending today. Sonny, you can start marking their names on these cups. We'll have some spare cups and black markers by the drinks table, which Sonny can man. And look, I've made a sign.'

Proudly, he holds up a white A4 sheet of paper with a black laser-printed message reading: PLEASE WRITE YOUR NAME ON YOUR CUP AND RE-USE IT. He is so pleased with this.

I look at his face for signs of grieving. I want to be angry with him for obsessing with cups when he should have been thinking about my mother and how miserable he made her for most of her life. I want to whip up my resentment against him, to remember the scoldings he gave her over her consumption of cups, the way he treated her like an errant child in front of everyone. I want to think that his concern with cups demonstrates his callousness towards his wife, to be convinced that he never really loved her.

I want somebody to blame for my mother's death. I want to blame him, the way Sonny does.

'You fucking bastard,' says Sonny. He drops the tea towel to the floor and walks out.

The Patriarch stares after his son, who hasn't spoken to him since Mum died. And slowly, he slides down the sky-blue wooden cupboard door. He melts vertically along its surface, sucked down by grief and gravity, until he slumps into a squatting position. His face crumples, tears seep from his eyes and his black-rimmed Buddy Holly glasses fog over.

I want to blame him, but I can't now. I can't make him the scapegoat because lately, sometimes when I look at him, I don't see the Patriarch anymore. I just see Jonah Tay. Jonah Tay, who had been attracted to Pandora Lim because she was everything that he was not. Who married her and then tried to force her into becoming everything that he was. Who loved his wife but didn't know her. Who gave her everything she didn't want and couldn't get along with the son she adored.

He is a good husband and father, she used to tell us, as if we all needed convincing—herself included. He tried his best and was even heroic in that attempt, for the very act of immigration had terrified a man afraid of change. To have crossed the boundary of the familiar into the foreign had been no easy feat for this reluctant Chinese Odysseus. He took a deep breath and did it—then he never stopped complaining about it for the rest of his life, reminding his family of the sacrifices made and the opportunities lost. Migration had exhausted him; after his initial euphoria, he made no attempt to root himself into his new country, content instead to burrow and hide himself in the home he was certain he would share with his wife long after the kids were gone. Now, perhaps for the first time, he faces his life alone, without her taken-for-granted presence, and he washes the multitude of cups he had so begrudged her using when she was alive.

Slowly, he straightens to his feet, takes off his heavy-rimmed glasses, pats his pockets and pulls out a handkerchief. He wipes the tear smears off the convex curves of glass, mops his face and blows his nose—a fierce trumpeting sound like a bugle announcing war.

'Everybody at the wake gets one cup and one cup only,' he announces.

My family. We are all so absurd in our grief.

SONNY, THE COD
GOD KILLER

When Sonny Tay was conceived in 1968, momentous events had been taking place around the world: the Prague Spring, the Paris May Days when trade union workers struck and students proclaimed that it was forbidden to forbid, civil rights marches and the death of Martin Luther King, the My Lai massacre in Vietnam, and the slaughter of protestors in Mexico City just before the '68 Olympic Games. On the day of his birth in May 1969, violence broke out once again—in Malaysia this time. Malay Muslims, incited by the youth of the United Malay National Organisation, went on a jihad against Malaysian Chinese and Indians, murdering some and maiming others. The killing spree had been organised according to a precise cafe colour scheme: after *susu* (the milky-white Chinese) then *kopi* (the coffee-coloured Indians).

The Patriarch and his wife were living in the one state in Malaysia where the Sultan forbade violence against any ethnic group. This may have been because his dentist and tennis partner—the Patriarch—was Chinese, while his

physician and golf partner was Indian. The Patriarch was
especially favoured because he was in possession of a rusty
tub of a boat in which he would chug upstream to the
various *kampong* villages along the river, tending to tooth-
aches, enduring halitosis, extracting teeth and plopping
them into a small Kraft peanut butter jar he kept for that
purpose. The teeth would later be sold to the universities
to supply dental students with real teeth to work on.
('Those Malays had real long curved roots to their teeth,
I tell you,' he'd say admiringly. '*Ai-yo*, real hell to extract.')
The Sultan used to hijack the dental boat for occasional
fishing trips because it was the only vessel in his state with
a tiny toilet on board. The Patriarch was naturally invited
to join the Sultan's fishing parties. There was little skill
involved; some of the Sultan's servants would be sent
upstream with explosives. By the time the fishing party
arrived, dead fish would be floating side-up on the muddy
ripples of the river. The Sultan would then take his royal
fishing net and grandly scoop out of the river the desired
number of corpses before the whole party floated back
downstream. The Sultan's dependence on the Patriarch and
Dr Gupta for his dental and physical health, as well as his
recreational enjoyment, probably led him to regard Chinese
and Malays sympathetically. Whatever the reason, while
Chinese and Indians were being sliced with sharp-bladed
*parang*s in the streets of Kuala Lumpur and Petaling Jaya,
my mother was screaming from the pain of childbirth,
safe under the Sultan's protection, while my father hunted
durians.

She thrust her child into the world and was delighted
to find it male. She immediately assumed that her son,
conceived and born in the crucible of social change, in the

Chinese year of the cock, and in the western astrological month of the bull, was destined for great things. She name him Augustus Tay. When the Patriarch returned from his durian hunting, he was instantaneously and incurably jealous of the little Great One. He immediately shoved Augustus back into his proper filial place by calling him Sonny.

Everyone assumed that, like most Chinese fathers, the Patriarch would have been ecstatic that his child was a son. But the Patriarch didn't like other males. He had grown up in a household where he had always been the centre of all female attention. He was the first-born son and heir and, until he was sent to an exclusive Anglican boys' school in Singapore, he had no conception that he might not be the sun around which other worlds revolved. At school, he instantly felt that other men were in competition with him for every woman's attention, though he would learn to overcome this sense of threat and form fragile friend-ships in his sober student days. Even when he met and courted his wife, he rapidly became the favourite male in her household. But when his son popped into the world, he immediately recognised that he no longer held first place in his wife's life. It was an intolerable situation, even if only a temporary one. How such an Oedipal situation could have arisen in a Chinese household always remained a puzzle. For a man who venerated his Chinese culture, this rejection of his first-born son was distressingly un-Chinese.

But in corrupting Augustus to Sonny, the Patriarch had either demonstrated great prescience or a characteristic determination to predestine his first-born to a life of ridic-ulous banality. There were to be no great surgical skills nor sporting prowess, no gifted musical abilities nor even the comfort of middle-class mediocrity for Augustus. The only great thing Sonny ever accomplished was when he slew Uncle Winston Lim's priceless, much-revered, prosperity-producing Amazonian cod on the second day of our mother's wake. Sonny's genius lay not in the actual cod-killing, but in ridding himself of the burden of half of our relations, and alienating the rest for many years, in one spectacular stroke.

The Lim clan mostly professes to be Buddhist, but superstition is the main religion. They avoid addresses and car number plates with '4' in them if possible, because it is a bad number. Phonetically, 'four' is a homonym for 'death' in Cantonese and might bring bad luck. Similarly, they paid through the nose to drive around in a car with '888' in the registration number because the word 'eight' is a tone variation for 'prosperity'. My grandmother Lim had once won a cheap porcelain statue of Kuan Yin, the goddess of mercy, in a raffle to raise money for the Anglican Chinese girls' school in Singapore. She immediately associated mercy with money and set up a makeshift altar in the kitchen, festooned it with red crêpe paper streamers, and placed a dish of mandarins, cups of tea and a jar for joss sticks in front of it. Each day she would knock smooth wooden rods together, clasp smoking joss sticks in her hands, and bow up and down in front of the goddess, chanting and praying that she would win at mahjong that night. My generation was not exempt. The Lim cousins encouraged the breezes of fortune to blow through their high-rise offices by calling in the geomancer to move around office furniture and determine the correct *feng shui* for their interior decoration. They scried the future in spinning spears of tourmaline crystals, consulted the local

Chinese fortune-teller, visited the *Fu Kay* practitioner for automatic writing prophecies, and read the *Financial Times* on top of all that.

These were our relatives who worshipped and bowed down before the Amazonian cod for no other reason than its sheer monstrosity and diabolical ugliness. Uncle Winston had bought it for five hundred and eighty dollars, and it had grown and grown and kept growing until it was now worth about four thousand dollars. Surely something that big, that black and that beastly must be evil and, hence, possess dark powers. As such, it had to be appeased with the usual plates of mandarins and small bronze urns of smoking joss sticks. Appeasement gradually transformed into cautious petition when it was seen that no actual harm had come to Uncle Winston as yet. Uncle Winston's petitions were trivial at first: finding the only pair of nail clippers in the flat; praying that his wife Shufen would miss her bus so that she would be late in getting home; curing his constipation as he strained and heaved over the toilet, full of sound and fury signifying nothing; and granting cosmic enlightenment as to how to program the new video recorder so that he could tape the weekly variety show and surreptitiously watch slim and beautiful Malay boys swaying and lip-synching to Boy George's 'Karma Chameleon' when Shufen was not around. Then he pushed his luck and petitioned the Amazonian Cod God for a twenty-dollar win at mahjong. Twenty grew into fifty, a hundred, two hundred until, finally, Uncle Winston won seven hundred and thirty thousand dollars in an illegally run bookmaking syndicate.

For a while, exhibitionist pride warred with miserly discretion and fear of the taxation office. He agonised for months over whether he should move into a new semi-detached house in Yio Chu Kang, or perhaps a pristine ninety-nine-year leasehold luxury apartment. He yearned to display his newly acquired wealth and success visibly, triumphantly. On the other hand, he thought that he should perhaps hide all signs of his wealth in case his numerous siblings, cousins, nieces and nephews suddenly tried to be nice to him and sponge off him. In sheer desperation, he went to the temple to pray to the gods. He bought holy oil from the monks to be burnt, offered joss sticks and fruit to his favourite black-faced god, then shook the container of fortune sticks until one fell out. The Chinese hiero-glyphics decreed that he was not to move out.

Auntie Shufen begged and cried, she threw his favourite set of golf clubs out the window—the first of many objects to fall from that apartment block—but Uncle Winston was adamant. Instead, he gave her a gold credit card to shop for new furnishings, thereby appeasing her desire for ostentatious display. Then he secretly bought a small, one-bedroom apartment on the west coast of Singapore and moved his latest mistress into it. In his Housing Develop-ment Board apartment, he built a huge aquarium for his Cod God and set up a gilt altar before the glass wall of the tank. Rumour of his good fortune spread and the relatives flocked from the ends of the earth—Sydney, Melbourne, San Francisco, London and Jakarta—to prostrate them-selves before this monstrous marvel.

Meanwhile, the Cod God stared unblinking and unmoving from behind his glass prison, only showing signs of animation when Uncle Winston climbed up the alumin-ium ladder beside the aquarium to throw in scraps of raw meat and smaller, undeified fish. There was no doubt that

Uncle Winston shared a special, privileged relationship with this fish, for the Cod God would even, on occasion, allow him to caress its slimy black back. Proudly, Uncle Winston perched atop the ladder and thrust his right hand into the tepid water, feeling the silky current of water sliding against his hand as the Cod God stirred itself and paddled to the surface to rub its scaly ridged back against those water-wrinkled fingers.

It was against this Amazonian Cod God that Sonny struck on the second day of our mother's wake. The Lims had dominated the first day's activities, going to the Chinese temple to organise a ritual burning for my mother. They had gone to great lengths to purchase from the monks colourful wads of Bank of Hell money, and papier mâché houses, cars, stereo systems, microwave ovens, mobile phones, computers, VCRs and Sony play-stations. These they then burnt in a solemn ceremony led by the monks, sending them off to hell where my mother now presumably resided, so that in death she would be surrounded by all the technology that had bewildered her in life.

Donald Duck had also organised for everyone to wear white cotton shirts and white shoes, with white bandannas wrapped around their foreheads so that they looked like photo negatives of Ninjas. This he did because he was convinced that it was the tradition of their unknown and largely unremembered ancestral village in China, from whence his grandparents had emigrated to Singapore at the turn of the century. How Donald Duck found out that this was their village custom was a mystery to everyone since none of their clan had ever bothered to return to China to rediscover their roots. Still, they obeyed because he was the Eldest Brother and Head of the House of Lim.

The Patriarch saw this ceremony as an outrageous challenge to his fundamentalist Christian beliefs, which is why, on the second night of the wake, we now sit, reluctantly and uncomfortably, at the interminably dull prayer meeting he has organised. Sonny shifts restlessly beside me, clutching his heavy bronze trumpet for comfort, expertly fingering melodies that only he can hear. I slap at mosquitoes and think about the conflagration in the temple courtyard yesterday. Christian hellfire and holiness have not the hypnotic attraction of heaving papier mâché Porsches into terrestrial flames.

And then it happens. I am jerked awake by sudden commotion. I don't know what Sonny has been doing, but all at once he grabs his trumpet, roars with incoherent rage and rushes over to the lift, stabbing maniacally at the 'up' button. The lift door opens and he disappears.

'Sonny, where you going, uh?' someone calls out inanely to the closed lift doors and winking floor indicator lights. Someone else jabs the button uselessly.

'How 'bout the stairs?' Cousin Adrian suggests.

'*Ai-yo*, my knees,' one of the aunties moans.

When we finally get up to the eighteenth floor, we can hear the destruction before we rush into the flat.

Sonny is magnificent in his rage. He lifts his trumpet and heaves it repeatedly against the glass wall of the Cod God's aquarium. Crack, crack and smash. Dank, turgid water floods out and drowns the pungent joss sticks and rotting oranges. He lifts his battered trumpet and smashes more glass. The outraged Cod God slides out with the dark tide, thrashing wildly, and impales itself on one of the gilt spires of its altar. Sonny flings aside the trumpet and tries to grab hold of the Cod God. He hauls it off the spire.

It slaps him in the balls with its black tail and jerks out of his hands. Left hand massaging and clutching his crotch protectively, he dives onto the sodden leather sofa, right arm outstretched for that football of a fish. His fingers slide off that sleek body as it wriggles and leaps onto the camphor wood chest inlaid with mother-of-pearl. A mighty battle of epic proportions ensues as Sonny and the fish flop and slither and splash in the flooded living room. Those who are present—and most of the relatives have now crowded in—are stunned into a disbelieving stupor, only able to watch as, with another despairing bellow, my beanpole brother finally digs his bony fingers into the Cod God's slimy, well-fleshed body. Man and fish god wrestle wildly as Sonny staggers over to the open balcony.

'No! Wait!' Horrified realisation of Sonny's intent snaps Uncle Winston into belated action. He wades fatly through the muck of his living room towards the balcony, his chest pumping with painful sobs. '*Ai-yo, ai-yo*. Sonny, what are you doing? Stop!'

'Sonny, have you gone completely mad?' the Patriarch barks out rhetorically as we surge in a wave towards the balcony to prevent ichthyocide.

But it is too late. Panting hard, his skinny chest rising and falling quickly like an accordion, Sonny heaves and hurls the Cod God over the blue-tiled edge. We can only look down incredulously as the Cod God bounces off several colourfully painted bamboo laundry poles—complete with fluttering flags of underwear—protruding from the seventeen balconies below. Finally, the Cod God thuds onto the bonnet of a mustard-coloured Mercedes, dents it, bounces heavily once and rolls limply to fall off onto the asphalt and weeds of the car park.

Up on the eighteenth floor, the relatives watch in fear and growing outrage as Sonny the Cod God Killer punches his way through our ranks and steps back into the soggy apartment. The telephone in the kitchen begins to peal shrilly. Irate calls from the neighbours below, no doubt. He spies his trumpet, picks it up and shakes it free of water. He sinks down onto the broken glass, hiccuping with tears and laughter as he tries to dry the bowl of the trumpet with his soaked shirt.

We are silent. We don't know what to say.

When the convulsions of hilarity subside, he raises the battered trumpet to his lips and, in a moment of Chinese melodrama, he huffs out a discordant, waterlogged version of the 'Last Post'. And then he begins to cry, jerky, painful, coughing sobs that rack his chest like tuberculosis.

We stand there, up to our ankles in stinking water, in mind-numbed silence. Many of the relatives will never see Sonny again, so utterly and irrevocably has he wrenched himself out of the close-knit fabric of extended family life.

Auntie Shufen holds onto Uncle Winston's arm and unsteadily wriggles out of her bright red Ferragamo pumps. She hands the shoes to her maid, giving her instructions on how to dry them. Then, in her stockinged feet, the stiff black hairs bristling through the beige hose, she wades through the room and slowly turns around. She looks at the wreckage of her living room and she turns to Sonny.

'You are cursed, Sonny Tay,' she says. 'You and your mother both. Cursed from birth, cursed in death.'

PANDORA OUT
OF THE BOX

On an airless, muggy Singapore afternoon in February 1942, women gathered in an open concrete court-yard at the back of a ramshackle, flaking colonial terrace. Someone was chanting and praying, rhythmically clicking wooden rods together. Smoke from joss sticks curled in silvery-grey arcs in the hot, wet air, while the scent hung heavy and low.

The women's attention was focused on my grand-mother, Mei Ling, who lay spread-eagled like a sacrifice on the round granite table where the family usually had dinner. The plate of *kang kong* fried with chilli and shrimp paste, the fried fish and the tureen of white carrot and pork bones soup had been hurriedly swept away from the table when, in the middle of lunch, Mei Ling had suddenly grabbed her distended belly and cried out that her waters had burst.

'*Ai-yo*, so painful,' she moaned now, crying loudly. 'I'm going to die from this bloody child.'

Her younger sister, Madam Tan, scolded her in a sibilant whisper for jinxing herself and her child by voicing such thoughts. Bringing a child into the world was a difficult enough endeavour with mischievous demons hovering unseen everywhere, waiting to play a trick on the newborn baby by slashing the mouth with a harelip, adding an extra finger or toe, or maiming the child with countless other physical deformities. Demons' ears prick up at the faintest whisper of news that a human child has been born, but some-times they can be fooled if friends and family keep their heads and address the newborn as 'pig' or 'dog' or 'shitface'. But to invite curses openly as Mei Ling was doing—what folly!

'Keep your voice down, Ah Ling,' Madam Tan said urgently. She turned to the servant. 'Por-Por, get the Tiger Balm and rub it over her stomach.'

Por-Por grudgingly gave up her place by Mei Ling's side to Madam Tan, who dipped a grey towel into a small basin of tepid water and sponged Mei Ling's face. Madam Tan took a grubby, dun-coloured bolster from another woman and eased it under her sister's head.

Mei Ling fisted her left hand and thrust it into her mouth, gnawing on the knuckle of her thumb and whim-pering fretfully. 'I don't want it. Don't want this damned baby, rubbish child.'

'Talk nonsense! Your child is a gift from the gods. You should thank the goddess for it,' Madam Tan reminded her sharply. But she felt in her heart that the gods could have bestowed the gift on someone who would have the means to take care of the child. It wasn't Mei Ling's fault that their father had married her off to a timid shopkeeper of little stature and less wealth. Madam Tan had been more fortunate. She had been given to a tea merchant as his second wife and her status in her luxurious household was high because she was Mr Tan's favourite wife. She had done what she could to help her elder sister's family, but now there was another child on the way. She rinsed the cloth and swabbed Mei Ling's forehead gently. She could have tried harder to say no, especially during war-time, Madam Tan thought resentfully. And then she remembered.

Mei Ling hadn't wanted to get married. She wanted to learn how to read and write like the Chinese girls from middle-class Christian homes who went to church schools. She wanted to become a schoolteacher. On her wedding night she took off her red silk wedding dress, unwound the reeking bandaged stumps of her crushed feet and wrapped herself in her oldest, smelliest clothes. She sat on the celebratory red cotton sheets of her bed, watching the bedroom door. When her diffident, virginal husband crept into the bedroom and got onto the bed, she scrambled off it and crouched down on the floor, watching him with hostile animal eyes. Bewildered, he looked at her. He climbed off the bed and sat down on the floor beside her, his hands reaching out tentatively. She got up and climbed back onto the bed. He followed, and she rolled off the other side of the bed onto the floor. All night he followed her from floor to bed and back to the floor again until, exhausted finally, he gave up and slept on the bed while his wife dozed in the farthest corner of the room.

The same absurd pantomime occurred on the following night. She huddled in a corner of the room in her smelly rags and glowered at her husband. When he approached her, she scrabbled over the floor to another corner. All night he followed her from corner to corner, bed to floor, until once again he gave up, flopped onto the bed and slept. For nearly a month this nightly routine went on. Finally, he complained timidly to her father.

The father called the whole family before him. He made his recalcitrant daughter strip off the top of her *samfoo* and crouch down before his chair, her naked back a footstool for his elegantly slippered feet. He ordered a bond maid to bring a bamboo cane. Then with those black slippers, gorgeously embroidered with brightly coloured butterflies, he kicked his eldest daughter's breasts and torso. Once, twice, three times. Then he kicked her away and handed the bamboo rod to her husband.

'Now be a man and make your wife obey you,' he said.

Appalled, the shopkeeper let fly two tentative flabby whacks and faltered.

'Again,' the father said.

Two more red strokes slashed his wife's back.

'Again. And again. And again. And again.'

The shopkeeper lashed and struck and slashed until his wife's back was a map of red latticed lines and she was sobbing and pleading, battered and broken.

'Stop.' The father took the bamboo cane from the shopkeeper. Holding it disdainfully by the ends, he broke it in half. He turned to the bond maid. 'Dustbin.'

She hurried forward with a rattan basket. The father dropped the contaminated splinters of bamboo into it and waved the bond maid away.

'Bring me water and a towel.'

Another bond maid came forward with a porcelain bowl of scented water and a soft handtowel. With slow, deliberate motions he washed his hands and patted them dry on the towel. The maid took the bowl and towel away.

The father stood up and looked at the shopkeeper with contempt in his eyes. 'Next time, break your own wife yourself and teach her to obey you.'

The first months of my grandmother's marriage have gone down in the annals of Lim family history, passed on from woman to woman, handed down from mother to daughter, aunt to niece. Nobody was ever quite certain about the point of this story. Was it meant to be an instance of proto-feminist resistance? Or a fable about a Chinese wife's duty of submission to her husband? Or about the eternal cycle of generations of Lim women struggling against their husbands, only to succumb to the inevitability of disillusionment and defeat? But at any gathering of Lim women this story was told and retold until we women understood that ours was a family conceived in violence and rape, raised in sullen resentment and unspoken grief. By the time my mother was born, Mei Ling had already given birth to five children, three of them girls, all of them unwanted.

In that tiny courtyard in Singapore, afternoon shaded into evening and unbearable humidity soaked the growing dark and drenched the lengthening shadows. The air stank of sweat and the sharp aroma of that ubiquitous panacea, Tiger Balm, rubbed into Mei Ling's temples and swollen belly. And then the soupy torpor of twilight was splintered by shrill screams. Women squawked and fluttered in voluble alarm.

Madam Tan stepped forward authoritatively, bending until her mouth was level with Mei Ling's ear. Her polished fingernails scraped into her sister's sweating skin.

'Stop screaming,' she ordered. 'Show a little self-control for once.'

'I can't,' Mei Ling sobbed. '*Ai-yah*, *ai-yah*, I'm going to die.'

'It's coming,' the midwife said excitedly. 'I've got the head now. It's coming out. Not long to go.'

Mei Ling screamed again.

'Shut up!' Madam Tan hissed viciously, the clawing of her nails drawing blood from Mei Ling's forearm. But it was too late.

They heard it then: the drumming of boot steps in the dirty alley outside the walled courtyard, followed by the thundering on the door, as though iron balls were being bowled against it. Flakes of faded paint dislodged from the rotting wood and snowed down onto the dark grey concrete of the yard. The women shrank back in alarm.

'Now look what you've done,' Madam Tan said angrily. She grabbed the rag that the women had been using to sponge Mei Ling's forehead and body, twisted it into a ball and shoved it venomously into her sister's open, drooling mouth. 'Shut up, damn you!'

Her neat head lifted as the door thundered again. 'Por-Por, go let them in before they break down the door.'

But the rotted wooden bolt placed through the rusting iron brackets on either side of the door splintered under the barrage of blows. The door exploded open. In an instant the courtyard was swarming with Japanese soldiers, rifles raised in readiness to shoot, stab or strike. The women screamed in terror. A short, squat captain in full dress uniform muscled his way to the stone table, his long ceremonial sword drawn.

Mei Ling gave out a muffled groan through the sodden rag in her mouth and the midwife called out, 'I've got the child.'

Excitedly she held up the bloody, shining, slippery mess of a baby. Then she raised her eyes and saw the upraised sword of the Japanese captain pointing at Madam Tan, and she cowered back against the granite table, muttering, '*Ai-yo*, scared me to death.'

Mei Ling shoved thumb and index finger into her mouth and pulled out the dirty rag. With an effort she raised her head, her eyes red from weeping and her facial muscles slack from exhaustion. She cleared her throat and spat at the ground. Spittle landed on a black boot. A Japanese soldier slapped her. She looked at him, then turned away to look at Madam Tan.

'Well?' she said.

Madam Tan stepped warily around the Japanese captain and inspected the wrinkled baby. The midwife was tying off the umbilical cord. Madam Tan parted the baby's limp, putty legs and slid her finger between the mucky thighs.

'Another girl,' she said, resigned.

Mei Ling's head fell back onto the sweat-drenched bolster and she began to laugh. 'Kuan Yin, Goddess of Mercy, I curse you because you have none. Sky God, I curse you too. You knew I didn't want another child. I knocked my belly until my knuckles were red and sore and my guts ached, but you kept it there and now you've given me another girl.

'Another fucking useless cunt of a girl,' she said bitterly as my mother drew breath and began to wail under the sharp shadows of raised rifles and a drawn sword.

SYONAN, LIGHT OF THE SOUTH

My mother honestly believed that she was cursed from birth for, that day, disaster struck that tiny terrace household in Singapore—or *Syonan*, Light of the South, as the Japanese now called the island. All the women gathered there in the courtyard—sisters, second cousins, neighbours and friends—would never congregate in that same group again.

Mei Ling's childbirthing screams had attracted the attention of Japanese soldiers looking for *kuniang*s: 'comfort women' they would take away to the *Yoshiwara*, or red light district, for the duration of the occupation. Even after the war some of those women never returned to their families or friends, so ashamed were they of what they had been forced to do during the war.

Madam Tan was fortunate. As the wife of a wealthy *towkay*, she had some protection. All she lost were her pearl earrings, her gold necklaces and rings, and a thick jade bangle. The bones of her left wrist were crushed like twigs when the tight bangle, which she'd worn since she was a child, was dragged over her hand. The loss of her jewellery vexed her until the end of her life, and she never ceased to remind her sister that her screams had brought disaster and loss to the women gathered in the courtyard that day.

Mei Ling, spent and filthy, looked at the sobbing women being taken away. She glanced at her daughter and hated her for the pain of childbirth and the humiliation of having had her legs spread wide open before the Japanese troops. When the midwife tried to place the baby in her arms, she slapped it away feebly and called to Por-Por.

'Here, take it away,' she said, pushing the baby towards Por-Por. 'I don't want it. Get rid of it.'

Frightened and bewildered, all the women looked helplessly at Madam Tan. She nursed her broken wrist with her right hand, tears of pain leaking from her eyes. With a huge effort she put aside her own agony and took charge, as she always did. 'Clean up the child,' she said to Por-Por.

'No water,' Por-Por whispered. In mid-February the Japanese had cut off the pipe carrying water into the city. For over a week toilets had been choked with sewage and the stench was overpowering. Each day the women put out large tin pots, pans and buckets in the open courtyard to collect water from the afternoon thunderstorms. It was usually enough to cook with but now there was none left over as the last few days had been dry.

'Then find something else,' Madam Tan said, annoyed and frustrated that the women all seemed immobilised by fear. Turning to the Japanese captain, she slowly mimed the action of cleaning the baby. He nodded. 'Go on, Por-Por.'

The servant sidled past the soldiers warily and stepped into the kitchen, holding the baby in her left arm. She rummaged through the cupboards and found a three-quarter full bottle of rice wine which she emptied into a bowl. She grabbed a tea towel and dipped it into the rice wine, swabbing the baby with it, conscious of the tense silence behind her, the vibrations of terror clashing with barely leashed violence. When she had wiped away the stickiness of blood and amniotic fluid, she gave the baby to Madam Tan to hold in her right arm, then Por-Por began to sponge Mei Ling. Meanwhile, the midwife surreptitiously slipped the afterbirth into a glass jar to keep for medicinal purposes. When Mei Ling was cleaned and clothed in a cotton print dress, Madam Tan once again approached her with the baby. Again she turned her face away.

'Give it to Por-Por. I don't want that devil child. For nine months she has dragged me down, body and soul. At the moment of birth she brings disaster and shame to this house. Give it to Por-Por. Or throw it in the dustbin. I don't care.'

In the end Madam Tan took the child home—the only girl among her two sons. It would be good to have a daughter, she thought. Someone to look after her in her old age, to tend to her ancestral altar when she was dead. But the child was a nuisance, fretful, colicky, often whimpering. Her incessant squalling saw her exiled to the servants' quarters where she was looked after by bond maids already irritable from overwork. Nobody could make her stop—neither by stern scoldings nor cajoling jiggles in work-wearied arms. Once the cook stuffed torn rags into her mouth to stop her crying. She nearly choked to death before another maid dragged out the rags and slapped her hard to make her breathe again. Throughout this time she never once saw her real mother.

Mei Ling rarely left the Lim household after the birth of her fourth daughter. Por-Por was sent out each day to the wet and dry markets to buy food. She scuttled along the streets with her head bowed and her eyes cast to the ground. Once, early in the occupation, she had accidentally looked a Japanese soldier in the face. He slapped her and kicked her to the ground. After that she was careful to cross the street whenever she glimpsed soldiers hanging about. Then one day Por-Por didn't return from the markets. All afternoon and evening the Lims waited anxiously. They ate leftover fried noodles and snacked on peanuts roasted with salt and sugar. They wondered whether one of the boys should go out and look for her, but they didn't dare to break curfew. When she still had not returned two days later they accepted, fatalistically, that Por-Por was gone. It was better not to make a fuss or ask questions—nobody could help anyway.

But the Lims' efforts to keep a low profile were un-availing. They had no wealth with which to ensure their security, no property worth taking except for their bodies. The Japanese soldiers returned one afternoon as Mei Ling was plucking the brown tails off bean sprouts and the younger children were playing in the yard. All the Chinese families along their street were expelled from their homes at gunpoint, allowed to bring with them only whatever food they could carry easily in their hands or pockets. During the Great Roundup the Lim family was separated— the shopkeeper and the two sons were marshalled into football fields and sports stadiums with other Chinese men while Mei Ling and her daughters were herded into nearby terrace houses. In a surreal replay of her wedding night, Mei Ling made her daughters rub dirt over their faces and bodies and comb excrement through their hair. Abject filth earned them contemptuous kicks and globs of spittle but kept them safe. Unless they were teenagers and pretty, the women were largely left unmolested and allowed to care for their children. Other young women were rounded up and taken to the brothels.

Mei Ling and the remaining women were eventually permitted to return to their ransacked homes after three days. The street had changed, many of the young women were missing. Nobody ever knew how many women were forcibly recruited as prostitutes during this period. Even after the war was over and the perpetrators of war crimes were being prosecuted, parents and relatives were reluctant to testify for fear of harming their daughters' chances of marriage by revealing what they considered their family's shame.

The Chinese men disappeared for days during the Great Roundup. The shopkeeper was forced to sit cross-legged in an orderly row with other men. He craned his neck for a sight of his sons and was kicked for moving. While Japanese soldiers paraded up and down the rows looking for any excuse to abuse, his joints cramped painfully and his flesh became as numb as stone. Bewildered and disorientated, he pissed and shat in his pants and the tears of shame pooled in the corners of his reddening eyes. By the end of the first day he was dehydrated, stinking and suffering from heat-stroke. The daily thunderstorm cracked in the afternoon and he sat in the drenching rain throughout the evening, sleeping in the puddles of water during the night. Dawn came and he shivered in the moist air, feeling dampness creep from the sodden earth into his thin bones. By the middle of the second day, he had run out of food, and hunger gnawed at his belly. He thought longingly of the tightly packed rows of biscuit tins, stacks of salted fish and sacks of rice in his little shop, and he yearned for home.

Eventually the men were divided into two groups. The shopkeeper saw his eldest son singled out into the first group—the young and physically fit—who were then sent away to work for the Japanese. He looked into his son's eyes as he was marched away, but said nothing. He himself was shoved into the second group of men, who were being given slips of paper with the word 'examined' written on them. They queued before the officer handing out the passes, but by the time he stood in front of the table the Japanese officials had run out of paper and the word was being carelessly inscribed onto visible parts of the men's bodies. He had the word 'examined' written on his sallow chest and was then allowed to return home. During the following days he went without a bath in order to preserve the cheap ink imprint. His wife would not come near him but they both came to be thankful that he was physically branded, for other Chinese men attacked each other in the streets to grab those precious slips of paper that would safeguard them against further selection attempts.

The shopkeeper came home to find his premises had been looted. The Japanese had taken away all the valuable goods and much of the food, Mei Ling told him. They had left the shop in a mess with broken glass, spilled rice and crushed biscuits all over the floor. It had taken her hours to clean it all up. They could not possibly continue their business. What were they to do now? she asked desperately. He did not answer her. Instead, he closed the wooden doors to his shop, locking and barring them carefully. Then he climbed upstairs to spend the rest of the war—and much of the rest of his life—in his bedroom while his wife looked after the remaining children and bartered for food on the black market or begged for it from Madam Tan.

Years passed until, one evening, the neighbours began to feel a change in the air. They realised that they could no longer hear the sharp clatter of Japanese boots echoing in the alley, nor the reverberation of rifle butts on old wooden doors. There were fewer soldiers in the streets and, eventually, they seemed to disappear altogether from the hawker stalls, the markets, the docks and back alleys. People began to reappear. The eldest son was the first to stagger into the courtyard through the back door one day, emaciated and ill with malaria. Shortly after, Por-Por came home. She had shaved off the black hair that used to fall to her waist when she undid the tight bun from its perch on her head. Her scalp was stubbled with greying hair, but she walked to the market with her head held up once more.

Singapore was no longer *Syonan*, and all the Lim and Tan children were renamed by Madam Tan, who insisted that English names and English education would be the route to advancement and prosperity in postwar Singapore now that the British had returned. My mother, now four years old, was renamed Pandora. Madam Tan had picked the name from a Reader's Digest condensed book of Greek and Roman myths. She had not understood the stories, only recognised the names. The other girls were renamed Lida, Daphne and Persephone or, as they pronounced it, Percy-phone. The boys were renamed Donald and Winston by the local Anglican priest.

About a year after Donald and Por-Por reappeared, Pandora sat in the kitchen of the great mansion and spooned rice porridge, salted duck's egg and dried anchovies into her mouth, smearing her upper lip with a gooey white moustache. Exciting events were happening upstairs in Madam Tan's room, and all the relatives, neighbours and their maids were rushing about. But she had been banished by Mei Ling, whom she knew as 'Auntie', to the kitchen, with only Por-Por and the other maids for company.

'Is Mama having a baby?' she asked Por-Por idiotically, knowing the answer already.

Por-Por looked at the pretty child dressed in a white silk pantsuit, her hair tied up with drooping pinks bows in slipping bunches over her ears. She glanced at the jade studs in Pandora's ears and the gold anklet flopping onto the red wooden clog. She touched her own fuzzy hair, still growing back. She felt spiteful and wanted to make the little girl cry.

'Stupid girl. Madam Tan is not your mother. She is having another baby and then she won't want you any-more,' Por-Por said.

The child blinked and stared at her, slowly spooning more porridge into her small mouth.

'Are you deaf, dummy? Are you stupid? Did you hear what I said? Madam Tan is not your mother.'

Still the child said nothing. She thought about the woman lying in the bed upstairs, pictured her in her usual attire: glamorous and exotic in a finely embroidered red silk top with ivory buttons, black silk trousers, gold neck-lace with a jade pendant of a dragon breathing fire from her neck, new jade bangle around her deformed left wrist, heavy gold rings that could cut your face when she slapped you for being naughty.

'Don't you know that your Auntie Mei Ling is your real mother?' Por-Por said, watching Pandora closely. The child blinked hard at her but said nothing. 'Madam Tan took pity on her sister and adopted you because she already had two sons. Don't know why she wanted a daughter. Girls are useless. A woman needs sons. Your real mother didn't want you and now that Madam Tan has a new baby, maybe even a daughter, she won't want you anymore. Nobody wants you, rubbish girl.'

The child began to cry at last and Por-Por smiled, satisfied. She patted Pandora's head. 'Never mind. Don't cry or you will look ugly and nobody will want to marry you when you grow up.'

She fished out a handkerchief and held it over Pandora's nose for her to blow. 'You're a pretty girl, Pan-Pan. Maybe I'll look after you if you're a good and obedient girl. You can be my foster daughter and I'll take care of you. How would you like that, uh?'

Pandora did not answer. Please gods, she prayed to unknown deities, please let her have another boy.

Madam Tan had a baby girl after all.

THE MELODRAMA OF
LIFE AND LIMS

Soon after Por-Por's revelation, Pandora was summoned before Madam Tan one morning. She looked at the whimpering baby in Madam Tan's arms, mouth like a fish sucking fretfully at Madam Tan's swollen veined breast. Madam Tan told her that she would be going to stay with Mei Ling for a while.

'If you're a good girl and respect your elders and behave properly, then people will love you,' Madam Tan said. She pulled the baby away from her nipple and gave her to one of the bond maids. Then she undid the rest of the buttons on her blouse and took it off. She lay down on a woven bamboo mat. A bond maid started massaging her back, pummelling the bunched flesh under the skin with tight fists until the knots of muscle were tenderised and loosened.

'I don't want to go,' Pandora said.

'You can play with your sisters. Four of you together. Imagine that!'

'I don't want to play with them. I want to play here.'

'One of the servants will pack your clothes and toys and take you over to your mother's house this afternoon.'

Pandora knew then that she would not be returning as a daughter of the Tan household. Madam Tan had referred to Mei Ling as 'your mother' for the first time.

'Mama, don't make me go,' she said. 'Please.'

'You're a good girl, Pan-Pan,' Madam Tan said. 'So pretty. If you are good and obedient you will find a rich husband to marry you when you grow up.'

She waited until the servant had finished rubbing liniment into her tense neck, then she sat up and shrugged on her silk top. She looked at Pandora and smiled, beckoning her forward. She tilted her head, graciously offering up one cheek. 'You can give me a kiss, Pan-Pan. I have some sweet plums and a red packet for you. It has *two* gold coins in it! And I shall give you a pretty gold bracelet that you can wear around your wrist.'

After lunch one of the bond maids packed Pandora's silk *samfoo*s into a suitcase and put all her toys into another. When this was done she got the gardener to call for a trishaw. She helped the child into the seat and climbed in beside her. After giving directions to the trishaw cyclist, she settled back to enjoy the ride, knowing that she would have to walk back to the mansion in the wet afternoon heat.

'You will like living with your real mother, Pan-Pan,' the bond maid told the child comfortingly. 'There will be lots of children to play with.'

'Will there be boys?' Pandora asked.

'Lots of them,' the bond maid assured her. 'Your mother has been very lucky. She has three sons to carry on the family name. Your brothers Ah-Donald and Ah-Winston are older than you, and now you have your baby brother Henly to look after.'

Pandora thought about Madam Tan's large, quiet house with the green-tiled roof and the painted terracotta dragons guarding each apex. She thought about the cool marble floors that reflected her foreshortened running figure back to her. There were the inlaid pearl screens, the carved rosewood and gold-embroidered satin furniture, the antique Chinese vases, jade carvings and fragrant sandalwood jewellery boxes. The opulent room where the ancestors were worshipped and placated at the gilt altar, and the fat red columns surrounding the fish pond where expensive Japanese carp flashed red and gold as they darted among succulent lily pads.

Then she thought about the men in Madam Tan's household. She remembered the clogging opium fumes from Mr Tan's private rooms, where he smoked the war away. She thought of how she had to serve him thick black tea and hot rice buns stuffed with pork in the morning to show him that she was a humble, filial daughter. She would look up into those yellow eyes cracked with threads of red capillaries, stare at the pouches of mottled flesh under the lower lids. She thought of his wandering, groping, pinching fingers, his brown tea-stained teeth, his stinking breath pungent with stale opium smoke. Good girl, good little girl, he muttered each morning as he hauled her onto his knee and fondled her with his right hand while holding his pork bun in his left. He took great, hungry bites of bread and warm white crumbs snowed down onto her silk suit to fall inside her panties.

She also remembered the bed she'd had in her room upstairs, and she thought of how her two foster brothers would sometimes sneak into her room during the night and snuggle up to her tightly, one on either side. They would rub themselves against her small body and snigger. She learned to squeeze her eyes tightly shut and lie perfectly still. If she complained, one of them would pinch her with long, powerful fingers. He would pull her halfway down the bed while the other brother farted into her face, giggling hysterically. They were boys—the little masters of the house— so they could do anything, get away with everything.

The trishaw stopped. The bond maid got out and haggled over the price, then she pulled Pandora out of the seat, grumbling about being cheated by thieving trishaw-men while the cyclist cleared his throat loudly and spat into the red dust near her feet. The bond maid jumped back with a startled exclamation and screamed curses after the cyclist as he pedalled away. Grasping Pandora by her chubby hand, she knocked on the back door. Por-Por opened it, smiling widely.

The servants chatted for a while, exchanging extravagant compliments, uncertain of the exact hierarchy of their status. Por-Por was a servant, free to come, go and marry as she wished, but she was attached to a poor terrace household in the city slums. The bond maid, on the other hand, was to all extents and purposes a slave attached to an important and wealthy household, and she could only marry if her mistress consented to the arrangement. To complicate matters, the mistresses of both households were sisters and Madam Tan was the younger of the two, so Madam Lim had the advantage of seniority. Eventually, however, sufficient 'face' was given and the exchange of gossip exhausted. Por-Por took Pandora's suitcase, led her into the cracked courtyard and closed and bolted the new wooden door that had replaced the one the Japanese soldiers had kicked in five years before.

All the Lim children, except Donald, were ranged in order of age in the courtyard: Lida, Winston, Daphne and Percy-phone. Eldest Sister, Second Brother, Second Sister, and Third Sister. Donald Duck, Eldest Brother, had moved out to share a rat's nest apartment with friends in China-town. Little Henly (or Henry, depending on who was pronouncing his name) was nowhere to be seen. The Lim children stared at Pandora curiously, insolently, and whis-pered among themselves. Daphne giggled because she was a giggler. Then Winston stepped forward with a big grin on his face.

'Welcome home, Youngest Sister,' he said. He grabbed her hand and pressed something into her palm, stepping back quickly.

Pandora felt the pulse of a scaly wriggle. She opened her hand and screamed when she saw the slime-green gecko blinking up at her. She dropped the reptile and thrust her hands behind her back as Winston slapped his thigh, doubled over with laughter. He glanced around slyly at his siblings to see whether they were sharing the joke. He felt piqued that their smiles were merely lukewarm. Lida looked bored. He wanted to get Lida's attention, make her laugh. He ran to Pandora and pinched her hard on her forearm, howling with hilarity when she squealed and her eyes spurted tears.

'Welcome home, Youngest Sister,' he gasped again be-tween gusts of exaggerated mirth.

Pandora was born to be a victim and everybody knew this. She had already been rejected by the Tan household, easily replaced by Madam Tan's baby girl. Now she was terrified that the Lims would not want her either. She set out to make herself indispensable. She helped Por-Por around the kitchen, slicing ginger, chopping chillies, mincing garlic, nipping the straggly brown ends off small hills of bean sprouts. She washed her father's and brothers' clothes, hosed and scrubbed clean the bathroom and outhouse after they left it soiled. Excess flesh melted off her frame until her silk *samfoo*s no longer fitted her. Mei Ling packed them away and she never saw them again. She wore Daphne's hand-me-downs and was embarrassing in her gratitude.

Later, she tended the shop whenever her father wanted to take a mid-afternoon nap upstairs, and she got caned for items that subsequently went missing because the other children had stolen them. Loyally, she kept silent. She needed to be needed, and plain-looking, thick-headed Percy-phone was the only member of the family who really needed her. She did Percy-phone's homework and defended her elder sister against Winston's taunts and tricks. In return Percy-phone accepted her into the family and gave her unconditional love and friendship all her life.

She never got to know her eldest sister very well, for Lida left the terrace house shortly after Pandora returned. She had become the mistress of a rich man and she moved into his house along River Valley Road.

'Lida was a real character, one of a kind,' Percy-phone would reminisce many years later, half-admiringly, half-disapprovingly. 'Real beautiful and real smart, but very wild. Remember the jewellery she used to come home with? She flaunted them in front of our mother. Mr Fu was besotted with her, the dirty old man. She used to take Pan and me to see the Chinese opera and *wayang* shows once in a while. Then afterwards she'd buy us some ice-cream from Cold Storage. Only the white people—the *ang mohs*—or very rich Chinese people shopped at Cold Storage during those days. We used to pass by the supermarket and look inside, but we didn't dare to enter because it was an *ang moh* supermarket. But Lida was very daring and she would go anywhere. That girl had no shame. She got bored with Mr Fu after a while and, after her first abortion, she ran away with Tom the English Sailor from Newcastle-upon-Tyne.'

For Pandora and Percy-phone, Eldest Sister Lida remained an exotic character in a melodramatic Chinese opera; a glamorous figure for whom the rules of respectability did not apply. During their childhood she had staged before the family—before the whole neighbourhood, in fact—emotional tantrums, tragic posturings, loudly screamed accusations of neglect and misunderstanding, and thrilling scandals. Before any household in the neighbourhood had scraped together enough money to buy a black and white television set to watch the soap operas from Hong Kong, the neighbours lived vicariously through Lida Lim's life. Arch-enemies became grudging and wary friends as they sipped tea, clicked mahjong tiles and exchanged the latest gossip about poor Madam Lim's intractable eldest daughter. Lida Lim became the bonding agent, not only of the Lim family, but of the entire neighbourhood. Huddled next to each other in bed, Daphne, Percy-phone and Pandora learned to become siblings through the exchange of awed whispers about Eldest Sister.

Proximity to perversion cloaked them with fame and attached them to friendships at school; it paved the way for Mei Ling into the houses of the wealthy, whose appetite for delicious morsels of scandal was as great as that of their poorer counterparts. Mei Ling no doubt enjoyed playing the tragic role of the disgraced, lamenting mother to the hilt.

'*Ai-yo*, what to do? Always she so stubborn and rebellious. All my children so naughty. Bring me nothing but heartache. Lida won't listen to me. She brings shame to the whole family but she doesn't care. I tell her father to beat some sense into her but he won't do it. Lida, she snatch the stick from his hand and break it into two. What can you do with a girl like that? Bring me so much pain only.'

The final confrontation was played out two years after Pandora was sent home to the Lims. That was when Lida left Mr Fu, who made his chauffeur drive the creamy white Mercedes around to the tumbledown terrace. He eased himself out of the car, an old man dressed in a white suit and a white Panama hat, clothes perfectly coordinated with his car. He rapped on the front door with his cane and Mr Lim ushered him through the shop and into the house, bowing and scraping before him. Mr Fu had come to beg Lida to be his third wife. Such an honour, such a great honour. But it wasn't to be.

What made it especially humiliating at the time—and farcical afterwards—was that Mr Fu's first and second wives followed after him and begged Lida to leave their philandering husband, the father of their collective three sons, alone. Mei Ling thought that the position of third wife was as respectable as any her eldest daughter could attain. Anxious to marry Lida off, she strongly urged her daughter to accept Mr Fu's proposal. But as Por-Por always said, Lida had been born with 'itchy feet'. She was bored and restless; she wanted to escape Singapore and travel abroad. Illiterate and uneducated because she had grown up during the

Japanese occupation and had not been sent to school—
no-one thought it worthwhile educating her afterwards
since she was a girl and would presumably marry and raise
children—she nevertheless wanted to witness first-hand the
world that Hollywood had translated for her on the flickering screens of the local cinemas.

Lida refused to marry Mr Fu. She told him and his
wives that she had fallen in love with Tom the English
Sailor. Mr Fu was too old and too staid for her. Sex with
him was one step away from necrophilia. His prick was too
flabby and, besides, she could no longer tolerate the dis-
colouration of his teeth from years of chewing tobacco and
smoking opium. His breath made her gag and she could
count on the fingers of one hand the number of orgasms
she'd had with him.

Desperate love raged into hate at this humiliation.
Mr Fu and Wives Numbers One and Two marched off to
find a medium to curse Lida Lim. When the local Chinese
medium refused because she was a friend of Lida's, they
sought out a Malay *bomoh* to avenge the flippantly delivered
insult to the House of Fu. Many years later, when Lida
started to go blind from retinitis pigmentosa, all the Lim
relatives remembered the Fus' threat to visit the Malay witch
doctor and they were convinced that the steady deterioration
of Lida's eyesight—from night blindness to full blindness—
was a result of her careless offence to the Fus. When the
same disease emerged in Pandora a few years before her
death, they were unshakable in their belief that the *bomoh*
had cursed all the Lims. They spent a fortune trying to undo
the curse before they themselves fell prey to it.

On the afternoon that Lida rejected Mr Fu and his
wives, a fierce and tear-wrenching screaming match ensued

between mother and daughter in the courtyard. Daphne, Percy-phone and Pandora huddled together in the boys' bedroom next to the kitchen, listening in round-eyed, fearful delight. The neighbours gathered on their balcony overlooking the courtyard to watch the showdown and comment loudly, occasionally shouting down advice to the unheeding protagonists. Nobody was disappointed. Tempests of tears were followed by lightning-hurled accusations of ingratitude, lack of filial piety or mother love and, finally, mutual repudiation of kinship between mother and daughter forever.

Lida packed her belongings, hocked the jewellery given to her by Mr Fu and ran away with Tom the English Sailor. Thus she became the first member of the Lim family to emigrate from Singapore. She never came back.

That night Mei Ling called Pandora to her room and looked her in the eye for the first time since she had returned to the terrace house two years previously.

'My eldest daughter is dead to me now,' she said. 'You have come home to take her place. If you are an obedient and respectful daughter, then Mummy will love you.'

All of Pandora's life, love would come with strings attached and conditions to fulfil.

THE BUSINESS ACUMEN
OF DONALD DUCK

In the Lim household adult melodramas and childish games all took place in the open courtyard adjoining the kitchen. Two balconies overlooked the courtyard, one of them being a sort of mezzanine floor of the Lim terrace, the other belonging to the neighbour's house. By mutual consent of the shopkeeper and the neighbour, long bamboo rods were placed across the balconies, and the laundry of both families was hung out to dry over the courtyard. On the dull and listless weekends after Lida Lim's departure, Winston or Daphne would go up to the Lim balcony, draw in a bamboo pole, tie a raffia rope to the middle and push it out again so that the rope slithered down to the courtyard. They went downstairs and all the children took turns swinging on the rope, hollering bloodcurdling imitations of Tarzan calls.

This was a favourite game until the bamboo pole cracked under the flabby weight of Winston. He sailed up into the air only to tumble, at the apex of his pendulum swing, and crash onto the concrete, breaking his wrist and being buried under a flurry of drying women's underwear. His fear of punishment was far less than his terror that he was now cursed by bad luck because he had actually been touched by women's defiling garments.

All the children were walloped by Mei Ling, who bolted the back door and chased them around the courtyard until she caught them with flying whacks and whipped them soundly with the bamboo cane. After each child was red-striped and sobbing loudly, she followed her family's tradition, breaking the bamboo cane in half and throwing it into the dustbin.

'See what you've done,' she said to them. 'Your worth-less hides have contaminated the cane. Good for nothing now but to be thrown into the sea.'

Most of Pandora's childhood memories ended with the walloping and the disposal of the bamboo cane in the same dramatic manner. Her stories were parables of imaginative mischief followed inevitably by harsh and painful retri-bution. In the world of the Lims, delights had to be stolen and happy endings were impossible.

After the demise of Tarzan, their hours after school were spent playing rounders with the neighbours. These games usually ended in rancorous hostility as each family accused the other of cheating, swore vicious vengeance and vowed never to play with the other again. Sometimes, when it rained, they tore up their homework and folded paper boats to float in yacht races along the open stormwater drains outside the crooked rows of terraces. They chased each other around the streets, taking terrifying leaps across these gigantic drains which swelled and roared with rainwater during the wet season. Before the water eventually became too polluted, they'd spot tiny fish darting up the drains as they leant over to peer into the muddy water. Sometimes they fell in and were hauled out by Por-Por, only to be embraced by the unending supply of bamboo switches bought from the peddler who visited the house every week. But most of their games were harmless until Donald Duck came home when Pandora was eight and taught them the new game of stealing.

Donald Duck had still been at school when the Japanese rounded him up and took him off to a work camp, and he couldn't be bothered returning to his studies after the war was over. In later years he fiercely resented anyone who was more educated than him, and his bilious ire was reserved especially for anyone with a university degree. The Grads, he called them contemptuously as he tapped himself on the chest and proclaimed to anyone who would listen that he himself had been educated in the University of Life, and that was the one that really counted. In his garrulous old age he came to believe that there existed in Singapore a Conspiracy of Grads who aimed to destroy ordinary, non-university educated people and grind them into poverty. In the business world, he would proclaim impressively, you couldn't trust the Grads. They were sly, tricky, ever ready to stab you in the back, trample you while you were down, kick you in the head, slit your throat, slice off your balls and generally dish out all other kinds of corporeal violence.

Donald Duck first went into Business—and you could always hear the capital 'B' in the word—during the war. When he was conscripted by the Japanese to work for them, he made himself useful by obtaining women, antiques and rare food delicacies for his Japanese masters. He learnt to speak Japanese and became their interpreters as they

stormed their way around the city streets. (This skill, inci-
dentally, served him well when he started a dubious under-
ground company trading organ parts with the Japanese after
the war, craftily selling out to another associate who was
then arrested and imprisoned for twelve years—some say on
the information supplied by Donald Duck.) He led Japanese
troops into the dark, densely populated wormholes of
Chinatown and brought them safely out again, richer for
the expensive herbal medicines, jewellery, watches and pens
they'd acquired. He stole for them and kept a substantial
commission for himself.

Towards the end of the war, after its cessation in Europe,
he contracted malaria and was allowed to return home.
While the Americans were bombing Hiroshima, he tossed
and sweated feverishly in bed, and was nursed back to health
by his loudly lamenting mother. He lay exhausted and
wasted as the Japanese were driven out of Singapore and the
Allied troops returned. By the time he had regained his
health and slipped out onto the streets again, there was
no-one to point him out as a Japanese collaborator. Instead,
he made himself useful to the Allies, continuing his black-
market and pimping business. He eventually abandoned all
these activities for a nine-to-five job in a warehouse import-
ing soft drinks from America.

While Lida Lim was busy causing a local scandal, he
had been living with some friends in Chinatown, but now
he returned home because he was flat broke and deeply in
love. Donald Duck should have been rich, but he was an
incorrigible and unlucky gambler. Most of his profits from
the war had dribbled into the hands of the bookies, and
he was in love with an expensive, high-maintenance
eighteen-year-old woman who was famous for winning that

year's Miss Singapore Telecom contest—which basically
meant that she was a beautiful woman who could answer
the phone in a pleasant tone and smile dazzlingly while she
dealt with the flood of tedious questions and complaints
then pouring in as Telecom rolled out cables and connected
phone lines to homes.

Wendy Wu came from a background even poorer than
the Lims. Her father had been a rickshaw-man. But she
had a stunning face dominated by large black eyes with the
desirable epicanthus fold, soft white skin greased with Oil
of Olay, a slender, long-limbed body and big firm breasts
before the age of affordable implants. Those breasts, prom-
inently paraded with the help of a state-of-the-art Maiden
Form bra under her tight cotton *cheongsam*, were objects
of desire among men and envy among women, the Lim
girls and their female neighbours included. Not only did
she have big breasts, Wendy Wu also had a veneer of femme
fatale poise borrowed from years of watching Bette Davis,
Mae West and Lauren Bacall films, for although sex was
always a priority with her, Hollywood was her first and
truest love.

Donald Duck was in love and, confidently, he thought
he had a good chance with Wendy Wu because he was a
handsome man. The Lim sisters used to say that in his
youth he looked like a Chinese version of George Reeve
as Superman. He was tall for a Chinese man, he had
developed his upper body and biceps with weights and
martial arts, and he slicked his thick black hair back into
a James Dean pompadour using Brylcreem. He strutted
cockily around the city streets and posed on red plastic
stools in the markets as young women sidled up to flirt.
But he needed money to push his case with Miss Telecom

so he came home to recruit his siblings into Business. He taught them how to steal and sent them to practise in their father's shop. When they were proficient he assigned them to various shops around the city and they stole for him successfully for months before Mei Ling discovered what was going on.

Daphne was caught stealing a radio from a shop one day and threatened with prosecution. She cried with terror and wet her pants, a sour puddle forming on the green square-tiled floor of Lee Hong Ting Good Luck Electronics. Someone, Lee Hong Ting presumably, called Mei Ling. Then Daphne, holding her skirt carefully so that the damp patch didn't show too much, was dragged home to be walloped until she couldn't sit down for a fortnight. Mei Ling snapped the switch in half and threw the two parts into the dustbin. Henly rummaged through the rubbish until he found the pieces, rescued them and used them to make a frame for a kite which never got off the ground. Disgusted, he abandoned it, and the kite was later seen floating dismally down a stormwater drain.

After that, nobody dared to steal again, even in the face of Donald Duck's dire threats. Donald Duck eventually wheedled his way back into Mei Ling's good graces by offering to babysit Pandora after school. Mei Ling was thrilled. Her first-born son had changed. What a dutiful, caring son I've got, she bragged to the neighbours. He takes such good care of Pandora. So nice to see them together. He'll make such a good father to my grandsons, you just wait and see. Donald Duck helped Pandora with her home-work and indirectly got himself an education. When she came back with good report cards, he smiled smugly, as proud of himself as he was of her.

'You study hard, Pan-Pan,' he told her when he took her to the goldsmith to get her ears pierced and bought her tiny gold sleepers. 'Don't be a lazy dumb-dumb like me. You study hard and get a good job. Then some rich man will want to marry you one day.'

In his own selfish, limited way, Pandora was the one person in his family he genuinely loved even though he exploited her whenever he could. She was the embodiment of everything he could not possibly be. Years later, despite his hatred of Grads, he would encourage her to go to university. When she dropped out of her course, his disappointment was so acute that he did not speak to her for a year.

In the afternoons, when school was over, Donald Duck took Pandora to the hawker centre near Bugis Street. Big Brother will give you a special treat, he promised her. Just outside the market he pulled a pot of rouge from his canvas knapsack and smeared a pink blob over each of her cheeks. Then he took a used tube of Wendy Wu's red lipstick and spread it thickly over her lips so that she looked like a clownish China doll. Isn't this fun, he said to her. Just like Mummy. He tied back her hair with colourful pink and red ribbons. Then he took her by the hand and brought her around the hawker stalls, watching her pretty eyes growing round with desire as she sniffed the savoury air and looked at steaming dishes of fried noodles, rice vermicelli, *roti prata*, green and pink Nonya cakes, red bean soup, ice *kachang*, juicy stalks of freshly cut sugarcane, fat pillows of curry puffs and crisp fried banana fritters.

'Do you want a special treat?' he asked. She nodded. 'Big Brother will give you a special treat, but first you have to do something for me. Deal?'

Before she could answer he pulled her over to a crowded coffee stall where unshaven men in white singlets, dusty black trousers and brown plastic slippers sat on red stools, sipping muddy coffee from huge glass tankards. Donald Duck slipped his hands under Pandora's armpits and hefted her onto a stool.

'Sing the song I taught you for all the nice uncles,' he coaxed. She ducked her head shyly and looked uncertainly at him. 'Go on, sing.'

She just looked at him and his hard palm hovered near her rouge-smeared cheek.

'Do it,' he said.

In a thin, reedy, off-key voice, accompanied by Donald Duck on the harmonica, she sang a doleful song about how the flower of her youth would soon be plucked. She faltered to a halt and a smattering of bored applause broke out. Donald Duck smiled mournfully and bowed obsequiously to the listless patrons of the coffee stall.

'Uncle, may I?' He pulled a stool up to a table where four men lolled and sat, cradling Pandora lovingly on his lap. She turned her face away from the men, burrowing into Donald Duck's light blue shirt, smearing it with her face paint.

'Your sister?' A man with white stubble on his head and shrivelled arms the colour of cooked liver. Watchful eyes over a thick curve of glass as he slurped coffee.

'*Ai-yah*, yes. My only surviving family.' He pulled off his cap and sighed gustily. Looking the man in the eye, he recounted the pathetic story of how she was his beloved sister and the only surviving relative left in the whole world, the others having been struck down by malaria, dysentery, tuberculosis or the Japanese—the means of death varied each day and mattered little as nobody believed him anyway. He tried his best to look after Little Sister, he said, but they were poor, had only the clothes on their backs and a small corner of a room in Chinatown. Poor little sister, sometimes she needed the comfort of a father. He paused and looked hopefully around the circle of cynical eyes until, finally, the white-stubbled man offered a father's comfort to the poor little girl for a while.

'I have two little girls of my own,' he grinned, playing along. 'Little girls need their fathers.'

'See how kind Uncle is to you, Pan-Pan? What a lucky girl you are.' Beaming broadly now, Donald Duck lifted Pandora off his lap and made her climb onto 'Uncle's' lap. Then he stretched, yawned and sauntered off to buy himself a beer, settling down at another table to chat, smoke or roll the dice for an idle half-hour until the uncle had had his fill of playing father and Pandora, now teary-eyed, was allowed to slip off his lap.

'Uncle, are you going already?' Donald Duck said. 'Pan-Pan, are you hungry? Kind Uncle, my little sister is hungry.'

'Then buy her something to eat,' the man said. He pulled out a few grubby, crumpled notes, tossed them down at Donald Duck's feet and walked away.

'Bastard,' Donald Duck muttered as he stooped quickly to pick up the money and count it. 'There, Pan-Pan. Don't cry anymore.'

True to his word, Donald Duck would then buy Pandora a small treat, tapping his foot impatiently while she slobbered it down, eager to be back home sprucing himself up for his date with Miss Telecom.

'Finished?' he demanded. She nodded, cramming the last bite into her small mouth, her smeared red lips studded with crumbs. He grasped her hand and walked briskly to the bus stop to take her home. On the bus, he pulled out his handkerchief and scrubbed her face painfully clean of makeup until she cried out.

'That dirty old man,' Donald Duck said contemptuously. 'Fucking prick.'

As the bus wound its way into the city he grabbed Pandora by the shoulders and turned her to face him. 'Listen to me, Little Sister, and listen well. You're my favourite sister, yes? Big Brother loves you, yes? Don't you *ever* let me catch you letting a strange man put his hands all over you if Big Brother is not around or else I'll wallop you until you wish you were dead. Understand? Dirty old men like him can't be trusted. Someone ought to slice off their balls and feed them to the pigs.'

Hanging around the hawker centre, Donald Duck soon developed another enterprise. He went into partnership with a hawker who sold roasted meat served with steamed rice and water convolvulus stir-fried with chilli, all arranged decoratively on a banana leaf. Donald Duck guaranteed the cook a cheap supply of good quality meat in return for thirty-five per cent of the takings.

He came home with his wallet bulging with notes and made Winston jealous.

'Where you get all that extra cash?' Winston demanded, for he worked at the same company as Donald Duck. 'How come you all of a sudden got money to splash around?'

'Business acumen,' Donald Duck said smugly. 'I got Business acumen.'

Winston saw Donald Duck selling meat to the hawker, but he couldn't figure out where Donald Duck was getting his supply from. He decided to tail Donald Duck. He sat in a darkened cinema sucking on the straw of his Fanta, craning his neck to peer across the aisle to where Donald Duck wriggled in his seat, his left hand stroking up the hem of Wendy Wu's skirt until he could slip his fingers between her stockinged thighs. Irritably, she slapped his hand away and stared at Humphrey Bogart on the screen. Donald Duck tried it again, and again she slapped his hand away, then pinched him hard for good measure. He turned away sulkily and shifted restlessly. After a while he turned back to Wendy Wu and took her right hand, romantically linking his fingers with hers. 'I love you, Wendy,' he told her.

She smiled at him and let her hand lie passively in his. He stroked her forearm lightly and she snuggled closer to him. He inched their hands towards his crotch, then unlinked their fingers and pressed her palm flat against it. He covered her hand with his and began massaging his crotch slowly, cautiously. When her gaze remained firmly fixed on the screen, he looked around him surreptitiously and Winston quickly ducked his head. Everyone was staring at the screen, elbows bent and hands moving rhythmically from mouths to popcorn boxes and back again. Donald Duck slowly unzipped his trousers and started to ease her stroking palm between the slit of material. Wendy Wu heaved an exaggerated sigh and glanced at him. Looking down, she pushed aside the flap of material. Her fingers grabbed his cock impatiently and began to knead it mechanically. 'Happy now?' she said in a savage whisper as her gaze returned to Lauren Bacall staring at Bogart. Donald Duck subsided into satisfied silence.

After the movie Winston trailed behind Donald Duck and Wendy Wu as they meandered through the night market and shared a late supper, Donald Duck gobbling down most of the plate of fried noodles since Miss Telecom was watching her weight. They wandered down to the waterfront, found an empty trishaw and climbed into it. Bored, Winston imagined what it would feel like to fondle Wendy Wu's plump breasts. Then, because he had very little imagination and could not get a hard-on from his thoughts, he lit a cigarette and stared at the dark shadows of boats gently rolling over the streamers of moonshine on the water. His mind fell into its pleasant and natural state of blankness.

Donald Duck and Wendy Wu emerged from the trishaw, giggling and straightening their clothes. Winston tossed his third cigarette into the river and followed them back to Wendy Wu's flat in Chinatown. After dropping her off, Donald Duck disappeared into a small shop and emerged a few moments later carrying a cage with a hissing cat tied to the bars with a piece of raffia. He flung his dark grey coat over it and began to wind his way north towards the wealthier neighbourhoods. In a back alley, he uncovered the cage and opened the spring-door. The mystery of his meat supply was solved. He was using a cat on heat to entice tomcats—both feral and pedigreed—into the cage. He then slaughtered the tomcats, skinned them, chopped them up, arranged them attractively on a tray and brought them to the hawker to be barbecued with garlic, ginger and soy sauce.

Winston tried to edge his way into the Business, but he had no acumen. Stupidly, in typical Winston fashion, he approached Donald Duck's supplier of cats on heat. A few days later Daphne and Percy-phone dabbed Mercurochrome on Winston's wounds and bandaged his ribs, but he still required three stitches to his left temple where the skin had split open and a lot of blood had gushed out.

'Tell anyone and you'll be swimming with the fish,' Donald Duck told him toughly, cocky in his aggression.

Eventually Mei Ling found out about Donald Duck's Business ventures. Por-Por came across Donald Duck and Pandora on one of her afternoons off. She was buying straw brooms in Bugis Street market. She heard Pandora long before she saw her, an unmelodious squawking of a vulgar Chinese song. One glance at Donald Duck, Pandora's painted face and the 'uncles' was enough to send Por-Por racing towards them, upraised broom in hand. She chased Donald Duck through the hawker centre like a demented witch, calling out, 'Stupid boy! Arsehole! I'm going to chop off your fucking prick and fry it in hot chilli!'

They slipped in and out of food stalls and knocked over rickety tables laden with steaming soups and curries. They kicked over aluminium stools and left outraged diners in their wake. Finally, Donald Duck ran into the stinking darkness of the wet market. Por-Por ran in after him. Her wooden clogs slipped on the slimy entrails of a recently butchered rooster. She skidded, clawed the air frantically and smashed down onto the mucky concrete floor, dislocating her hip, jarring her elbow painfully and staining her clothes with blood and gore. Donald Duck ran out of the market and lost himself in the narrow streets.

But when he came home that night, Mei Ling was waiting up for him. She held no bamboo cane in her hand. He was too old to be walloped, too big even to attempt it. Instead, she tossed his things at him, stood on tiptoe and, catching hold of his left ear, twisted it hard. You've broken my heart, she told him with typical Lim melodrama. She threw him out of the house and forbade him to come home until he had repented of his evil ways and changed for the better.

She couldn't find it in her to disown him. When he got married to Miss Telecom nearly a year later, she welcomed him back to her house with a wide smile and proudly displayed to the neighbours the matt black and white photographs of her eldest son's wedding. They were a beautiful couple, the tall man in the dark suit and the bride in her novel white wedding gown, for Wendy Wu's family was Catholic and they'd had a western wedding. For weeks after, Mei Ling would take out the photographs and stroke them lovingly until they were smudged with fingerprints. She bullied her husband into letting the newlywed couple inhabit the master bedroom until they had enough money to move into a home of their own. She and the shopkeeper moved into the small dark room between the kitchen and the shop, while each night the other two boys carried their canvas beds with resignation into the shop and set them up there. What Donald Duck had done to Pandora was easily forgotten.

'Mei Ling was never a mother to us, but nothing could shake her devotion to Donald Duck,' Percy-phone often said years later. 'He was, after all, her first-born child, and a male at that. Boys are good, girls are not. Some things you learn early on in life, and then you just learn to live with it.'

QUEEN OF THE KITCHEN

Por-Por was dying. The Lim children squeezed hours of morbid entertainment out of the melodrama of her slow death. The winces of pain followed by sighs of suffering. The disbelief in her suddenly discovered, imminent death. The angry, panicky denials. The bursts of frantic, futile activity. The pleas and prayers that were tossed up desperately to the gods, only to come smashing down on the broken cement yard that was her domain. This was a new development in the soap opera of their lives and they loved it.

Nothing exciting had happened for years. Not since Donald Duck went into another of his shady Business ventures, acquired a wealth as mysterious as it was substantial, and moved himself and Wendy out of the dilapidated tenement into a new apartment along the Tiong Bahru Road. Business and Wendy kept him busy; he rarely visited anymore. Winston and Daphne were busy courting and being courted. That left Percy-phone and Pandora to keep each other company, for Henly—a loner all his life—had little to do with them.

Pandora led a schizophrenic life throughout her school years. She was a dutiful Chinese daughter at home and an absurd lampoon of an English schoolgirl outside. Because of Madam Tan's fervour for all things British after the Japanese occupation, the Lim girls were sent to an Anglican school for Chinese girls. Here they were taught to play hockey, indoctrinated with stirring choruses of 'Land of Hope and Glory' and given elocution lessons which helped them to efface the local Singlish patois under a borrowed veneer of pseudo-BBC English.

The Chinese principal was an ardent imperialist; one of the successes of the colonising and Christianising missions organised by those formidably intrepid English spinsters who had come out to the colonies and found a purpose in their lives by leading the Girl Guides. Coming from a wealthy Chinese family that traded in silk from Shantung and Thailand, Miss Liu had been sent to England to study English literature at University College, London. During her four years there, she called herself Doris and picked up a BBC accent, which she carefully cultivated and maintained all her life to the point of caricature. The accent and the London university background—not quite Oxbridge but sufficiently impressive in Anglophilic Singapore—could have been her passport to a prominent position in many newly developing Singaporean businesses which sought English-educated graduates to interact with their British trading counterparts. But the Girl Guides exerted a strong influence on Doris Liu long after she left their uniformed ranks, and she had decided to dedicate her life to teaching.

She became the principal of the Anglican Chinese girls' school and did her best to transform it into St Clair's or Malory Towers, with herself as the wise, benevolent head-mistress lending an understanding ear, meting out justice and instilling the proper 'tone' into the school. The pay was meagre but she was independently wealthy. All she required was regular correspondence with Queen Mary's—and, later, Queen Elizabeth's—personal secretary. Each year she informed the Queen, via her assistant, of the various sporting and swimming carnivals, musical evenings and Shakespeare performances with which she tried to uplift the cultural tone of these colonial Chinese girls. The Queen was told that the school had started a Girl Guides' associ-ation and that a team had gone camping along one of the east coast beaches and had learnt to recognise important constellations on this trip. (Years later Pandora tried to point them out to her children but the sky looked different in Sydney; all she could make out was the Southern Cross and Orion's belt.)

The Queen received Christmas and Easter cards, and effusive wishes on her official birthday. In return, Miss Liu received each year an official Christmas card from Buck-ingham Palace and a brief, civilised letter written by the Queen's secretary. She read them out with quivering pride to the assembly of schoolgirls, shuffling and wilting in the equatorial humidity. It was enough to keep the colo-nials happy; enough to keep Pandora an ardent royalist, a Princess Diana watcher, a women's magazine devourer on the side of God, the Queen and Bruce Ruxton until the day she died.

In other ways those Singaporean schoolgirls tried to transform their Chinese beings into English souls. To be English was to live in a world of Enid Blyton books where young middle-class children underwent all manner of predictable adventures, demonstrated their resourcefulness and constantly outwitted dimmer working-class adults. They told each other to 'buck up', exclaimed 'I say, how super!' in Singaporean accents and did their British best to be Bricks. They formed Secret Seven clubs, played at being the Famous Five, and talked about midnight feasts with ginger beer, potted meat, tinned sardines, exotic tinned pineapple and ham sandwiches. Then they went to the school canteen and bought lunches of spicy *laksa* or *mee goreng* and slurped them up with chopsticks and ceramic soup spoons.

But at home Super Bricks were forgotten as Pandora continued to do her best to uphold the tradition of Chinese filial piety. Every evening she ran tepid water into the grey cement tank in the bathroom for her father's bath. When he went into the bathroom to splash water over himself with a blue plastic pot, he threw his divested clothes over the top of the corrugated steel door. She collected the clothes, washed them that night and hung them out to dry on the bamboo poles over the courtyard. After his bath, she fetched his brown plastic slippers and knelt down to fit them to his feet as he peered into the small, green-tinged mirror in the corridor and raked his hair into neat, oiled furrows. Por-Por would have cooked dinner by then and it would be waiting, steaming hot, on the round granite table in the courtyard.

'Papa, come and eat rice,' she chorused dutifully each night, then trailed after him down into the courtyard where all the family stood around the table, waiting for the shopkeeper to take his place on the most comfortable stool—the only one with a padded seat. He cleared his throat and motioned them to be seated.

Her chopsticks squeezing and gripping like tweezers, Mei Ling plucked up the fattest, choicest morsels of meat and the most tender green vegetables for her husband, laying them deferentially in his rice bowl. If he was in a generous mood he would then transfer some chunks of meat from his bowl to one of his sons'. Henly was a favourite, but Winston often stole from Henly when nobody was looking. One of the daughters would keep a watchful eye on her father's teacup to ensure that it was constantly filled to the brim with the cheap jasmine tea they drank. Once the shopkeeper had been served, Winston and Henly were given the other medium-sized chunks of meat, leaving scraps of bones and vegetables for the women to fill their rice bowls and stomachs with.

After dinner the shopkeeper retired upstairs to read the Chinese newspapers by the flickering fluorescent light of the goose-necked desk lamp. He did the day's accounts with deft clicks of the abacus beads. He practised his tai chi, pushing his palms slowly against the weight of the humid air. Then, when he was hungry again, he thrust his head out of the bedroom door to call for his nightly supper of soft-boiled eggs. It was the role of the eldest daughter to prepare the eggs and as each daughter moved out (or ran away with English sailors called Tom), the next in line would take over the nightly duty. Until Percy-phone, that is. She was so abysmally untalented at cooking that the eggs she made were sent back several times because they were undercooked and the albumen was still runny, or overcooked and the yellow yolks had congealed.

Because of the huge wastage that accrued, Pandora took over the nightly preparation of soft-boiled eggs. She took two eggs from the wire basket, plunged them into boiling water and timed them perfectly—just under three minutes. They were then cracked with military precision into an ugly pink-flowered porcelain bowl with a gilt rim. Pandora took great care not to pierce the golden yolks with the jagged edges of the shells. She then dribbled soy sauce over the eggs and dusted the mucilaginous surface with pepper. She set the bowl on a tray and climbed upstairs while the eggs were still hot. She knocked on the bedroom door and was permitted to enter and present them to her father. With both hands. A nightly offering of daughterly love and duty.

Eventually Mei Ling would join the shopkeeper in their bedroom. Percy-phone then did her part of the daughterly chores, bringing up to the bedroom a tray holding two glasses brimming with Guinness. Presented, once again, with both hands. She left them on a table and shuffled out, closing the door softly behind her. Sometimes Winston and Henly joined the two girls upstairs. They listened outside the bedroom door, just to hear the sound of their parents' voices. Not that the shopkeeper talked much. He had nothing to say. He worked hard in his shop all day, sold the same stuff, saw the same people, led the same monotonous life which satisfied him after the upheaval of the war years. Mei Ling was always chattering about her day, gossiping about the neighbours. The children smirked at the sound of light laughter as Mei Ling set out to amuse and seduce her husband. With both hands. Her wifely duty each night. Laughter subsided into tense silence, punctuated by the occasional creaks of the rattan bed, the slap of skin against skin and the sucking noises of sex.

Por-Por sometimes caught them listening by the door and her bony fingers would then shoot out to grip the nearest ear she could find. She'd haul them downstairs, scolding in a furious undertone: 'Stupid kids! Dummies! Stinking arses! Wait till I get the cane and whack you hard. Then you'll know.'

When the Lim children were in their teens, such occasions became rare because Mei Ling had become addicted to mahjong. Singapore began to prosper during the 1950s and the shopkeeper's business thrived. He squirrelled away his money, spending nothing on himself and his children except for new clothes and shoes every Chinese New Year. In the habitual austerity of his life, however, Mei Ling was his one great indulgence. After his authority and right of access to her body had been established in the early days of their marriage, he had gradually relaxed his autocratic treatment of her. They even became friends. As long as sex was readily available, there was little he would not do for her. Once a month he went to the local goldsmith's shop with her and she came back decked with twenty-two carat gold chains, bracelets, charms, bangles and earrings. These she slowly gambled away. Bored with her life, she stimulated herself by mainlining with mahjong.

He was powerless to punish her, for as he grew older and more reclusive, he came to depend heavily on her for human contact. Need made him weak, and this she realised quickly. Sex was a bargaining chip she used to cover her losses at the mahjong table. He mortgaged the tenement, paid her debts, and never questioned her fidelity. Simply didn't want to know anything as long as she came home each night and talked to him before they went to bed and made love.

So absorbed were they in each other, in Mei Ling's need to gamble and his need for her body, that they didn't realise for a long time that Por-Por was ill. Percy-phone and Pandora were the first to notice the deviations in Por-Por's normally rigid and unchanging schedule. During their school holidays, Por-Por often took them with her to the servants' club when she had a day off. These gloomy pigeonholes for domestic servants were squeezed into the ramshackle buildings in Chinatown above shops selling bolts of cheap, brightly patterned cotton cloth, dark green waxed paper umbrellas, gold and silver jewellery, spices, herbs and medicines, padlocks, firecrackers, red lanterns, scrolls of calligraphy, cheap porcelain statues of Chinese gods, joss sticks, wooden clogs, tea, Wrigley's chewing gum, and Chinese comics and pornographic magazines from Hong Kong. The rooms above were partitioned by bead curtains, flimsy bamboo screens, panels of cheap wood, scavenged sheets of corrugated iron, or grubby net curtains. They were rented out by some sort of servants' union to provide leisure space for servants on their free days. Por-Por brought Percy-phone and Pandora there even when they were in their teens because they never went anywhere with their mother and she felt sorry for them. While she and her friends played mahjong, drank tea and gossiped, she left the girls to leaf through magazines with glossy photographs of pouty-lipped Hong Kong film stars with big breasts and hard brown nipples, or to follow the histrionic adventures of Chinese heroines in comic books filched from the shop downstairs.

Then one afternoon, instead of going to the servants' club, Por-Por took them to the Thian Hock Kheng Temple between Amoy and Telok Ayer streets. The girls stood in front of the bright red railings, stared uncertainly at the colourful dragons dancing over the ridge of the green roof, and thought of their religious lessons at school and the missionary's rantings against Buddhism and ancestor worship.

'Why are you standing there? Are you girls stupid or something?' Por-Por demanded. 'Come inside and pray to Ma-Chu-Po or I'll knock your heads together.'

They followed her inside and bought joss sticks and oil from one of the monks.

'*Om nee tor phat*,' he said, inclining his shaved head benevolently. Por-Por beckoned him aside and spoke to him. She pulled some dollar notes out of her small red silk purse and thrust them at him. He nodded again and went to the main altar. He took a smooth cylindrical wooden stick and began to hit the wooden *nah mor* drum with it, chanting and praying to the heartbeat of the tap-tap-tapping stick.

Por-Por made the girls kneel in front of an altar laden with oranges. They offered oil, lit the joss sticks and, clasping the smoking sticks in both hands, began the slow, fluid, seesawing prayer motions of the upper body, bending in supplication and rising again. They knelt there until the prickle of pins and needles in their knees ceased and all feeling in their legs grew numb. Joss stick after joss stick was lit to smoulder away in the small brass urns in front of the altar.

Finally Por-Por allowed them to get up and hobble away painfully.

'What were we praying for, Por-Por?'

For a moment she looked as though she might tell them. Then, 'For prosperity, happiness and longevity, of course, stupid girls. What else does anyone pray for?'

There were no more trips to the servants' club after that visit to the temple. No more surreptitious peeks at girlie magazines. No more awed gasps at the huge melon breasts of glamorous Chinese films stars and resigned glances at the small bumps on their own adolescent chests. No more stories about Chinese princesses dressed as peasants who went on long journeys through the mountainous countryside to escape cruel stepmothers; who fell into the evil hands of lascivious warlords; who were rescued by princes—similarly in disguise—on unspecified pilgrimages. No more stolen packets of foil-wrapped spearmint gum. No more casual gifts of watermelon seeds and roasted peanuts from the other servants in the club.

Por-Por's days off were spent trudging from one temple to another all over the city. When she had exhausted all the Chinese temples, the churches and cathedrals followed: Cathedral of the Good Shepherd, the white wedding cake of St Andrew's Cathedral, even the Armenian church of St Gregory the Illuminator. Often they would not be allowed to enter the Christian cathedrals, so they stood outside and prayed. Por-Por wouldn't set foot inside a mosque or a Hindu temple. She despised the Indians and hated the Malays because, during the Japanese occupation, the Chinese had been singled out for the most brutal treatment while a few Indians and Malays had served in Syonan institutions. The deep distrust she had of them was extended to their gods. In between visits to grand temples and cathedrals—working on the premise that the more opulent the building, the greater the power of the gods therein—they visited Chinese herbalists, acupuncturists and mediums.

Neither Percy-phone nor Pandora knew what was wrong with Por-Por. On each visit, they prayed for prosperity, happiness and longevity. They sighed and groaned with her and enjoyed their religious tour of the city's temples. They never mentioned these trips to their parents because they simply didn't think of it. 'Papa, come and eat rice', 'Mama, here is my school report'—that was the extent of their conversation with their parents. The shopkeeper had always reserved his words for Mei Ling, and she in turn spoke to them through the ubiquitous bamboo cane. Gradually, Percy-phone and Pandora took over all of Por-Por's chores around the house: the cooking, cleaning, scrubbing, scouring, sweeping, laundry and shopping.

One day, fifteen months after the temple visits had started, Por-Por sat listlessly on a wooden stool in a corner of the kitchen with a red plastic bucket beside her, saving her energy to retch and spit, listening to Nat King Cole demanding back those lazy, hazy, crazy days of summer on the transistor radio. Mei Ling stepped into the kitchen and suddenly seemed to notice that Por-Por had shrunk. Folds of slack skin sagged off her bird bones. Her glossy black hair had turned grey and limp. Her eyes looked like those of a dead fish: flat and filmed over, with hummocks of loose flesh underneath. She shambled. She was old. She was sick.

'What's wrong with you? *Ai-yah*, why you didn't say anything?' Mei Ling cried out in an access of acute remorse.

The white doctor was summoned, despite the expense and, after examining Por-Por, he showed the women the baggy flaps of Por-Por's breasts. Percy-phone and Pandora stared in fascinated loathing, mentally comparing the full ripe breasts of film stars with this thing—the mottled flesh, the stiff, starched pad of skin under the shrivelled and weeping left nipple.

'Stop staring, stupid girls,' Por-Por said dully. But mostly she was beyond modesty and beyond caring.

They kept her in the household as long as they could, wheezing, moaning and vomiting on her coconut fibre mattress on the kitchen floor. She became a fixture there, like Kuan Yin, the goddess of mercy, smiling in blooming porcelain health on her altar in the opposite corner. On her better days, Por-Por sat up on her mattress and scolded the girls for cooking and cleaning badly.

'Are you blind, stupid girls? Can't you see the dirt under the sink? Do you want the kitchen to be invaded by rats and cockroaches? Do you want to see me eaten alive, dummies? Useless and good for nothing, you are.'

The Lim family told friends and neighbours rather proudly that Por-Por was dying. The white doctor had even confirmed this. Everyone flocked through the back door into the kitchen to have their curiosity satisfied. Yes, yes, they said, shaking their heads sadly. She was certainly dying, they told each other. Everyone could see that; so sad, you know.

Por-Por loved the melodrama of her death. She was the daughter of schoolteachers in China and had grown up in a Methodist mission school, but she had failed her parents. She had foolishly squandered the opportunity of education, she lamented regularly in later years when she chased the

Lim children around the courtyard with a bamboo cane, forcing them to do their homework. She had grown up among books and knowledge, yet she remained illiterate. Instead she had preferred to enjoy herself with men at the local coffee house until her mother had had enough and kicked her out of the house. Then she was forced to migrate to Singapore and find work as a servant. So let that be a lesson to you all, she scolded the kids.

Por-Por had hoped to marry after she had saved up enough money from working as a servant. She was beautiful and smart, and she ran the household efficiently. But then the war had come along and when she returned from the *Yoshiwara* after the Japanese occupation, she knew that she would never be able to marry. No man would want her anymore. Perhaps it was just as well, she used to say. Years of living with the shopkeeper and his sons had bred in her a deep contempt for men. All her grudging affection was reserved for Pandora first, then Percy-phone. But they were women and they hardly counted. To the shopkeeper, she was invisible; a nonentity even though she kept his house running smoothly and brought up his children. All her life she saw bitterly the insignificance of her existence in the eyes of others, and felt the horrific stain of having been a Japanese *kuniang*; a stain which could never be washed away no matter how often and meticulously she scrubbed herself each day.

Now, dying had made her the undisputed queen of the kitchen and courtyard. Pandora propped her up on bolsters and pillows and Por-Por granted neighbours and friends an audience. She was temporarily revivified by the attention, succoured by sympathy and gratified by the loud lamentations that swelled in the courtyard each day as she rehearsed for a different audience the trials and tribulations of her life: the parents who had loved their Christian god more than their only daughter; the missionaries in China's Fukien province who had abandoned their flock when the communist guerrillas came and stole her grandparents' chests of jade and gold; her stupidity in not studying harder when she'd had the chance; the rich men who'd wanted her when she was young and beautiful, and who would have married her at the snap of her fingers; her devotion to the House of Lim, especially Pandora, her foster daughter; and finally, the long story of her sickness. She honed her tale, adding more tear-jerking pathos to each retelling.

For a brief moment, she made them all feel as though they were players in a larger drama with an obscure but significant meaning, something absent from their pedestrian lives. The process of Por-Por's dying was cathartic for the neighbourhood. People went away shaking their heads sorrowfully, wiping away their tears, feeling glad they had visited, feeling somehow nobler.

Eventually, tired of the incessant flow of people through his backyard, the shopkeeper moved himself to exert his authority, the only memorable instance that decade, by decreeing that Por-Por should go away to the Longevity House on Sago Lane—also known as the Street of the Dead—in Chinatown. The Longevity House was a hospice of sorts where the indigent went to expire. The Lim women's protests could not budge him. He suddenly remembered that he was Head of the House, and all the years of Por-Por's servitude and devotion counted for nothing against the pleasure of exercising power and the prospect of regaining domestic peace and solitude. With that one decision, he repaid the years of subtle insults and

mocking comments heaped on him—and on all men—
by Por-Por.

So she lay exhausted and silenced on an old soiled bed,
covered incongruously by a new patchwork blanket the girls
had sewn her from the scraps of material left over from their
Chinese New Year dresses. They went to visit her twice a
week, bringing her jellies and porridge, and once, when they
had saved up enough money for it, bird's nest soup with
slivers of ginseng root. As she wasted away before their eyes,
she grew hungry for the little details of their lives, especially
Pandora's.

'What's happening, stupid girls?' she asked each Wednesday or Saturday afternoon when Percy-phone and Pandora
visited.

'Pan-Pan has a boyfriend,' Percy-phone volunteered.
'His name is Jonah Tay. He's from a rich Hokkien family
in Malaysia and he's studying dentistry at the university.'

'Why didn't you tell me before, dummy? What does he
look like? Handsome or not? Bring him to see me.'

But Pandora didn't. Subsequent Wednesday and Saturday afternoons came and went without any sign of Jonah
Tay. He was helping his mother at home. He was working
at the dental hospital. He was studying for his exams. He
was never free.

'What's the matter, stupid girl? Are you ashamed of me,
stinking arse? Are you afraid that he won't want to marry
you when he sees me? Have you forgotten who I am? I'm
your foster mother. Who took you in and looked after you
when Madam Tan abandoned you and sent you back?
You could have died in the streets if it hadn't been for me.
Ungrateful girl. You're useless! Don't come and see me anymore until you bring him. I curse your black cunt and all

the children you will push through it. May they give you as much heartache as you've given me.' She turned her face to the wall and shut her eyes.

Pandora went away and cried, resolving to bring Jonah the next time she went to visit Por-Por.

It was so dark and lonely in the Longevity House, Por-Por felt as though she were buried alive in a catacomb. The darkness accrued a suffocating weight. All around her she heard the moans, the wracking coughs, the wheezing gasps from fluid-filled lungs. She wanted to scream, 'Shut up! Shut up!' until she realised that the sounds were squeezing out of her own lungs. The air was foetid with the stench of putrefying flesh, the decay of the body inside and out. Most denizens of the Longevity House were dumped there and forgotten until they died. Then the over-crowded rooms echoed with the loud wails of the bereaved, many of whom were professional mourners paid for by guilty relatives so that the corpse would have a noisy send-off to the underworld. Buddhist monks from a nearby temple sometimes appeared in their grey robes, chanting prayers monotonously and marking time by beating on wooden blocks or cymbals. The keening wail of hired mourners would rise, rise, rise and then crescendo, fading away as the shock of iron nails sliced into the cheap wood of the coffin lid. The box would be hoisted onto wiry shoulders with the ease of familiarity, like crates of ripe, heavy fruit, as the noise and life trickled out of the door-way, leaving the house still.

Por-Por lay dead on her bed. The sheets were soaked with urine. She had shat in her pants from the terror of impending death.

DOGFISH AND
GOOD DEEDS

Pandora met Jonah Tay because Percy-phone—on her way back from work and laden with brown paper parcels of *nasi lemak* for dinner—fell into a swollen stormwater canal during the monsoon season and was washed down towards the estuary of the Singapore River. Terrified and half-drowned by murky water, she was fished out of the drain by a skinny young dental student who'd been cycling over to a classmate's home with biology books in his canvas satchel and a dead dogfish in a plastic bag so that they could dissect it to study for their zoology exam.

He helped her, limping, coughing and lamenting loudly, onto the muddy red bank, steadying her as she slipped and slid in the squelching clay. She thanked him over and over again, gripping his hand hard and pouring out words of gratitude in a Chinese dialect he didn't understand. He looked away and tried to disengage his hand, embarrassed by her effusion of thanks. She stank of river sewage.

Cautiously, he lowered his chin to sniff at his left shoulder. His nostrils quivered in revolted reaction. He stank as well.

'*Ai-yah! Ai-yah!*'

Percy-phone had discovered the loss of her brown paper parcels of food. Her tears of gratitude transformed into terrified wails as she thought of the neatly wrapped packages of fragrant coconut rice, crisply fried anchovies, cucumber chunks, boiled egg slices and chilli *sambal* paste now swirling out to sea. Fish food. There would be no dinner for the Lim family that night because Mei Ling would be out gambling and Por-Por was no longer there to cook. The shopkeeper would be furious.

'Please,' she begged in English when she saw that he didn't understand her dialect. She dropped to her knees, slumped in the mud in an appropriate supplicatory posture, one hand grasping the grey material of Jonah's trousers as if it were the sacred hem of a god's robe. 'Please, you have to come home with me and explain what happened to my father. He will believe you.'

Rising irritation at this pathetic, stinking, sobbing woman warred with reluctant compassion. For a moment he wished that he had just stood on the bank and watched as she was swept out to sea. But pity won, for his heart was soft in those days, as yet unpetrified by the accumulated disappointments of a lifetime. He gently helped Percy-phone to her feet, promising to take her home and ensure her father understood that it wasn't her fault the parcels of *nasi lemak* had floated away.

At this point, her terror banished by a total stranger's casual act of humanity, Percy-phone fell in love with Jonah irrevocably and forever. It was a love that stood staunchly by her brother-in-law even as she wept with Pandora over the daily throb of marital pain years later. A love that heaped no blame or guilt onto him after Pandora's death, even as the other relatives stabbed him with accusing glances to salve their own consciences and quieten the insistent whisperings of impatient neglect in their hearts. A love that helped her to understand dimly the tangle of kindness and cruelty, the tug-of-war between duty and domination, tenderness and tyranny, that made up Jonah Tay. And, in understanding, to forgive.

Now, Jonah picked up his bicycle and mounted it, encouraging Percy-phone to seat herself on the flat wire tray over the back wheel and to hang on to him as he cycled laboriously through the narrow rain-slicked roads to the ramshackle shophouse. He rang the bicycle bell as stray dogs, sniffing the river stench of the sodden couple, loped into the streets and barked loudly. People turned their heads to stare, point and comment openly. This would normally have annoyed him, being the focus of so much embarrassing attention. But he was buoyed by the afterglow of altruism: an English-educated Chinese knight in stinking armour who had rescued a damsel in distress. Percy-phone wrapped her chubby arms around his skinny body (it was like hugging a chopstick, she thought dreamily) and felt the first stirrings of sexual desire as she pressed her suddenly erect nipples to the wet cotton shirt plastered to his back. She thought, with a quick thrill of shame that mottled her face, that only a few layers of material stood between her naked breasts and the flesh of this man who had rescued her twice.

Concentrating intensely on keeping his balance on the bicycle—the heavy, smelly woman behind him was leaning slightly to the right and her arms were clamped around

him like pincers—and sweating profusely with the exertion
of pushing the stiff pedals of the bicycle with his bandy
legs, Jonah failed to notice the woman's arousal through
her thickly padded bra. His jaw was clenched tightly, his
heavy brows dipped into a frowning V as he counted from
one to twenty in all the languages he knew in order of
familiarity: Hokkien, English, Cantonese and Mandarin.

One, two, three, four, five . . .

At each count he pushed a recalcitrant pedal with
quivering calf muscles, resolutely refusing to think of the
distance he had yet to go before he reached her house.

Seventeen, eighteen, nineteen, twenty. Pause. Breathe.
Yat, yee, sahm, sey . . .

Inhale, exhale.

Then finally, the welcome tap on the aching shoulder.
'The blue door over there.'

The counting slowed, the pedals stopped, two pairs of
feet—one in red Bata sandals, the other in mud-caked black
leather shoes—dropped to the dirty paving of the alleyway,
and the bicycle sagged against the cracked wall. Gasping
painfully, Jonah raised a tremulous fist and rapped weakly
on the blue door. His chest was on fire and his muscles
were liquefied. No answer. He rapped again, harder this
time, and he heard the sound of raucous shouts and the
echoing slap of slippers on concrete.

The bolt was slammed back and Pandora wrenched
open the door. She saw a skinny man in grease-smeared
Buddy Holly glasses, a grubby long-sleeved cotton shirt that
had once been white, and muddy grey trousers. Sweat
beaded his forehead and his thin chest pushed in and out
in ragged respiration. The rotten stench of the river rose

from his sodden clothes. She recoiled and was about to order him away when Percy-phone loomed into the light.

'*Ai-yo!* What happened to you?'

Loud, solicitous exclamations were exchanged with equally loud and piteous explanations. Wooden doors along the alleyway began to open as neighbours stuck their heads out in blatant curiosity to see what was going on.

Pandora turned to look at Jonah, ineffable gratitude prompting her to overcome her habitual reserve and shyness with strangers and seize his hand. She shook it warmly. 'Thank you, thank you,' she said, pumping his hand up and down.

He stared into her long-lashed brown eyes, took in her slender figure dressed in a pink *samfoo* and, in that dark and foetid alleyway, on that hot and humid Singaporean evening, Jonah promptly tumbled headlong into love.

'No problem,' he said nonchalantly, trembling limbs and pain-racked chest now forgotten in the glorious glow of first love. Jonah Tay, the hero. 'Don't mention it.'

Introductions were made, thanks offered again, graciously waived again, and Jonah was then ushered into the house, making his first acquaintance with the broken concrete courtyard that was the backdrop to so many momentous occasions in the Lim lives. He was introduced to the shopkeeper and the men fumbled awkwardly as they groped for a dialect both could understand. In the end, Pandora translated for them. With the gravity and authority that came so naturally to him, Jonah explained in concise but respectful terms exactly what had happened to Percy-phone and the brown paper parcels of *nasi lemak*.

'Eh, Percy-phone. You all right or not?' The shopkeeper was moved for the first and only time in his life to express open concern for his third daughter. Then, without waiting for an answer, he clapped Jonah on the shoulder, ignoring the slime on his shirt. He led Jonah away to pour him a glass of Guinness and to press on him six mandarins and a jar of peanut brittle to take home. Mei Ling came in from her mahjong and explanations were repeated. The Lim women hovered over Jonah and fussed flatteringly while the shopkeeper made unexpected conversation. At last, his heart warmed and his ego puffed by the regard of the Lim family, Jonah stood up to leave.

'Come again, ah?' Mei Ling cried hospitably as she showed him out the back door. 'Don't be shy, you know.'

The shopkeeper, too, called out his approving invitation as he shuffled upstairs to his abacus beads and Chinese newspapers while waiting to eat. 'Don't be a stranger. Always welcome.' Then, without a glance at the girls, he ordered: 'Call me when dinner is ready.'

'Thank you, Uncle,' Jonah said. 'Goodbye Auntie, Pandora, Percy-phone.' He paused to give Pandora a meaningful look which she missed because she was busy scrabbling in the kitchen cupboards for leftovers to make some sort of dinner. Goodbyes were returned, hands were waved and then he stood alone in the alley as the door shut and the bolt was slid home. He stared at the blue door for a moment, his heart thrumming with love and desire. Pandora, he thought euphorically. Then he turned to scan the alleyway once, twice, and realised that his bicycle was gone. Stolen.

His satchel lay in the gutter, next to broken Tiger beer bottles and empty Camel cigarette packets. His biology book had been flung down carelessly near the satchel, falling open at elaborately labelled diagrams of the human respiratory system and the gastrointestinal tract. A large shoeprint was visible across the crumpled pages. Belatedly, he remembered that he had been on his way to Beng Chee's home to study for their next day's zoology exam.

First love was temporarily flooded by the swelling tide of panic. He bent down and picked up his biology book, smoothing out the creases and brushing away the dried mud from the pages before putting the book carefully into his satchel. He now remembered that he had left the plastic bag containing the dogfish by the canal bank when he had pulled Percy-phone out of the water. His heart thumped painfully with fear and futile hope as he jogged back to the river, desperately praying, 'Please God, please God, please God.'

But there was to be no second miracle that night. Love had been given and, in the eternal law of compensation, something had to be taken away. He found the plastic bag lying where he had dropped it when he waded into the canal. It had been shredded to ribbons by stray dogs. The remains of the mauled dogfish lay three feet away, a few slimy scraps of flesh clinging loosely to the polished bones that gleamed pearlescent in the bright moonlight.

And, like the terrified woman had a few hours ago, twenty-year-old, five-foot-ten Jonah Tay sank to his knees in the mud and sobbed in the certain knowledge of the brutal beating that would be meted out by his thirty-eight-year-old, four-foot-nine mother when he did not do well in his exam the next day. No Tay children could ever be too old to be beaten into better behaviour by their loving parents. He bore the stripes of his mother's love for weeks after that, a reminder of the costly act of compassion and his fall into love.

PRIVILEGED SON

Jonah Tay had been born in Malaya on the day when, far away in Europe, Hitler's panzer divisions rolled into Poland and mowed down the cavalry that rode out valiantly to meet them, sabres waving uselessly against the crushing tanks.

The Second World War passed by the Tay family, casting barely a ripple in their daily lives. Their village was located in too remote a region of the hills to be of much interest to anyone. Decades later, the few remaining Tay relatives who'd stayed on in the village long after most of the family had left would tell visitors that under the stubby spikes of emerald grass in the football field were buried dozens of skulls and bones of villagers executed by the Japanese and ploughed under. Their ghoulish stories were false, a mishmash of myth and other people's truths. Japanese troops *had* appeared out of the jungle one day. They made a desultory search for radios in houses which barely had working electricity, helped themselves to sacks of rice, a few glittering trinkets and the odd serving girl, then disappeared down the dusty road again.

The real threat to the village would come after the war when, during the 1950s, the British colonial government declared a state of emergency and tried to flush out communist guerrillas from the jungles of Malaya. Jonah would then be taken by his mother to Singapore to be educated in an Anglican school, safely away from the communists. The Tay family feared that they would be targeted by communists because they were a Christian family who not only owned four large rubber estates but who also traded rubber and rice with the British.

My son, the doctor, Madam Tay wished to say nonchalantly to her neighbours when she and Jonah returned to the village for a brief visit. She choked on disappointment and spewed forth bitterness when Jonah failed to get sufficient marks to enrol in medicine and had to settle for dentistry instead. In the early years of his childhood, however, before the rubber market collapsed with the invention of synthetic polymers, Jonah had not been intended for either the medical or dental professions. It was assumed that, as the eldest son, he would inherit and run his father's rubber estates, living a life of indolent luxury, driving around in his silver Mercedes-Benz, wearing a gold Rolex watch on his wrist and carrying a Mont Blanc fountain pen in his checked cotton shirt as he hobnobbed with British businessmen and colonial officers in the larger neighbouring towns. Still, he was not spoilt as a child. Because of the wealth that he would one day inherit, he was made to work with the poorest Indian rubber tappers from the age of eight, so that he would appreciate his good fortune and remain suitably grateful and obedient to his parents.

Some of the rubber estates had been neglected during the war. The trees were over twenty years old and many of the neat paths between them were overgrown with rampant vegetation that supported teeming ecosystems of insects, frogs and snakes. The rubber tappers were afraid to venture into these parts of the plantation. A few years before, a conscientious Indian rubber tapper from a neighbouring smallholding had risen early one morning and entered the dense, ill-kept plantation belonging to a wealthy tea merchant who commuted between the village and Kuala Lumpur. The tapper never came out again. His wife raised the alarm and, the following day, a team of men from the village hacked their way through the undergrowth until they came across a huge, six-foot python lying utterly silent, utterly still in the long grass. Its elastic jaws were massively stretched around the head and upper torso of the dedicated Indian rubber tapper, whom it was very slowly swallowing and digesting.

The Malay peanut seller from the village lifted his *parang* and slashed it in a downward arc, slicing at the python's lower body. The other men hacked at the now vulnerable python—with its jaws and upper digestive tract gloved around the corpse, it was unable to writhe or coil in defence. When it had been dismembered, somebody prised the powerful jaws apart and two men dragged out the limp, crushed-boned body of the Indian rubber tapper. Faces were turned away in horror and an old cotton sarong was quickly used to shroud what was left of the partially digested face. The corpse was carried back to the rubber tapper's wife on a blanket for burial. That night, in different homes across the village, fearful prayers were made to various Christian, Muslim, Chinese and Indian gods to avert the evil that such a monstrous snake must inevitably portend. Meanwhile, the Malay peanut seller, armed once again with his *parang*, snuck back into the plantation, carved up the python's body into manageable chunks, stuffed them into a raffia sack and dragged them home. His wife curried the meat the next day and fed it to their malnourished children.

Since then, none of the rubber tappers who remembered the incident would enter plantations that were too densely overgrown. Mr Tay decided to raze two of his old-growth estates and replant. For days the sky was choked with a blanket of thick grey smoke as fire ripped through the plantation. Finally the burning subsided to a sullen smoulder and was washed away by an afternoon thunderstorm which turned the dark grey ash into sodden slush. The soil was turned over, fertilisers added and rubber seedlings planted in orderly rows. In all this activity, Jonah was made to participate from dawn till dusk. Mr Tay wanted his son to experience first-hand the backbreaking work involved in maintaining a labour-intensive rubber estate. Side by side with the Indian workers, Jonah dug holes for the seedlings and patted soil and manure into place. Sweat ran down his face, flies and mosquitoes circumnavigated his body and dive-bombed his flesh. The skin of his palms hardened and cracked.

Even when the seedlings had been planted and he was back at school, he did not escape the life of the rubber plantation. Each morning, if it had not rained during the previous night, he was woken up at five-thirty and sent to one of the other two Tay rubber plantations in the silver Mercedes-Benz. He joined the two Indian families who lived in wooden huts on the estate next to the rubber smokehouse, hurriedly eating fried bread and scalding his palate with thick black coffee. The tappers then handed him a bucket and they filed into the dark, silent rows of trees.

When dawn broke, thin blades of sunlight slashed down surreally through the canopy of large waxen green leaves. The rubber latex which had collected overnight in the tin cups tied to the trunks of the trees were emptied into the buckets. New lines were cut diagonally into a different section of the trunk and the tin cup retied to the bottom of the sloping lines to catch the fat white beads of latex as they bled out of the trunk and trickled slowly down the grooves. A thin, sticky residue would often be left on the lines of old cuts. It was Jonah's job to collect these rubber tailings, which could still be sold to make inferior quality rubber. When necessary, he lugged around a can of weedkiller and squirted it along the rows of rubber trees to keep the paths free of undergrowth. Later that morning, his young muscles throbbing and his body aching, he would return to the Indians' huts where the silver Mercedes-Benz awaited him. The chauffeur took him back to the house for lunch before he changed into his uniform and went to school in the afternoon.

Jonah loved school. It didn't take long for the Tays to discover their son's intelligence. 'My son got an A plus in spelling,' Madam Tay boasted to her fellow church members on Sunday. 'Top of his class, you know. Very good. Still, I walloped him so he won't become proud and stop studying.' Eventually, she persuaded her husband to let Jonah stop working in the rubber estates so that he could concentrate on his studies. In the afternoons, he came straight home from school and sat in the living room under her watchful eye, doing his homework. He was not allowed to play with or talk to his siblings. Each morning, she woke him at five-thirty so that he could read ahead for the day and surprise his teachers with his advanced knowledge. If he couldn't wake up immediately, she fetched the cane and savagely beat him out of bed.

'On looking back, I see that perhaps she was a stern disciplinarian, but she meant it for the best,' Jonah would tell his children years later in a rare moment of confidence. 'She wanted us to excel in life, to be prosperous, you know, and to have the education that was denied her in our ancestral village in China because she was female. Yes, she beat us often, and hard. You call it child abuse, but she did it out of love.'

Poor Jonah, who oscillated between the blows and briberies of love until he could understand it in no other terms. After dragging him out of bed, his mother fussed over him, bringing him a hot drink of Ovaltine and rice porridge with anchovies, peanuts and pickled vegetables for breakfast. She engaged a tutor to come to the house and give Jonah lessons before he went to school in the afternoons. She loved her son and there was nothing she wouldn't do to help him be the best in his class. And, always terrified of slipping below third position in any of his subjects, he excelled.

Jonah's privileged position as the first son was further strengthened by the prestige of his academic achievements. Madam Tay, lavishing her love and cloying attention on him when she wasn't beating him in order to keep him humble and filial, segregated him from his other siblings. As in many other families, the children had grown up sharing one big bed, but Jonah was untangled from the kicking, struggling limbs of his siblings and given a bed of his own when he excelled at school. For Jonah was reserved the best room in the large house, furnished with a huge antique bed and carved rosewood desk and chair. He was given the first radio in the village, and then the first turntable. At meal times, after Mr Tay had eaten, Madam Tay heaped into Jonah's rice bowl the choicest, juiciest morsels of suckling pig, braised duck, fried fish, barbecued pork, stir-fried liver and roast chicken. He remained stubbornly thin despite her efforts to fatten him. His brothers would then devour whatever pieces of meat remained, while his sisters were left with the gristle, bones and untouched dishes of stir-fried vegetables. Meat was a sign of wealth and privilege, and Jonah paid for his parents' favour with chronic constipation, a condition he was to suffer from all his life.

One day the tea merchant's rubber smokehouse was burnt to the ground. His children's pet Maltese dog had been decapitated and disembowelled, then flung at the iron gates of their large house. The British soldiers searched the jungle for the communist perpetrators and eventually found some suspects. They tried and executed them. Madam Tay tamped down her hysteria and grimly informed her husband that she was taking Jonah to Singapore to enrol him in an English school there. In any case, he would have a better chance of gaining a place at university if he didn't come from an obscure village in Malaya, she reasoned, for by now she had set her heart on Jonah becoming a doctor. Medicine was a safe and prestigious profession, she argued. The world would always need doctors whereas the price of rubber fluctuated wildly. Servants were sent to scour Singapore for a suitable house. Two months later, when Jonah was thirteen, mother and son moved into a small semi-detached house on North Bridge Road.

How she loved him, this clever, handsome son of hers. Sometimes she could hardly bear to have him out of her sight, away from the house. Where are you going, why are you so late, where have you been, what are you doing, what are you thinking? she asked him constantly. She had furnished a room at the back of the house, away from the noisy traffic along the road, so that he could study in luxurious peace, but she was constantly invading his territory. She sat on his bed and sighed loud, gusty, long-suffering sighs while he tried to concentrate on geography. She twisted her translucent green jade bangle, played with her gold rings and demanded to know what he was studying.

'Deserts.'

'Which ones?'

'Sahara, Gobi, Simpson.'

'A fine education this is,' she scoffed. 'What have deserts got to do with Singapore or Malaya? Why don't they teach you something useful in that expensive school we send you to, ah?'

Jonah did not answer her. He concentrated fiercely on the small black and white photographs in his geography textbook and imagined himself tramping across the empty sands, swaddled in layers of clothes that wrapped and flapped around him, cocooning him from the harsh heat of the blinding sun overhead. He stared at the blur of black text on the page until he fancied he could see the atoms skating quickly over the surface of his eyeballs. He felt as though he were shrinking into a small black hole somewhere in the middle of his body. First he felt his spirit being sucked into this pinpoint void, then his muscles, nerves and bones, and then the hole would close up. He would disappear from this world.

One night he felt the soft brush of light black feet on the back of his neck, then the hard blow of a thick mathematics textbook that left his ears ringing and his head reeling in shock and pain.

'*Ai-yah!*' his mother exclaimed as she edged a piece of paper under a squashed black bug and tipped it into the wastebasket. 'How did that cockroach get in here? It was crawling up your neck, you know.'

Madam Tay was bored. She brought Jonah to the tailor to have two new suits of clothes and several shirts made. In the evenings, after he had finished his homework, she made him play card games with her, the way her husband used to. Sometimes she took Jonah to the hawker centres to buy him yellow bean soup, durian, ice *kachang* or curry puffs. She made him accompany her on weekends to the wet and dry markets to shop for food which a servant would then prepare into a meal too sumptuous and excessive for mother and son. She made friends with the neighbours and forced Jonah to go with her when she visited them to drink tea and gossip. She turned him into a surrogate husband and wept tears of rage and betrayal when he slipped down to eleventh in his class.

'You made me go out with you,' he said sullenly. 'I didn't have time to study.'

She brought out the cane—now rarely used—and beat him for his stupidity in the exams and for his insolence in answering back his mother. But she left him alone to study after that, and he learned that he could carve out pockets of solitude if he sat at his desk and opened a textbook. Later, when he was sixteen, he wheedled her into giving him permission to visit his friends on the pretext that they had group assignments to complete. Most of the time she granted her permission, but occasionally she refused out of a capricious need to demonstrate her continuing power and authority over this, her first-born and most beloved son.

Jonah had many acquaintances with whom he studied; other boys from school with whom he sliced and diced rats, frogs, cockroaches and geckos, lifting out their circulatory systems or teasing apart skin, muscle, bone and cartilage to reveal skeletal and exoskeletal structures. But he had no real friends. His mother saw to it that he didn't have the time to develop friendships. Occasionally he resented her for this, but mostly he was resigned. His bony shoulders were bowed by the weight of her terrifying and obsessive love that manifested itself in new clothes he didn't want to wear and a hundred delicacies he had no wish to eat. Loudly she lamented her sacrifice in having given up her friends and other children so that he might have the opportunity to study in peace and safety, away from the dangers and back-wardness of their village. Some evenings, she wept noisily, missing the company of her husband. Then she dried her tears and wrapped her arms like shackles around her son, sighing that she would sacrifice all this and much more for him, just so that he could get a good education and make something of himself. He comforted her, poured her another cup of her favourite Lung Ching tea, and fussed over her. He felt the chains of guilt and obligation, forswore his resentment and vowed to be a more obedient son.

She had his complete love and loyalty until he rescued Percy-phone from the river, abandoned his dogfish, carried her home huffing and puffing, and met Pandora at the back door of the broken cement yard.

'Mama, I've met a girl and I want to go steady with her,' Jonah told Madam Tay a few weeks after he failed to do well in his zoology exam. She hadn't spoken to him for days after the beating, but her favour was grudgingly and gradually restored by his remorseful assiduity as he showered attention on her, accompanied her to visit neighbours he had no wish to see and ventured into shops that held no interest for him. 'I really like her. Her name is Pandora Lim.'

'*Ai-yo*, very painful. Jonah, come and knock the pain out of my back.' Madam Tay lay down on the silk-covered sofa of their North Bridge Road home and closed her eyes. Rapidly she cast her mind back over all the girls she knew from their clan, only to reject them one by one. Too short, too fat, bad physiognomy, unlucky moles, too wild, too delicate, not hard-working enough, too ugly, too pretty, too stupid, not submissive enough, no respect. She would have to see a matchmaker about finding a wife for her son. 'Hey, you useless boy, do I have to ask you twice?'

Obediently her son knelt by the sofa and began pummelling her back viciously with his clenched fists.

'I love you, you know,' Madam Tay said, eyes closed and voice vibrating from the drumming of her son's white-knuckled fists. 'I only want what's best for you.'

LOVE AND VERTIGO

Pandora wanted to fall in love and she wanted it to be forever, just as Nat King Cole had pledged. She knew about love. She saw it enacted on a flickering screen every Saturday afternoon when she went to the movies with Wendy Wu and Percy-phone. They sighed together in the cinema and learned to recognise the postures of love: the kiss of fingertips, the yearning gazes of mascaraed eyes, the twining embrace of waltzing lovers, the thirty-second lip-lock. At the movies, chubby-cheeked Gordon Macrae warbled a warning that people might think he was in love, while Gene Kelly splashed in puddles and tapped his way into various heroines' hearts. MGM made people do ridiculous things for love; they made Clark Gable don his tap shoes and sing about puttin' on the Ritz so that, in another movie, Judy Garland could write him a letter to tell him that he made her love him though she didn't want to do it.

Love was two-dimensional in images and words. With her index finger Pandora traced the language of love over the pages of Renaissance poetry that she was studying for her Higher School Certificate exam. Each afternoon she pored over fragments of sonnets, nutting out their meaning painstakingly for she knew she was not a bright girl. 'Good-for-nothing dummy,' Por-Por used to sneer.

Pandora had not always done well in her studies. The Anglican school that she and her sisters attended had baffled her at first. The English language, the ringing bells, the orderly rows of neat, navy-uniformed girls with their white socks and white sandshoes practising parade drills each morning—all this repelled her initially. She was slow at mental arithmetic and blurted out panicky wrong answers. The Chinese maths teacher, armed with a sharpened HB Staedtler pencil, handed back class tests scored with red crosses and drilled the pencil tip into Pandora's scalp.

'Stupid girl,' she jeered contemptuously. 'What are you doing at school?'

She made Pandora stand on a stool in a corner of the classroom with her skirt pulled up over her head for all the other girls to see and mock her shame. Daphne, who was the head prefect at the time, found out about it and threatened to report the maths teacher to the principal. Pandora was allowed to lower her skirt but she had to sit facing the corner for the whole lesson. She went home that afternoon and told Winston that she'd give him her gold bracelet if he slashed the tyres of Mrs Ng's car. He went further and flung pig shit all over the windscreen. Then he went to a goldsmith and sold the bracelet, caught a bus to Chinatown and bought himself a prostitute for the night. After that, Donald Duck helped her with maths and they struggled through it together.

But it was English that had most terrified Pandora. She stumbled over the unfamiliar words and disturbing syntax. Her tongue tripped over the outlandish consonants, vowels and diphthongs. Each night Daphne impatiently helped her with her homework, correcting her grammar, testing her spelling and teaching her new English words. Each morning, under the petrifying gaze of Miss Liu, the principal and English teacher, English words flew out of her head like the diseased street pigeons Winston tried to catch and sell. Eventually Daphne gave up and Pandora begged Donald Duck to pay for her to have private tuition with Miss Liu.

One afternoon a week Pandora caught a bus to Cairnhill Road and walked up the driveway to the white, low-slung colonial house with its drooping eaves and deep verandahs, where Miss Liu lived with her father. It was such a romantic house, but its grandeur awed Pandora for she had assumed that only the *ang moh*s lived in such mansions. Around the house, towering monstera plants reared alongside hibiscus bushes heavy with passion-red flowers, their large waxen petals framing golden, powdery stamens. Slender coconut trees waved and dipped in the afternoon breeze as, inside the library, Pandora and Miss Liu pored over mouldering leather-bound books of English poetry.

'There was a man who loved me when I was young,' Miss Liu said. 'He picked me up from my hall of residence and carried my books to the British Library. In the rain he unfurled his black umbrella and sheltered me. On winter mornings when the air was clouded with the puff of people breathing, he placed hot bags of chestnuts in my cold gloved hands to warm them. So long ago, it was. And then I lost him in the war.'

'He died?' Pandora asked.

'No. He was with the Allied occupation forces in Germany and he came back to London with a Berlin bride. I should have fallen in love with a Chinese man,' Miss Liu sighed. 'But they never spoke to me the words of love. Now read.'

Pandora picked up the book, ran her finger down the middle crease and read aloud.

> *Why didst thou promise such a beauteous day,*
> *And make me travel forth without my cloak,*
> *To let base clouds o'ertake me in my way,*
> *Hiding thy bravery in their rotten smoke?*

'This is love,' Miss Liu said. 'False promises that we can't help believing.'

On hot afternoons interrupted by rumbling equatorial thunderstorms, she taught Pandora about lovers who were compared to summer days; whose eyes were nothing like the sun. Week after week Pandora learned about the painful wrench of love on the emotions, the swing from exhilaration to depression and back again. Lovers were not blinded by love; rather, they chose not to see, hear or believe— *When my love swears that she is made of truth, I do believe her, though I know she lies . . .* Love was the marriage of true minds, she discovered one week, the one still spot of the universe that did not change. The following week she learned of fickle love and bitter rejection from Thomas Wyatt—*They flee from me, that sometime did me seek*—and from Michael Drayton the impossibility of goodbyes: *Since there's no help, come let us kiss and part.* Each lesson they untangled the knotty syntax and arcane vocabulary until the poet's meaning blazed clear and seared the ideal of romantic love onto a soul that hungered for affection.

What had sixteenth-century English love poetry to do with this unwanted fourth daughter ('Rubbish girl, picked out of the dustbin,' Por-Por used to say) of a reclusive Singaporean shopkeeper and his mahjong-addicted wife? Precious little, her family and friends would sneer. Poetry was for the *ang moh*s. It didn't put food on the table or clothes on the back. It could neither help her to make an auspicious marriage nor to get a decent job as a clerk until she was lucky enough to marry. Poetry was a luxury of the West, not a necessity for the East. But week after week, those poetry lessons changed Pandora. Suddenly, a world of love, a way of loving outside the usual matchmade marriages of compatible astrologies, crude sexual attraction and similar socioeconomic status, was opened up to her. Like Miss Liu, she climbed the dizzy heights of poetry and fell in love with the language of love. Was Miss Liu wrong to have introduced her to such impossible ideals of love that life would always disappoint? The ideals they cherished together—chivalric romance, Petrarchan fidelity, companionate love, the meeting and melding of two minds as well as two bodies—destroyed her marriage in later years. In Pandora's neediness, love, like vertigo, pulled at her and she was at once terrified and tempted by the void below.

Pandora was studying for her HSC exams when she met Jonah Tay. She wanted to go to university to study English, to become a teacher like Miss Liu. Education was a lifeline thrown to her; a ladder she could climb to get out of the vulgar, violent pit-life of the Lims. She watched love and studied it, longed to be in love, but didn't know if she wanted to be in love with Jonah. Didn't know if, in all her plans for escape through education, she could fit him in just yet. She didn't even know if she liked him very much. This thin, earnest Chinese man in black Buddy Holly glasses scarcely matched her vision of romantic heroes fashioned by characters as disparate as Mr Darcy, Rob Roy, the Scarlet Pimpernel, Humphrey Bogart and Cary Grant. But they were forever fixed on the screen, contained within a page.

Jonah Tay, on the other hand, was always hanging around the house, bringing gifts of food. Never flowers though. Each afternoon she heard the bolt on the back door pulled back and her name shouted out. From her book-laden desk in front of the bedroom window, she peered down into the courtyard to see Jonah below, waving parcels of fried noodles up at her. Her parents welcomed him and treated him as one of the family; the favourite son, in fact. For his sake they stumbled over simple Singlish phrases while he began to learn their dialect. When words failed, they beamed and nodded at each other.

At first Pandora thought that Percy-phone liked Jonah, but Percy-phone denied this vigorously. Jonah is interested in you, Percy-phone told her, and began to praise his many qualities to her imperceptive younger sister. Pandora felt that the romantic narrative was all wrong. Percy-phone was the one who had been rescued, and by all the conventions of chivalric romance, Jonah should have fallen in love with her.

'*Hi-yah*, this is real life, not storybooks,' Percy-phone said impatiently. 'You want to live in one of your nineteenth-century novels or what?'

Eventually she gave in to the strong urgings of her parents and siblings (even Winston liked him because Jonah was generous with both food and finance) and started going out with Jonah. His real attraction, in her eyes, was that he took her out of the crowded, noisy tenement where they were constantly breathing each other's stale air and invading each other's space. He was English-educated, like herself, and because of their different dialects they conversed in the local Singlish patois. He urged her to study and helped her with her science and maths. He seemed proud of her academic achievements. Like Miss Liu's young English lover, he carried her books to the library and bought her plastic bags of coconut juice to sip throughout the sweaty afternoons.

The early days of their courtship were overshadowed by the death of Por-Por and the subsequent rites of mourning that the shopkeeper, burdened with guilt and fear of the puissant dead, insisted on carrying out. Mourners had to be organised and an elaborate feast prepared for the return of Por-Por's spirit on the seventh day after her death. Pandora oversaw the entire operation and was stunned at the end of it all to find that Por-Por had left her enough money to put her through a year of university.

That night, after Por-Por's will had been disclosed, her hand shook with nervousness as she ate the four eggs that she had first under- then overcooked. Finally, she made the perfect pair of soft-boiled eggs. Peppered and soy-sauced, she brought them up to her father in the pink-flowered porcelain bowl. She bent towards him and served it to him with both hands.

'Papa, eat,' she said submissively.

He grunted, eyes not lifting from the newspaper page, accepted the eggs and waved her away. She retreated to the doorway and stood in the shadows, watching silently as he gulped the eggs and washed them down with black tea. He wiped his mouth with the back of his hand, then wiped his hand on the white singlet top which he had tucked into his loose drawstring pyjama trousers. When she made a slight movement, he looked up, startled to find her still there.

'What is it?' He was vaguely annoyed at having his concentration interrupted, at his daughter's unexpected demand for his attention. She came and stood before him, eyes cast down, and told him that she wished to go to university to study for an arts degree. She wanted to become a teacher like Miss Liu. She asked for his permission.

'The money?' he demanded.

'Por-Por left me some and Eldest Brother has promised to help me out.'

'God knows the family could use some help,' he complained. She said nothing and he contemplated her bowed head. 'What will you do after university? A degree is no use to a woman. Are you going to marry Jonah Tay?'

She felt the old familiar vise clamping shut around her. To escape one trap you had to put your foot into another.

'Yes, Papa.'

'All right, then. Do what you like. It's got nothing to do with me.' He picked up the newspaper and raised it like a barrier between himself and his daughter. 'Take my bowl to the kitchen. I've finished.'

'Yes, Papa. Thank you.' She took his empty bowl and left him alone with the Chinese news. Would his permission and approval always be tossed to her with such apathy? And when would she herself cease to care? Yes, Papa. Thank you, Papa. Thank you for caring for me so little, for thinking of me so little, that what I want and what I do is a matter of complete indifference to you as long as you're not inconvenienced by any responsibility for me. She resolved to study harder than ever so that she could get out of the tenement house.

A week before her HSC exams she sat perspiring at the tiny table upstairs in the girls' bedroom, in front of the metal grille window overlooking the colourful wrinkled shirts, skirts and trousers flapping away on the bamboo poles. The window was open because of the unbearable humidity. Teochew opera whined from the neighbour's portable radio. In the courtyard below, Winston practised his karate with screaming exhalations of 'hah!' as he massacred rickety chairs and chopped planks of wood in half. Downstairs, a gaggle of noisy women gossiped and laughed raucously, calling for more tea and steamed rice buns over the tapping of mahjong tiles. Mei Ling was having another mahjong party and two tables had been laid out in the room behind the shop. The women had come over just after lunch and would not leave until they ran out of money or their husbands came to drag them home to cook dinner.

Frustrated, Pandora slammed the thin bedroom door bad-temperedly, but the cacophony leaked through the cracks and pounded her brain. Mei Ling came upstairs to admonish her for slamming the door and making such a lot of noise.

'I'm not the one making all the noise. I'm trying to study,' Pandora cried out in irritation. She could feel tears of self-pity gathering at the edges of her eyes, threatening to spill over. 'Why must you have all the aunties over when I'm studying for my HSC? Don't you know how important this is to me? Can't you go over to Auntie Jin's for a couple of days until my exams are over?'

'Don't be so rude to your mother. Be grateful that I don't call you to pour tea for your aunties. What kind of daughter is this, always talking back to her own mother, ah? Good-for-nothing girl.'

Pandora sat helplessly in the sauna of a room and felt dark bitterness seeping into her bones, filling her with violence towards her mother and the aunties who came to play mahjong; the same aunties who would leave a few hundred dollars richer that night with the winnings from the gold earrings Mei Ling had pawned that morning. Study was impossible. The aunties' screams of cackling laughter echoed up the stairwell over the clicking and clacking of the mahjong tiles. Pandora bowed her head and wept in panicky frustration as concentration fled once more.

There was a knock on the door. Hurriedly she dried her eyes.

'Yes? What is it?' she called out.

The door opened and Jonah Tay came in.

'Hi. I thought you might want to come to the university library with me to study. Your exams are next week, you know,' he said, indulging his penchant for stating the obvious—a habit that would irritate her no end in the years to come. 'I've asked permission from your parents and it's all right with them. I said I'd bring you home on the bus safely so there's no need for them to worry. You need to study, you know.'

Pandora squeezed her eyes shut. 'Jonah, at this moment I could really love you.'

He beamed happily. 'Hey, I love you too,' he said. Already, he heard only what he wanted to hear from her.

Much later, when she got engaged to Jonah, it crossed her mind that she might have made a mistake. But it was too late, she had succumbed to vertigo, taken the fall and must live with the consequences. By then, her HSC was over and she was learning that one couldn't—and shouldn't—expect an incarnation of Renaissance courtly love in 1960s Singapore anymore than one could expect a Chinese shop-keeper father to take an interest in his fourth daughter, let alone love her.

THE GENESIS OF
CHRONIC CONSTIPATION

Madam Tay ambushed the lovers and hijacked the wedding. She had done her best to prevent it, to steer Jonah's interest in some other direction suggested by the matchmaker she had consulted back in the village. A number of wealthy, cultured, beautiful Singaporean and Malaysian Chinese girls had been brought to the North Bridge Road house and displayed like heifers, but Jonah wasn't interested.

To her bewildered annoyance, he was bewitched by the shopkeeper's daughter. He was entranced by Pandora's rowdy family, mistaking the volume of noise for the depth of familial affection. Denied contact with his own family, he basked in his acceptance by hers. He loved the laughter, the silliness, the anecdotes of daily life Pandora shared with Daphne and Percy-phone. He was amused by the rough teasing and swaggering machismo of Winston and Henly. He enjoyed the volubility of Mei Ling and the gossip of the mahjong aunties. He wanted to share all that with Pandora. Compliant to his mother's wishes all his life, he was suddenly intransigent on the choice of his bride. Scoldings, tears, cajolings, disavowal of family ties and threats of suicide made no difference. He was firm on this point. He would marry Pandora.

They got engaged in her second year of university. She was reading Walt Whitman and discovering her own sensuality. He came to find her in the library one evening, long after everyone else had returned to their homes or colleges for dinner. She looked up at him, her eyes dazed and unfocused, With the quick proprietary stab of a lover's pity, he scolded her gently for working too hard and forgetting to eat.

'Let's go. I'll buy you some *Hokkien mee*. You're not doing yourself any good by starving your brain of protein, you know. And you need carbohydrates to give you energy.' He pulled her up and peremptorily swept her books into her bag, hefting the strap over his shoulder, already taking charge of her life. He sat her on the back of his new bicycle and pedalled to the nearest hawker centre. He found a free table under the swinging coloured lanterns and made her sit down on one of the plastic stools while he went to order a plate of steaming Hokkien egg noodles fried in thick black soy sauce with salted fish, sliced pork, prawns and vegetable pieces. He brought it back to the table, together with two glasses of the black grass jelly drink that he didn't know she disliked intensely because he'd never asked.

'Come on. Eat,' he bullied her kindly. 'You need to build up your strength to study for the exams, you know.'

She felt light-headed and exhilarated, scarcely in need of food. Still, obediently she ate, paying scant attention to him as he talked about a difficult root canal case that he had seen at the dental hospital that day, about the coming exams, about his mother's poor health—about the minutiae of their everyday lives that had long ago ceased to interest her with its repetitive banality. She looked up at the gaily bobbing lanterns and beyond them to the star-dusted skies.

She walks in beauty, like the night
Of cloudless climes and starry skies;
And all that's best of dark and bright
Meet in her aspect and her eyes . . .

Pandora looked at Jonah, utterly stunned that he had just voiced the fragment floating in her mind. For a moment, she felt connected to him; a sticky web spun between her heart and his. Why, he does understand after all, she thought, and love devastated her. She looked down at her half-eaten plate of *Hokkien mee* and felt overwhelming gratitude for his constant solicitude. And she loved him because suddenly, in that particular moment, she realised that he really loved her; that finally, in her life, a man had chosen her, wanted her, adored her, needed her. She closed her eyes and hugged the moment to herself. She let go and flailed helplessly in the awed revelation of their love for each other.

'Jonah,' she said as she leant over and kissed him on the lips impulsively—the first time she had ever done so. 'I love you.'

He flushed brightly and gripped her hands. 'I love you too, Pan. Let's get married.'

'All right,' she said, drunk with love and lyricism. And then she heard it again.

And on that cheek, and o'er that brow,
So soft, so calm, yet eloquent,
The smiles that win, the tints that glow,

But tell of days in goodness spent,
A mind at peace with all below,
A heart whose love is innocent!

Slowly, Pandora turned around. A young Eurasian man with light brown hair and a ragged beard was perched on a stool directly behind her, a giggling Chinese girl squirming on his lap. She recognised him from her English literature classes. He had open a book of Byron's poetry and was reading it aloud to the woman, feeding her spoonfuls of sweet yam soup in between stanzas.

The spider web snapped. It hadn't been Jonah after all. The Eurasian man looked up and stared into her eyes. A perfect split second pregnant with impossible possibilities, swiftly followed by the intrusion of reality.

'Pan, you're not eating. What's the matter? Aren't you well?' Jonah demanded.

Pandora turned her back on the Eurasian man and gave Jonah her full attention. She loved him, yes she did. She loved his many kindnesses to her family, his patience with Daphne and Percy-phone, his gentleness towards her mother. She loved his generosity, the way he was always bringing bags of *tah mee* for her mother, brown paper packets of *char kway teow* for her father; the way he would go hunting for the biggest, ripest durians during durian season and lug the smelly, thorny fruit to her house for Winston and Henly. She loved the way he never opposed her dream to be an English teacher like Miss Liu. She had made the right choice; she was sure of it. She had made the only choice she could make after 'going steady' with him for nearly three years. Unless she wanted to gain a reputation like her eldest sister Lida Lim. She was sure of that too.

Once the engagement was announced, Madam Tay concentrated all her efforts on salvaging this disastrous turn of
events. She summoned Pandora to her house and, for her
son's sake, instructed his future bride on how she was
to behave and what would be expected from her. At the
same time she made it clear that, in her opinion, Pandora
was sly and opportunistic, taking advantage of Jonah's infatuation to connect herself to a wealthy family with a silver
Mercedes, four rubber estates, and as many business interests
in Malaysia. Then she proceeded to plan her son's wedding
without consulting the Lim family. They were surprised
and mildly insulted, then resigned and indifferent.

'Be a good wife to Jonah and always obey your mother-
in-law. Then we will never be ashamed of you,' Mei Ling
told her daughter before she went back to her gambling.
The shopkeeper appreciated the fact that the meticulous
routine of his life had not been disrupted by wedding
preparations. His only irritation was that Percy-phone, on
whom the nightly daughter's duty now fell, still could not
cook soft-boiled eggs properly.

Strangely enough, it was Wendy Wu—the Lims continued to call her either that or Miss Telecom to the end of
her life—who objected to Pandora's marriage. Wendy Wu
fell in love with Pandora after her marriage to Donald
Duck. She came round to the shophouse at least once a
week to visit, even when she was pregnant, and she often
took Pandora and Percy-phone shopping at the more
expensive department stores. She invited them over to her
house, taught them how to put on makeup and bought
them MaidenForm bras to shape and lift their small
breasts. She'd been the one to introduce Pandora to her
passion for Hollywood films. They nourished their love

affair with MGM musicals by swapping fan magazines. She persuaded Donald Duck to help put Pandora through university, and she was deeply upset that Pandora was getting married.

'I'm telling you, you're throwing away your life, *lah*,' she told Pandora. 'Look at you, so pretty, got so much brains and so many opportunities. Not a dummy like me. What for you want to get married to that skinny dentist, ah?'

She had met Jonah and Madam Tay, and she realised that the son bent only to the mother. Towards all others he displayed, kindly but firmly, the conviction that his was the right way, the only way. Though he claimed to hate it, he had spent too long being the centre of Madam Tan's attention and devotion; he would demand the same from his wife. Wendy Wu was the only one who recognised that Pandora would be too weak to stand up to Jonah. She was also the only one who guessed that, at times, Pandora privately thought she was making a mistake but didn't dare to break off the engagement.

After a while she gave up trying to dissuade Pandora from getting married and turned her efforts to counter-acting the effects of Madam Tay. She decided that Pandora should at least have a bit of fun before she was sequestered in marriage. Under the vague pretence of preparing for the wedding, she whisked Pandora away from Jonah's side. She taught Pandora how to dance and flirt a little, then she took her to various tea dances and nightclubs. They cha-cha'ed and rumba'ed and giggled and felt like both sisters and best friends.

'Make him wash your panties,' Wendy Wu advised Pandora as they listened to the latest Platters album in the Cathay music store. 'That's how I trained Donald to mind me, you know. I told him that if he wants to keep messing up my silk panties with sex, then he has to hand-wash them for me.'

But they both knew that Pandora wouldn't do that. Pandora had spent her life in service to the Lims. She was the one who hand-washed soiled underwear and scrubbed out toilets. She would continue to do so in the Tay household after her marriage.

In the end the wedding was a combination of two bizarre ceremonies—one Chinese and one Christian— followed by an enormous banquet. On the night before the wedding, Madam Tan came over to the Lim's house to act as the 'good fortune' woman, combing prosperity, longevity and happiness into Jonah and Pandora's hair. Pandora, fresh from her bath, sat by the window and stared at the moon.

'You're a good girl, Pandora,' Madam Tan said as she ran a red comb through her niece's long wet hair four times. 'Good girls get good husbands. I told you that a long time ago.'

The wedding day began early the next morning, when Jonah—dressed formally in a grey wedding suit—and his best-friend Beng Chee arrived outside the Lims' terrace and began the traditional bride-bargaining process.

'You pay how much for Pandora?' Winston hollered jovially through the padlocked grille bars of the shop. 'One million dollars or what?'

'You got to be joking,' Beng Chee exclaimed. 'Where anybody got that much money?'

'Make him do something to show how much he loves Pan-Pan then,' Daphne said, enjoying the game. 'And maybe we lower the price. Make him eat ten really hot chilli *puddies* or do push-ups in the street to show how strong he is. Or make him sing a song. Blueberry Hill.'

So poor Jonah stood out on the street, slowly simmering away in his wedding suit, wailing out how he'd found his thrill on Blueberry Hill. Eventually he satisfied Winston and Daphne's desire for sophomoric pranks and was allowed inside the terrace. He distributed the lucky red envelopes, stuffed generously with wads of money, to the Lim siblings, then Pandora came out and they both served tea to the proudly smiling shopkeeper. Finally, Jonah picked up Pandora, frothing away in white tulle, and staggered out of the house with her in his arms. She flung out her left arm to scatter rice and nearly bashed Winston in the nose before Jonah managed to dump her inside Beng Chee's car. He then hurried to his own car and drove to St Andrew's Cathedral, where the Christian marriage ceremony would take place.

Pandora's wedding banquet would remain a blur in her memory, a confused collage of buzzing conversation, dress changes (she had to change three times from white wedding gown, to red Chinese wedding garments, to formal evening dress), endless dishes of food, blinding flashbulbs going off and drunken shouts of '*Yum Sing!*' as guests toasted their health and happiness. The one thing she remembered quite clearly was the sight of Winston, chopsticks stuck up his nostrils, belching with laughter as he undid his belt to drop his trousers. She closed her eyes, gripped Jonah's hand tightly and turned away to smile at her new Tay family.

Many of the Tay relatives had come down to Singapore from Malaysia for the wedding, and there was not enough room in the North Bridge Road house to accommodate them all. Bedrooms had to be shared. Madam Tay and her husband squeezed into the newlyweds' bedroom, together with two of Jonah's sisters. Madam Tay looked at the bed, fitted with new sheets of lucky red.

'*Ai-yah*, we better sleep on the floor,' she told Mr Tay. 'My bones are not troubling me tonight.'

'Don't talk nonsense, Mama,' Jonah said tiredly. 'You've got arthritis. You and Papa sleep on the bed. Pan and I will sleep with the girls on the floor.'

'But the lucky sheets,' one of his sisters objected.

'Never mind, *lah*. We don't believe in that sort of thing anyway,' Jonah said.

'Jo, got room for you on the bed,' Madam Tay said. She huddled up to her husband and patted the narrow space beside her. 'Come.'

'No, *lah*,' Jonah said uneasily, looking at his wife.

'Come on, Jo,' Mr Tay said, rolling over and closing his eyes. 'We're all tired. Don't make a fuss. Just do as your mother says.'

And so it happened that on their wedding night, Jonah slept in the marital bed with his parents while his wife, stuffed with supper and suffering from the first pangs of dyspepsia and constipation that, like her husband, would plague her all her life, slept on a mattress on the floor between two of his sisters. In the dark, she listened to soft snores and gnawed on her knuckle to hold back the groans of stomach pain.

BOUNDARIES AND
BLACK HOLES

In her first year of marriage Pandora became pregnant accidentally and was forced to drop out of her final year of arts at university. They were staying with Madam Tay at the time, three individuals packed into unbearable proximity in the small semi-detached house on North Bridge Road. Pandora discovered that by accepting Jonah's proposal, she had also married his mother. Madam Tay fell easily into the time-honoured Chinese tradition of bullying her daughter-in-law.

Jonah was the alpha and omega of Madam Tay's life; the beginning and the end. On the finely balanced scale of her calculating affection, her love for stick-like Jonah preponderated over the combined weight of wifely duty to her husband and maternal feeling towards her six other children. This was the one that mattered. She might have to share him with his wife (not of her choice), but she would ensure that she had the largest share, the greatest dividend of his attention.

'*Ai-yah*, where have you been? Why you so late?' she demanded when they stepped in the door just after seven o'clock one evening. She got up from the rattan chair, fanning herself and flapping the pea-green patterned top of her *samfoo* to whisk the heavy air around her flabby body. 'I ordered Ah Lan to have dinner on the table by six-thirty and now it's all cold. After all the trouble she took to cook your favourite dishes too, you know.'

On the round glass lazy Susan were arrayed a number of roasted pork dishes, glass vermicelli fried with lotus flowers and black clouds' ears, a glistening, russet roast duck, and a tureen of turtle claw soup. Bowls of now-cooled rice squatted accusingly at each elaborately set place, red lacquered chopsticks laid neatly beside them.

'Be a good wife to Jonah and always obey your mother-in-law. Then we will never have any reason to be ashamed of you,' Mei Ling had told her. The one piece of advice passed on from mother to daughter in a lifetime together. So Pandora murmured soft apologies to Madam Tay and sat down at the table, waiting for her husband to help himself to the meal. Then it was her mother-in-law's turn. Sighing gustily in unspoken and implacable grievance, Madam Tay picked out the smallest, stringiest pieces of pork and scraps of duck where the crisp skin had torn away.

'*Ai-yah*,' she sighed again, drawing their attention to her meagre portion of food.

'Ah Bu, please let me help you to some more food,' Pandora said. 'You shouldn't be taking those pieces. They're not good enough for you.'

'Never mind about me,' the poor martyr said. 'As long as you two eat well, that's all that matters. I already took out the pieces. Can't put them back on the plate now.'

'Let me have them, Ah Bu.' And the dutiful daughter-in-law transferred the old woman's bony bits and gristly pieces to her own rice bowl. She plucked up succulent pieces of meat and heaped them into her mother-in-law's bowl, taking care to help her to most of the clouds' ears as well; she knew the old woman loved them.

'*Ai-yah*. No need, no need,' Madam Tay protested. 'You young people should eat these good pieces, you know. I'm just a nobody in my own house now. You come and go as you like and I'm all alone in the house all the time. I may as well not exist. I'm not wanted here. Maybe I should just leave the house and live out my last days in the Longevity House. *Ai-yah*.'

She sighed again and pushed her gold-framed glasses above the ridge of her nose to dab at her eyes with her mothball scented handkerchief.

Pandora ignored her words even as Jonah clucked soothingly to assure his mother that she was indeed a necessary part of their lives. She shouldn't mention this nonsense about the Longevity House, not when she had a perfectly good home in Singapore and another mansion back in their Malaysian village. And look how blessed she was to have lots of children who would all welcome her to stay with them. She had good sons and daughters who knew their duty to their mother. He ended by promising her he would be home on time for dinner the following night.

'Ah Bu, *chiak*,' Pandora said. Mother, eat. Eat and shut the hell up.

Soothed and petted, the mother-in-law picked up her chopsticks and began shovelling rice and roast pork into her mouth. Only then did Pandora pick up her own chopsticks and choke down the fat, gristly portions left for her. She felt her bowels constrict. It wasn't just the diet but the proximity of her mother-in-law. So much needed to be tamped down, sucked in and kept inside in front of the old woman, and her presence pervaded the house always. Pandora sat on the toilet and kept her ears pricked for the sound of her mother-in-law climbing and sighing her way upstairs to use the toilet, so that she could make quick preparations to flush the loo and vacate the room.

In her mother-in-law's house she was less than a guest and more than a servant. She lived in perpetual anxiety. She became clumsy overnight. She dropped vases which were then claimed to be irreplaceable heirlooms. She had to borrow money from Donald Duck to compensate Madam Tay for the loss. Washing the dishes one night, she broke a rice bowl and was accused of spoiling a special dinner set that had been given to Madam Tay by a close friend many Chinese New Years ago. She listened to Aretha Franklin on the radio one afternoon and woke Madam Tay up from her daily nap. She spilt some water and, before she could get a rag to mop up the liquid, Madam Tay nearly slipped in the puddle and fell. The woman sank onto her mustard-coloured velveteen sofa and patted her right hand to her fast-beating heart, moaning and scolding her daughter-in-law for her clumsiness.

'Are you trying to kill an old woman?' she demanded.

The bathroom upstairs had no lock on the door, although that was not usually a problem as the sound of splashing water alerted those out in the hallway that the bathroom was being used. Pandora was taking a bath one day and started in shock when her mother-in-law pushed open the door and flicked a scornful glance at her daugher-in-law's wet, naked body.

'Oh. You're here,' she said unnecessarily. 'I thought there was no-one here. I wanted to have a bath. *Ai-yah.*'

She walked away and left the door ajar.

There was neither the time nor place for Pandora to study. Because they had to be back by six-thirty for dinner, she couldn't stay late at the university. She wanted to do ordinary things with her husband, but the only time they had together was on the bus ride to and from the university. Madam Tay had bought a television set and she insisted that the two of them join her after dinner to watch the news and the various black and white programs about idyllic American family life. Later in the evenings, Pandora had to massage the aches and pains out of Madam Tay's back like a dutiful daughter-in-law, then rub Tiger Balm over the woman's flabby, liver-spotted flesh until her palms stung and burnt. She exchanged the soft-boiled egg making routine for brewing the various sweet bean soups that Madam Tay enjoyed for supper.

'You're a good girl, a good daughter,' Madam Tay said unexpectedly at dinner one night. She took from her pocket a small red silk purse and handed it to Pandora. 'Here. I brought this out of my bank box for you today.'

'Open it,' Jonah told his wife excitedly. Obediently, she opened it and lifted out a thick, twenty-four carat gold link chain with a round jade pendant. Its bright yellowness was almost obscene.

'Cost a lot of money, you know,' Madam Tay told her.

'*Wah!*' Jonah exclaimed. 'Mother is so good to you, Pan.'

'Ah Bu, thank you. You shouldn't have. I don't deserve to have this, but thank you very much.' Passively she let Jonah fasten the gold chain around her neck.

Pandora lost her time, her space, her privacy and her boundaries. She wanted intimacy with Jonah, for she still believed that she loved him. But she also wanted support from him against the subtle slights of his mother, the barbed insults that he couldn't or didn't want to see. And when that wasn't forthcoming, she wanted space to collect herself, to remember who she was. But personal boundaries were unheard of in that household where lives, personalities, tempers, needs and desires crisscrossed the bodily envelopes of individuals and blurred their solidity. Daughter-in-law kneaded, pounded and tenderised mother-in-law's back and rubbed liniment into it. Mother-in-law patted the stomach of daughter-in-law to see if the latter was pregnant. Hands touched, skins rubbed, bodies invaded personal spaces and overlapped individual lives.

Each night she let Jonah into her body, and each night she felt her sense of self slipping away little by little. He was a tender and passionate lover, but she most resented him when he pleasured her to the point of orgasm. In her new life where nothing outside herself was in her control, she could not forgive him for his erotic invasion of her body, for his breath-stealing, pulse-quickening lovemaking that wrested away from her what little control she had over her emotions and sensory responses. Even this belongs to me, he seemed to be saying as he ran his hands over her breasts and down to her thighs, as he slipped his fingers between her legs and caressed her. Pleasure is mine to give. Eventually she willed herself to lie still and unresponsive, watching impassively from deep inside herself as he redoubled his efforts to stimulate and arouse her desire.

Jonah recognised the familiar low frequency of panic. Pandora was slipping away from him. He loved her so much but he began to fear that he would never understand her or share real intimacy with her. She bewildered him. He thought his loneliness and isolation had ended forever when he married this woman. How he adored her. But something had short-circuited somewhere. Where was the sense of family he should have gained from marriage? He couldn't reach her; they didn't connect. He got the disconcerting impression, when he was talking to her— or talking at her, more and more—that she watched him from the other side of a red wooden bridge. He stepped onto the bridge and ran towards her, but the span lengthened as he ran. His feet pounded the wooden slats and more appeared in front of him, like barrelling train tracks, even as his long strides swallowed the distance and his thin chest heaved with used-up breath.

'Talk to me,' he cried in frustration. Then he buried his face between her naked breasts and wept from self-pity because he had not escaped the loneliness that lodged in his belly like a black hole.

'What do you want me to say?' she asked obediently, automatically caressing his hair with her fingers. 'Tell me what you want to hear.'

She closed her eyes and imagined that the flicks of rough hair between her fingers were the coarse feathers of an owl that would spread his wings and fly off, leaving her on a deep dark forest floor with bloody claw rakings on her white breasts. In her mind she stared at the silver plate of a moon swinging between the tree branches until her pupils shrank into the white moon globes of her eyeballs. She felt the detritus of damp undergrowth and rotting vegetation under her, the soft-legged scurry of insects exploring the slim expanse of her naked body, claiming it as their own. Her fingernails grew longer and clawed into the earth. She rooted herself blindly, blood and bone freezing, then pulping until she became a giant white mushroom, vegetative, still, silent, solitary in the forest dark.

He cupped his hand under her chin and twisted her face towards him. He searched her eyes for truth, but he could not see past the black opacity that kept her in shadow.

'Do you love me?' he asked.

'Yes,' she said, because she did. But not in the way that she had once thought she would love; not in the way that she once thought she would herself be loved in return.

Why did he invest 'love' with such significance, such life-changing power? Do you love me, he demanded, and because he asked—because she didn't volunteer it—he would never know. Ask, and you shall never receive. Seek, and you will never find what you are looking for. Knock and push the door open, and you run down the empty, echoing corridors chasing the hem of a skirt that slips up the stairs, the smooth mound of a shoulder that disappears around the corner, the pale crescent of a half-turned face that melts from the window and merges into the night. Do you love me? Yes, she replies. Can he believe her 'yes'? Has he pumped it out of her with the bellows of his need? Does she give him the answer he wants to hear out of fear or duty or even pity? Yes, she replies, but still he doubts her love. Do you love me, he asks over and over again. Each time she answers yes, each time he's back right where he started. He runs onto the bridge and the span yawns wider before his pounding feet. Love: the miraculous medicine for all his ills, for his eternal isolation. Love that will bind a man and woman together, that will banish loneliness forever. Love is the answer, but the question is wrong. If she loves him, why can he not feel loved?

He tries to connect with her through the only tangible thing left to him: her body. Each night he strokes, fondles and caresses her, willing, forcing her flesh to feel the agony of sexual pleasure, to welcome his intrusive thrusts. Did you like that? he asks desperately, panting and heaving with the night's heptathlon effort. Yes, she answers patiently. She sighs, and it could be from sexual repletion or utter weariness. You liked it? he checks again, as if truth were to be found in repetition. Yes. And he must believe her, even though he's ceasing to trust her. *When my love swears that she is made of truth, I do believe her, though I know she lies.* A woman's orgasm, like love, must surely crumble the bridge and close the chasm between them. If he cannot give her even this, then what can he offer her? So he strokes, fondles and caresses her more desperately, more urgently each night.

When he enters her, he spurts the black hole that is inside him up her body. She feels it growing within her now, that black forest where she metamorphoses into a white mushroom. Pluck me, eat me, die. That is where she hides as he manipulates her body. She tells him over and over that she loves him. The more she tells him, the less certain she is that she does. Not because he is unlovable, but because she no longer knows what love is.

As he suckles her breast and his fingers scrabble over her body like insects, she ticks off in her mind all the things she knows: hunger, pain, malice, betrayal, hurt, anger, hate. The sharp slap of a father's rejection. The accidental glance of a mother's indifferent eye. But also affection, laughter and the tears of hilarity. The texture of fine Chinese silk, the suppleness of soft leather, the picture of a snow-capped mountain in New Zealand which she secretly tore out of a geography book at school, the harsh hooter of the Malay peddler selling banana fritters, the delicious shiver of cold ice running down her gullet on a hot, humid day. Also dark silence. She ticks off her emotions and joins them with a child's wavy lines to their matching pictures. But there is no picture to match with love. Just the language of Wyatt, Shakespeare, Sidney, Marlowe, Marvell, Jonson and Donne, who were not Chinese women living in 1960s Singapore and therefore no longer count. Love has slipped its leash and floats in the ether of her unknowing; she cannot anchor it to anything. And if she loves Jonah, and love is a big black hole, then what she increasingly feels for Jonah is a big black 'O'. He tries to colour in between the lines, but he cannot colour fast enough and the borders keep stretching further and further away from his efforts.

Until one day he smudges her 'O' with a foetus. Their child, he tells Madam Tay proudly, but Pandora doesn't feel that it belongs to her. He invades her body and she has to make space for his colony. She throws up her guts every morning as a sign that she is jettisoning her self. Madam Tay recognises this sign. It's a bad pregnancy, she tells them both, and she insists that Pandora defer her final year at university. She is confined to her bed with this new 'I' in her 'O'. She drinks ginseng tea, bird's nest soup and chicken soup with herbs; eats pig's liver and braised pigeon. She vegetates and roots in her bed, in the darkness of her bedroom, her belly ballooning like a septic cyst. She will never be human again until she expels this foreign 'I' inside her. She wants to carve her belly out, beat it and pummel it into flatness. Now she knows how her mother felt, carrying her all those years ago.

Secretly she begs Percy-phone to buy her laxatives for her constipation. She purges herself until her body is wracked and bent double, until she is weak and trembling, her throat raw and her breath rasping. But the cyst just keeps growing in her. It swells and plumps her belly. She gives up and lies in her bed, exhausted in defeat. Her body is no longer hers to control. Pandora is lost and in her place as a wife, daughter-in-law and mother-to-be.

'Is it a boy?' Madam Tay demanded.

'No, it's a girl.'

'That wife of yours! What use is she if she can't even give you a healthy son? I curse that smelly cunt she's brought into my house.'

He wasn't sure whether she was talking about his wife or his daughter, but it didn't matter anymore. 'No need to. It's already dead.'

Jonah went upstairs and entered their bedroom. He looked at his wife's face, noted the lines of exhaustion, the grey tinge of her skin, and all at once he felt that he had never loved her as much as at that moment, when he could sponge her sweaty body, comb her matted hair and feed her nourishing ginseng tea. She was dependent on his care and he was completely happy.

'Well, you're safe and that's the main thing,' he said, caressing her dear, dear face. But she turned away from him and stared at the green wall. Her eyes were open but she didn't see. 'Don't you want the tea? Shall I bring up some chicken soup? What do you want?'

It was a red letter moment, the first time he had asked her this question. Pandora, showing herself to be drama queen Lida Lim's sister, said, 'I want to die.' But the delivery was wrong; it was flat and soft, squeezed out from putty, mushroom lungs. Where was the force of melodrama? It was a flabby performance for this audience of one.

'Don't talk nonsense,' he rebuked her sharply. An English education had proved inadequate in uprooting his deeply buried superstitious fears that malevolent spirits might overhear and grant her request. 'What do you really want?'

'I want to move out of your mother's house. I want to go far away.'

And so he struck a deal with his father. He renounced all his rights to the rubber estates as a first-born son and, in return his father bought him a dental clinic in a small village in Malaysia. Jonah left Singapore and moved his wife away from his mother. He did it because he loved Pandora, but he would never quell his resentment at the fact that she had made him choose between his mother and herself.

DURIAN SEASON

Jonah Tay and his dental partner, Beng Chee, nursed a passion for durians—those yellow fleshy globs of fruit wrapped around smooth brown seeds, cradled inside thick, spiky green husks. They loved to inhale the aroma— of old unwashed socks—and looked forward to durian season with drooling anticipation. One of the benefits of living in Malaysia was undoubtedly the abundance of durians. Every year from June to September, Jonah and Beng Chee emerged into the twilight to prowl the darkened streets and roadside stalls in search of durians. It was a lifelong love affair for both of them. The pungent scent hung heavy in the humid air, easily discernible through the thick layers of pollution, petrol fumes and rotting garbage in the open sewers and unswept streets of the town. It crept into their brains and incited their lust until their mouths salivated for the creamy texture and onion aftertaste of the fruit.

In 1969 Beng Chee's hunger for durians arrived a month early. He heard rumours that durians were already available in Petaling Jaya. The thought tantalised him and he could not keep his mind on his work. He sat his patients down in the dental chair, prised open their jaws and saw their gaping mouths filled with creaming durian custard. He extracted teeth and imagined he saw the silky stones of durian seeds. He was impatient for the swift passage of days. Each morning he came early into the dental surgery to tear away the wafer-thin pages of the calendar one by one. He wanted to rev his motorcycle through May and screech to a halt when he arrived at June.

'Hey, Jonah, let's close up shop, man,' Beng Chee said as he walked into the dental surgery on the morning of Friday, May 13, 1969. He shoved the appointment book under Jonah's nose. 'Look, no appointments today, *lah*.'

'What about walk-in patients, ah?' Jonah objected conscientiously.

'Got rumours of durians in Selangor. Big fat durians, man! Why not we visit my brother in Petaling Jaya? If got durians, he sure know where to get some.'

Jonah hesitated for only a moment. 'Better tell my wife. She's expecting any day, you know. Better make sure she's all right first.'

Pandora lay in a canvas hammock strung up between two banana trees in the garden. This pregnancy had been an easy one and she bore the alien weight easily, serene in the knowledge that this child would be the longed-for son; a child that would erase the guilt and atone for the death of the one she hadn't wanted. She sipped sugarcane water, chewed salted mandarin peels and read a Hollywood fan magazine featuring Grace Kelly. She looked up in surprise when she heard the drone of a car engine and saw Jonah parking his Mercedes at the edge of the garden.

She slipped her large Jackie O sunglasses down the bridge of her nose.

'Jo, *apa kaba*?' she asked, slipping into the Malay they used with their maid from the *kampong*.

'Hey, you know what? Beng Chee thinks that durian season has started in Selangor. We're going to drive up and get a few cases, okay? You'll like that, won't you? It'll be a quick trip. We'll just zoom up there, pick up some durians, and I'll be back before night.'

'Sure. Enjoy yourselves.' She patted his hand absently and returned her gaze to the glossy photos in the magazine.

Still he hovered hesitantly. 'You'll be all right, won't you?'

'Of course, *lah*. No need to worry. Drive safely.'

But they would not return that night. They drove off before lunch, these two Chinese knights in an orange Fiat, ardent in their self-imposed quest for the holy grail of durian. They made good time to Beng Tek's bungalow in Petaling Jaya, a sprawling suburb which had sprung up around the University of Malaysia on the outskirts of Kuala Lumpur. The drive was easy as the major highways and narrow sidestreets were clear of traffic. Beng Chee rolled down the window and as the wind whooshed past, he whistled and sang at the top of his voice to Jonah's cassette of the Best of the British Proms, Recorded Live at the Royal Albert Hall.

'Rule Britannia! Britannia rules the waves,' the two men carolled exuberantly, nostalgic for the sing-alongs of their schooldays. 'Britons never, never, never shall be slaves!'

But whatever waves Britannia still ruled over, they were certainly not Malaysian ones. Not since *merdeka*— independence—in 1957, when the Malay sultan Tunku

Abdul Rahman had presided over the Federation of Malaya's separation from the British Empire. Any hope that the Federation of Malaysia might be a multicultural society made up of three main ethnicities—Malay, Chinese and Indian—began to disintegrate by the late 1960s. The fear of Chinese economic and political power had already been demonstrated on August 9, 1965, when Malaysia kicked Singapore and its prime minister, Lee Kuan Yew, out of the Federation. Racial hatred against the immigrant Chinese population in Malaysia would once again be demonstrated on Friday, May 13, 1969.

Of these matters Beng Chee and Jonah were blissfully unaware. Their minds obsessed by the thought of early durians and their voices lifted in patriotic British song, they sped towards Petaling Jaya ignorant of the fact that in Kuala Lumpur, UMNO youth members and other Malays from the rural *kampong*s had smashed, looted and burnt down Chinese shophouses and temples. Armed with their *parang*s and knives, invoking the will of Allah, they slaughtered and disembowelled hundreds of Chinese men, women and children. Later estimates would place the number of Chinese killed at around two thousand. After *susu*, then *kopi*.

For years to come, the slightest whisper among the Chinese community of a possible Malay *jihad* would send shopkeepers scuttling into their houses, drawing close the accordion steel grilles and securing them with huge padlocks, pulling shut the wooden doors behind the steel grilles and barring them from the inside. The general air of terror would spread throughout the Chinese-dominated areas of Kuala Lumpur and Petaling Jaya, the panicked actions of one shopkeeper alerting the rest so that, within half an hour, whole streets would be deserted as Chinese families cowered behind closed doors and waited for May 13 to repeat itself.

For those who were caught away from home, the experience of driving, cycling or running down those empty, fear-filled streets was one which could never be forgotten, easily evoked by the evening news footage of Indonesian rioters burning and looting Chinese businesses after the Asian 'Tiger' economies toppled like dominoes in 1997. In 1998, a rumour spread among the Chinese communities in Malaysia and overseas that another *jihad* along the same lines as the Indonesian riots had been planned. Desperate phone calls were placed to family members from Chinese communities in Australia, the UK, the USA and Canada. Within hours of those phone calls, all flights out of Malaysia were fully booked and Chinese people left in droves to cross the causeway from Johor Bahru to Singapore. May 13 still has the power to conjure up blind panic and irrational fear among Malaysian Chinese three decades later.

But on that day in 1969, Jonah and Beng Chee thought only of durians. When they reached Beng Tek's house, they were surprised to find the steel gate closed and padlocked. Jonah tooted cheerily on his horn and Beng Chee got out of the car to rattle the gate.

'Ah Tek, ah! It's me, Ah Chee. *Ai-yah*, why you so like that, *one lah*? Come and open this gate, man.' He shook it violently.

Gaudy orange and purple flowered curtains twitched at the upstairs window and, a few moments later, a servant came scurrying out to unlock the gate. The car rolled into the driveway, stopping under the porch, and the gate was quickly locked again. The servant urged them into the house and the metal grille and heavy wooden door were firmly locked.

'Ah Chee, you damn fool! What are you doing here, *lah*? Don't you know that the prime minister has declared a curfew?' Beng Tek was furious as he cuffed his younger brother around the ears. 'You could have been killed, man.'

And it was only then that they learned what those strangely deserted highways and streets meant. According to the official news on the radio, Malay demonstrators marching to protest the Chinese post-election victory had been set upon by violent Chinese and had been forced to defend themselves with knives and *parang*s. But the Chinese grapevine was already at work and telephone lines buzzed with the news of atrocities committed and allegations of soldiers, called in to stop the riots, who shot the Chinese instead. Later, telephone lines were cut off.

'*Ai-yah!* Pandora.' Too late Jonah realised that in his craving for durians, he had left his pregnant wife to fend for herself and he had no way of knowing whether the riots had spread to their village. He sweated anxiety and was beaten down with guilt. When at last he managed to ring Pandora, he learned that she had gone into labour and had given birth to their son, attended only by Dr Gupta, the sultan's personal physician. She was perfectly safe, she assured him, for the sultan had immediately issued strict orders that no racial riots were to take place in his state. But the Malay maid had abandoned their household and returned to the *kampong*. Her mother had come around later to tell her that no Malay would work for a Chinese from now onwards—they would rather starve to death first. Pandora was alone in the house with her baby boy.

When curfew was lifted briefly the next day, Jonah and Beng Chee hopped into the orange Fiat and sped back towards Pahang. At each roadblock they sat in trembling fear as their identity cards were checked. They waited for summary execution and almost wet their pants with relief when they were waved on with surly motions of the automatic rifles. Finally they entered their state and it was then that Beng Chee noticed the roadside stall just outside the valley *kampong*.

'Jonah, stop! Look at that, man.'

And there it was, a pushcart with tray after tray of green-armoured durians, the air pungent with the ripe, cloying smell. A Malay man in a ragged white T-shirt and checked cotton sarong sat on a stool beside the cart, sipping Fanta from a bottle and fiddling around with his black transistor radio. Malay love songs with lots of clapping burst forth with a hideous screech of static. The orange Fiat slowed down and rolled to a halt. A windowpane descended cautiously.

'*Selamat pagi, pak. Apa kaba?*'

The Malay man looked up and his brown face split into a melon-slice grin.

'Fresh durians, finest quality, rock-bottom prices. You want to buy or not?'

Jonah and Beng Chee stepped out of the car, lured by the sight and smell of the mace-like fruit. To have travelled all that way in such danger, only to find their hearts' desire in a roadside stall so close to home. It was almost too much to bear. But Beng Chee got down to the business of bargaining.

'How come you got so many left if the quality so good, ah?' Beng Chee demanded. He picked up a spiky ball and sniffed, inhaling the enticing scent deeply. 'Can't be so good if nobody wants to buy.'

'*Allahmak!*' the Malay man wailed in exasperation. 'These riots, you know. They scared all my Chinese customers away. Now my customers think that all Malays are out to get the Chinese so they tell each other not to buy durians from Malays. What has it all got to do with me? I'm just a poor durian seller trying to feed his family. I'm going to go broke if the Chinese continue to boycott my durians. You want durians or not? I give you good price.'

'How do we know whether they're good?'

Both men gasped and jumped back in fear as the Malay whipped out his *parang* and slashed downwards with all his might. Sunlight glinted off the broad silver blade as it cleaved the rigid shell of a durian in two, exposing the crescent-shaped pods in which the custard-yellow arils snuggled, three or four to a pod. The durian seller dug out two pieces of durian and offered them to the men.

'Try,' he urged. 'Very sweet.'

Beng Chee bit into one and closed his eyes in sheer ecstasy.

'How much?' he asked.

They haggled over the price and ended up buying the entire cartload—some fourteen cases in all. Before money could change hands, the durian seller suddenly stiffened.

'Listen,' he said urgently. In the silence they could hear the distant sounds of marching and singing. The Malay looked significantly at the two men. 'You better run into the jungle and hide,' he advised them. 'You two are sitting ducks here on the main highway. Leave the car and run. Quick!'

They ran, hearts pounding and chests bursting. They crouched in the dark of the dank green foliage, waiting with dread in their hearts and sweat on their skin. The minutes crawled by and there was nothing but silence from the distant road. Jonah scratched his back and shifted to avoid an army of vicious red ants. Beng Chee glared at him and, with exaggerated gestures, placed a knobbly finger to his lips. They waited with numbed limbs.

And then they heard it—a loud explosion. Through breaks in the undergrowth they saw the bright light of an orange ball of flame and thick black smoke. The rage of a burning fire and then, much later, silence again.

'Hey! You can come out now. They've gone.' The foliage parted noisily as the durian seller peered into the green gloom.

'What the hell . . .' Jonah stumbled to a halt. In the place of his orange Fiat was a black, burning wreck. The durian cart was upset and the fruit had rolled all over the road.

'Sorry, *lah*,' the durian seller said. 'They were Muslims led by some UMNO youth members. They were on their way to KL. I told them that you had stopped to buy some durians but that you ran off down the road when you heard them coming. They knew that the car must belong to a Chinese because no Malay could afford one unless he's the sultan, so they burnt it.'

'Then what happened to your cart?'

'They overturned it and threw some cases of durians into the burning car to teach me a lesson for trying to sell

durians to the Chinese. What to do?' He shrugged fatalistically. 'You still want some durians or what?'

'No, no. Not now.' Jonah was horrified by the blazing
black shell of his car. He stared at it, mesmerised by the
thick smoke spiralling into the air.

'We don't have a car now. How to get them home?'
Beng Chee demanded.

'Well,' the durian seller pondered the question and
scratched his armpit. 'I can sell you the cart, then I'll help
you to wheel it as far as my *kampong*.'

'Done. How many cases can we salvage?' Beng Chee
peered at the fruit on the roadside and began counting. He
and the durian seller righted the cart and heaved durians
onto it. Money changed hands. They grabbed the wooden
handles and began pushing it down the road.

'Jonah! You coming or what?'

They made it back to their neighbourhood in the early
hours of the morning. They stopped at Beng Chee's house
first to unload his five cases of durians, then they wheeled
the cart to Jonah's bungalow and unloaded another five
cases outside the kitchen door.

'So, see you at work, ah?' Beng Chee called in farewell
as he staggered back to his house.

Jonah opened the first case and heaved out a durian.
He unlocked the door and slipped inside. His wife was
sitting at the kitchen table, suckling a wrinkled prune of a
baby. Immediately he felt the overwhelming weight of guilt.
He walked over to the table and carefully placed the durian
on it.

'Sorry, *lah*,' he said, and the words were inadequate to
his ears. She just looked at him and he quailed before the
condemnation in her eyes.

'Say something,' he pleaded.

'*Ai-yah.*' Jonah heard the familiar groan echoing from the front of the bungalow. Then the sound of a throat clearing itself violently, and the gentle ping! of spit hitting a metal basin. He looked at his wife questioningly and moments later his eyes bulged with shock as Madam Tay shuffled in weakly.

'Ah Jo! I thought you were sure dead.' She flung her arms around him and started crying, lamenting and thanking God noisily.

Pandora set aside her son in his small crib. She got up and poured a cup of hot tea for her mother-in-law. 'Come, Ah Bu. Sit down and drink this.'

'*Ai-yah*, my heart. I'm too old for all this. Come, Jo, help me to my room.'

He had no choice. He looked helplessly at his wife, who turned away from him. Then he put his arm around his mother and they shuffled back to her room together. He patted her arm, comforted, explained, comforted again, and dreaded the thought of repeating the performance for his wife when all he wanted was to take a hot bath and go to bed. Finally, Madam Tay dropped off to sleep, her pudgy white fingers still tightly clasping his long bony hand. He unlinked their fingers and rubbed his eyes. He went out into the corridor hoping Pandora might be asleep, but he saw the garish glare of fluorescent light from the kitchen, so he sighed and went in.

'I'm sorry,' he said again.

She said nothing at first, just looked at him with those eloquently accusing eyes. Then she bent down over the crib and picked up the baby.

'Even Malaysia's not big enough or far enough away,' he thought he heard her mutter.

'Don't you want to know what happened?' He was irritated that she hadn't asked.

'What, your wife gets an explanation as well?' She surprised him with her sarcasm. Then she sighed. 'All right, what happened, Jo?'

He narrated the last few days' adventures for the second time that night. 'But we managed to get the durians after all,' he said. 'Look. Shall I get you a piece?'

'You look,' Pandora said, pulling the baby away from her nipple and shoving him towards his father. 'This is your son Augustus. You haven't even asked about him or looked at him properly. Look!'

Jonah dutifully took the baby from Pandora and inspected his son, and felt—nothing. Tired. So tired. The baby began to squall. He wrinkled his nose at the smell and handed Augustus back to Pandora.

'Jonah, do you love me?'

He was surprised because she never asked. He was always the one seeking that reassurance.

'Of course I do. You know I do,' he said, but he felt annoyed that she had to ask him now, when he was grubby and sweaty from walking all the way back from Gombak. She didn't even care that he had been out of his mind with worry for her over the last few days, or that he could have been killed while buying durians. She didn't care, or she wouldn't make a fuss now.

'If you love me, you make damn sure my son grows up in a country where he never has to worry about something like this happening. I don't care where we go—England, America or Australia. But you make damn sure that he never has another birthday like this again. If you won't emigrate, then you won't have a family either.'

If he hadn't been so tired, he would have been furious that she was using his love as leverage for another impossible demand. But then he looked at his son and he remembered her last birthing experience, remembered the grief that had bound them together over their dead child. He was crushed by contrition. He should have been there for her, but he wasn't. He'd promised to take care of her, but once again he hadn't. What kind of a husband was he anyway?

'All right,' he said wearily. 'I'll look into it. Straight away. Promise.'

But Jonah had spent too many days in his youth slicing delicately into the trunks of rubber trees and watching in hypnotised fascination as white pearls of latex oozed, beaded and dribbled sluggishly down the trunk. He was a man who deliberated, pondered, explored options and came to decisions slowly. It took him six years to get his nerve up to let his mother know that he wanted to emigrate to Australia. For six years Pandora watched and waited, waited and watched. She gave birth to me during her time of waiting, when she reminded and nagged and felt her desperation grow. Then he finally announced one day that he had gone to the Australian High Commission in Kuala Lumpur and picked up application forms for immigration. The Tays were moving to Sydney—Jonah, Pandora, Sonny and me.

INTERLUDE TO
A NEW LIFE

There is a photograph, framed in tarnished Selangor pewter, of my mother, Sonny and me in 1978. The White Australia Policy had been phased out and Australia was in need of medical and dental professionals. The Patriarch had come ahead to find a house for us and to set up his own dental surgery before bringing us over. In this photo we are standing in the arrival hall of Sydney's Kingsford Smith Airport, holding beige jackets in our arms because the pilot announced on arrival that it was sixty-four degrees Fahrenheit outside, which was cold for us at that time. (Now sixty-four degrees Fahrenheit makes no sense to me; I'm so used to gauging the temperature in degrees Celsius.) We look confused and uncertain, out of place.

Sonny has his thick, spiky hair Brylcreemed down, but the long flight from Singapore to Sydney has dislodged the neatly combed furrows so that greasy strands now droop over his wide forehead. He is dressed in a sky-blue long-sleeved shirt—buttoned at the cuffs and right up to the throat—and dark blue jeans that, being too long for him, have been rolled up a few times at the leg cuffs. Grey lace-up shoes peep out from under those cuffs. He is gripping a red Qantas cabin bag with the white flying kangaroo on the side, hanging on to it for dear life. His eyes bore so intensely into the camera, his gaze must have shot laser beams right through the photographer's head. His lips are red and sulking. He is nine years old.

My mother is holding his right hand. She wears a loose purple, brown and yellow batik top and flowing brown polyester trousers. At her brown sandalled feet are scattered the collective detritus of our eight-hour stay in the cabin: a large black cabin bag; plastic bags with grubby soft toys and favourite tiny pillows and bolsters with blue ribbons and yellowing lace borders; one duty-free bag holding a box of Johnny Walker Black Label scotch; another two which are bulging but sealed, their contents invisible and unremembered.

My mother loved shopping, especially duty-free shopping. The idea of 'duty-free' was simply a licence for her to shop without feeling the guilt and accusation of extravagance pummelled into her by the Tays. She was alive and excited when she shopped, often indecisive but thrilled at the cornucopia of cosmetics, fresh fragrances, leather wallets, silk scarves, belts, handbags, watches, pens, hairdryers, Walkmans, batteries, rolls of 100, 200 and 400 speed film in 24 or 36 exposure packs, neck cushions, back cushions, padlocks, Samsonite luggage, winking bottles of whisky, scotch and wine, and even cigarettes, tobacco and glinting silver cigarette lighters, although she had never smoked. All duty-free, all potentially there for her to purchase, though her actual acquisitions were usually meagre: a box of Lancôme facial moisturiser, two tubes of Elizabeth Arden lipstick and a 100 ml bottle of Nina Ricci 'L'Air du Temps' that she would use once or twice a month, then carefully store away at the back of her closet (in darkness so that light would not denature it) because it was too precious and expensive to waste on herself every day. She laughed and looked interested in everything. She exclaimed over the prices, rummaged through stands, sought out bargains and chatted to the sales assistants. She became a person once again when she shopped.

Otherwise, she stared out at the world through those flat, blank eyes that reflected you back to yourself. Those same eyes that stare out of the pewter-framed photograph as she held me, a wrinkled, grumpy seven-year-old, by the hand. Those same eyes that viewed the suburbs of inner-western Sydney—that made a new home in a new land—without giving any clue to her innermost feelings.

I wanted to know her. I wanted to crack that black glass, to rip apart the opacity and find the person within. Like everyone else intimately related to her in her life, I wanted to do violence to her, to force her to surrender up her self to me. I wanted to take by force what would not be given voluntarily. That was no way of knowing anyone. But behind the shattered black glass lay another harder, thicker pane, and behind that yet another. For so much of my life, she looked at me with those vacant eyes that made me rage and cry.

FAMILY BONDING

Immigration forced us in on ourselves and moulded us into a family—fractious and often bitterly absurd, but a family nevertheless. Sacrifices were made, unasked for, and lifelong obligations were imposed. To us children, immigration was an irredeemable debt, but one for which we were grovellingly grateful at the time. And still are, I suppose.

Few could ever guess Sonny's relief at immigrating to Sydney. He hated school in Malaysia, for he was terrified of his teacher. She barked angry orders at him, contemptuously smacked his bony knuckles with her wooden ruler when he stuttered out wrong answers, and laughed at him when he tried to bribe his way into her favour with a clichéd apple (bruised and softened in his schoolbag) and a twenty-eight dollar silver ballpoint pen that he had stolen from the Patriarch's office drawer.

He was even afraid of the school monitors, especially Janet Lee, who was always immaculate even in the wilting heat, who paraded up and down the rows of schoolchildren with her white Dunlop sandshoes turned out at symmetrical forty-five degree angles because she learned ballet and took care to point her feet. Janet Lee, who stood in front of the flag and sang the Malaysian national anthem with her arms and feet in first position, as though she was about to dip into a plié at any moment. She watched Sonny fidgeting away, tapping his large shoes during the speeches and whispering to his neighbour, and she reported him to the principal. Then the Patriarch pulled him out of school in the middle of the year and sent us all to stay with Auntie Percy-phone in Singapore. It was the most unexpected relief.

We learned how to swim while we were in Singapore, for Mum was determined to transform us into good Aussie kids and swimming was part of the whole deal. Four times a week Sonny and I went to Big Splash for our swimming lessons with Mr Ting. He made us put our heads under the water and blow bubbles, gave us foam boards and taught us to kick. Sonny was great at swimming; he took to it naturally. I preferred to splash around and could hardly wait until our lesson was over so that we could play in the wave pool or slide through the plastic tubes. It often rained in the afternoons: fat, warm drops of rain that dimpled the rocking surface of the pool. If it thundered, Mum would call out in alarm, telling us to get out of the water in case we got electrocuted. We'd clamber out and shake ourselves like wet dogs before wrapping gaudily coloured towels around us—sarong fashion. Then we'd beg her to buy us little packets of Nutella, which we would peel open eagerly, scooping out the melting chocolate paste with the small plastic paddles provided.

A year later, when we were settled in Burwood, Mum enrolled us for swimming lessons at the Ashfield pool so that we could continue to be good Australians like Dawn Fraser, but it wasn't nearly as much fun by then. Tony, our swimming coach, was determined to train us to swim properly, even competitively. Technique, he said. It all comes down to technique. With the right technique you can last the distance. (This was what my lovers kept telling me years later too.) Tony dropped us into the fifty-metre pool and I half drowned myself as I tried to flap my way from one end to the other in what was supposed to resemble a free-style stroke. I sucked up chlorinated water through my nose and sneezed and spluttered. The meniscus of the water bobbed before my eyeballs and I stared in panic at the long stretch of blue before me. Sonny's head was decapitated, a bobbing ball receding into the distance; so far away that I would never catch up. The water was alternately cold and warm with patches where someone ahead of me had urinated. I stopped swimming lessons as soon as I could, although Sonny continued and even swam for his school. Somehow, once we started swimming competitively, the fun was taken out of it. There was no more time to be wasted blowing bubbles underwater as we'd done with Mr Ting. Singapore had been an interlude to real life.

One night, in Singapore, we went to the hawker centre with Auntie Percy-phone, Uncle Winston, Auntie Shufen and their children. We crowded around tiny tables piled with *char kway teow*, steamed fish with ginger and shallots, chicken and beef satay with peanut sauce, *gado gado* and *pohpiah*. Little dishes of sliced chillies drenched in soy sauce dotted the table. Chopsticks clicked and people chattered and slapped at mosquitoes.

'What's the matter with you, Sonny?' Uncle Winston demanded. 'How come you don't take chilli? You're not a real man unless you can eat the hottest chillies, you know. My father used to pick up those tiny chilli *puddies*—the hottest chillies you can find on this earth—and he ate them like sweet cakes. Here, have some.'

He spooned a generous amount of chilli into Sonny's bowl of noodles. Sonny picked up his chopsticks and ate. His eyes oozed tears and his nose dribbled. His larynx and tongue were on fire. Desperately, he sucked up coconut juice through a straw, then fished out the ice cubes to roll them around his burning mouth. Uncle Winston and the rest of the cousins roared with laughter while Auntie Shufen sat there, staring unblinkingly at Sonny and gnawing off pieces of satay with her teeth.

'What a sissy! Can't eat chillies. We'll have to make a real man of you before you go to Australia, huh, Sonny? Huh? What will your father say, you sissy boy, you.'

We worried about what he would say, but I think that Sonny and I have never loved the Patriarch as much as when we first saw him at the airport in Sydney. We hadn't realised that we'd actually missed him until we saw his familiar Buddy Holly glasses searching us out, a thin man in a grey polyester windcheater, navy trousers and a white shirt with a tie because those were the days when departures and arrivals were still important psychological as well as physical markers of passage, and Asians dressed up formally to go to the airport. He exclaimed happily—even spontaneously— when he caught sight of us. He picked us up and nuzzled our necks, then pushed our heavy trolley out to the car.

'You'll love the house,' he told us. 'It's got a rumpus room for you to play in and I've put a mini trampoline in there. Both of you also have your own bedrooms. There's a big garden out the back too. And just wait till I show you Sydney.'

The Patriarch was determined to make us fall in love with Sydney. He was going to take us up to the Blue Mountains on the weekend, drive us to Mrs Macquarie's Chair, make us walk around the Botanical Gardens to Bennelong Point, book us on a Captain Cook Cruise, show us the tourist face of the city. We'll have a *great* time, he told us. He took us to Pancakes at the Rocks and promised me a birthday party at McDonald's so that I could have an ice-cream cake and maybe meet the clown with the big red boots and the sinisterly smiling face. For those few weeks he was so happy to have his family with him once again. He wanted to do everything for us and everything with us. We hadn't disappointed him yet.

True to his promise, one weekend he decided that we should see Katoomba in the Blue Mountains and have a picnic in the park. When I think of family picnics, I hear the hiss of sizzling oil and the clang of the metal wok in the kitchen as Mum cooked rice vermicelli with pork, egg and vegetables. The Patriarch directed operations, packing green plastic plates and cups into a basket and searching for paper napkins. Sonny washed chillies, cut them into tiny pieces and wrapped them in plastic. The seeds stung his fingers and he dreaded the moment when he would have to confess that he could not bear the taste of chillies. The Patriarch did not know this because we never ate together in Malaysia. In the early evening the servants would cook dinner for Sonny and me to eat in the kitchen. Mum and the Patriarch had their meal in the dining room much later.

Immigration brought with it the novelty of shared family meals.

'Wait till you see Katoomba,' the Patriarch told us as he selected cassettes to play in the car on the way up to the mountains. He was nothing if not an organised man. 'You'll love it. You've never seen anything like it before. We've all got to get up very early tomorrow so that we can reach there before all the traffic gets on the road.'

All our lives we would arrive at the Royal Easter Show, the premiers of *Star Wars* and *ET*, Christmas parties and school speech nights a good hour before anyone else arrived, just so that we could avoid traffic and queues. The Patriarch was not a man who enjoyed the company of the general public. And although he made Mum take driving lessons and eventually bought her a car, he was the one who always drove when we went out together.

That night Sonny could not sleep. He tossed in bed and thought of the chillies. The following morning he worried about it all along the Great Western Highway up to the Blue Mountains, dreading the moment when his masculinity would be shamed before his father.

The Patriarch was oblivious to Sonny's pain. He drove us to Katoomba first so that we could gape at the petrified claw of the Three Sisters. We hollered across the valley—the first and only time in the presence of the Patriarch—and he smiled in benevolent approval. We listened to the hissing recording of the story of how the Three Sisters came into being and peered into the binoculars—I couldn't focus them properly and all I saw was a smudge of green at the bottom of the valley. We went into the souvenir shop and the Patriarch bought us a Three Sisters paperweight, a Sydney Harbour Bridge pencil sharpener and a plastic ruler with tiny photographs of the Blue Mountains glued along its length. This was our introduction to Australia before it became our home. Vast geographical and artificial structures were shrunk to fit a child's hand, commodified into the implements of education.

From the Three Sisters he drove us back to the town centre so that we could have a picnic lunch. From the car I looked at other families picnicking in the park. The smell of barbecuing meat and the hiss of fat sizzling on hot coals provoked stomach rumblings and mouth-watering cravings for meals as yet unknown and untasted. People were lying in the sun, munching on sandwiches, drinking Coke or beer or cups of wine from Coolabah casks.

Then out we got, the Tay family, with a huge Esky and a brightly coloured groundsheet because it had rained the previous night and the Patriarch believed in preventing rheumatism and arthritis decades down the track. We found a shady spot because Mum didn't like the sun and we unrolled the groundsheet. The Esky was opened, the ice-cream containers full of noodles removed. Paper plates were unpacked and dealt out like cards. Schweppes lemonade was poured into cups—what a novelty fizzy lemonade was to us back then—chopsticks paired up and handed round, and Mum started heaping noodles onto the plates. There we sat, cross-legged, solemnly shovelling noodles into our mouths with our chopsticks, sucking and slurping up the longer strands. They dripped from our lips like a tangle of worms. We were an incongruous sight in the park; we didn't fit into the picture.

'Where are the chillies?' the Patriarch demanded. Mum unwrapped the plastic film and laid out the chillies. The

Patriarch helped himself and offered them to Sonny. 'Sonny? Want some?'

Sonny was filled with shame. Slowly, hesitantly, he picked up a few pieces with his chopsticks and put them on his noodles. He took a deep breath and thrust a skein of chillied noodles into his mouth. Once again, his eyes watered, his mouth burned and the tips of his ears turned red. He reached for his cup of lemonade and guzzled noisily. He just could not do this. He tried to push the pieces of chilli to the edge of his plate but their hotness infested everything. He couldn't eat that contaminated plate of noodles but he couldn't go for a second helping until he'd finished the first plate. Waste not, want not, the Patriarch always admonished. Sonny's stomach growled hungrily and he hung his head.

'Sonny? Why aren't you eating?' The Patriarch had noticed his untouched plate.

'Can't eat it,' Sonny mumbled.

'What?'

'I said I can't eat it. The chillies are too hot for me. I can't eat chillies.' There. He'd confessed and his shame hung like a bright blade in the air, poised to strike him down before his father's eyes.

'*Hi-yah!* Then why did you want to take chillies?' the Patriarch said.

'I was trying to be a man. You're not a man unless you can eat chillies.'

'Who told you that?'

'Uncle Winston.'

'Talk nonsense! Chillies have nothing to do with being a man. I tell you what, Sonny, you've got no choice, you know. Sex comes from biology, not from chillies. When you study science at school and dissect rats, then you'll see. Give me your plate.' The Patriarch took a spoon and scooped Sonny's noodles and chillies onto his own plate. '*Nah*. Go and get some more *mai fun*. You have to eat or you won't have any energy left to hike down to Wentworth Falls.'

Later that afternoon, after a long bushwalk and the exotic experience of our first Devonshire tea, we drove back to Sydney, back down the Great Western Highway. The setting sun seared the backs of our necks and baked the vinyl car seats. We had to stop by the side of the road once, while I was sick, but I didn't get told off. The Patriarch was in a buoyant mood. His kindness was stunning in its breadth and duration. I loved my father so much. He pushed his favourite Carpenters cassette into the machine and turned up the volume. Music swelled in the car. The Patriarch warbled in joyful song, wondering, along with Karen Carpenter, why birds had suddenly appeared. Mum, Sonny and I joined in the chorus. Absurdly, happily, we flapped our arms like wings and assured the Patriarch that we too longed to be close to him.

A CURE FOR INSOMNIA

When I think of my first year in Australia, I remember long nights of insomnia followed by bedwetting that would arouse the Patriarch's wrath in the morning, earning me roars of rage and a burning twisted ear. Mum could not understand why, at the age of eight, I started wetting my bed when I had never done so before. Neither could she understand why I could not fall asleep in our new Burwood house.

'No ghosts to scare you here,' she told me. 'Everything's all right, isn't it?'

Her statement of reassurance became a plea for comfort instead.

My mother would make me a cup of Horlicks every night to help me fall asleep. There were no bedtime stories. Ours was not a storytelling household. Bedtime was signalled by the sound of the kettle burbling and the clinking of a teaspoon against china as Horlicks was heaped into the Colgate mug that the Patriarch had given me on my fifth birthday. A sales rep had given it to him, together with a pen and a black calculator. My nightly ritual of Horlicks ceased only when I was twelve.

It stopped for three reasons. Firstly, I discovered that the sugar content of Horlicks far outweighed its soporific effects. I was, by then, battling weight problems in my head, starving myself into skinniness, sloughing off my excess flesh. Secondly, by this stage my mother was Renewed, even Born Again. It would be a few years before she divorced our family and married God; still, the cup of Horlicks was no longer presented with a mother's love but with the fear of the Lord. Acceptance of my bedtime drink now entailed hours spent in repentful prayer, me on my knees on the carpet, admitting to and wrestling tearfully with a myriad of trivial sins before my mother confessor, while the cup of Horlicks cooled on the bedside table and the hot milk formed a wrinkled beige skin on the surface. Thirdly, and most crucially, the Patriarch discovered the longstanding crime that had been committed in his household and forbade me to drink Horlicks at night if I wasn't going to clean my teeth afterwards.

'It's a filthy habit,' he said. His shock was profound, his disappointment in us devastating. He had taken exquisite and unparalleled care of our teeth since the first raw stump had swelled painfully through reddened baby gums. When Sonny and I were old enough to clean our own teeth, he brought home from his dental surgery a large plastic model of lolly-pink gums and even, American-white teeth. Other kids, before they went to bed, might learn about Red Riding Hood: 'Grandma, what big teeth you have!' The Tay children learned the names of our individual teeth. Starting with the two front ivories of the First Incisors, the Patriarch rehearsed the awesome geometry of those large white plastic teeth which marched uniformly away from each other along the grinning arc of the antiseptic gums. First Incisors, Second Incisors, Canines (the dog teeth which were also vampires' teeth), First Premolars, Second Premolars, First Molars, Second Molars and Third Molars—also the Eighths, or Wisdom Teeth.

He taught us how to brush our teeth properly, the way he tried to teach his patients who trembled on his dental chair as they exposed maws of dirty, rotting teeth with the stale stench of decay and gingivitis. Always use a toothbrush with soft bristles so that you won't wear away the enamel. Don't brush too hard or vigorously or you may get abrasion cavities. We nodded solemnly. Move the brush in gentle but thorough circular motions, thus. And don't neglect the gums. Because of the fluoridisation of Sydney's water, dental problems are less likely to result from caries and tooth decay than from periodontal disease, which is a terrible consequence of improper and careless brushing. Yes, Dad. He brought home glossy A4 posters, supplied by the Australian Dental Association, showing soft, pulpy, reddened gums and stumps of yellowed teeth in various stages of disease. We had one each to Blu-Tack to our bedroom walls, in place of the INXS, Boy George and Duran Duran posters that other kids decorated their rooms with. But above all, he commanded us, we were to go forth from that day forwards and Floss.

For many years during our childhood, we lined up before the Patriarch every night and obediently opened our mouths for his inspection. He bent, he peered, he pushed our chins up to the light and flashed an orange Everyready torch at our uvulas. Pass, he said, and we were then allowed to go to bed. Imagine his consternation and outrage, then, when he discovered that the drill parade had been in vain, that his wife had undermined and betrayed the practice of good dental hygiene he had so carefully inculcated in us all these years, simply by bringing me a cup of Horlicks *after* I had cleaned my teeth.

My childhood nights were subsequently spent tossing and turning, gazing at the ceiling in the dark, listening to night trains grinding along the track to Burwood Station, watching through the window the occasional blue flash of sparks along the electricity cable overhead. Concentrate, I told myself. If only I could concentrate hard enough on the soothing monotony of the train, I would be able to tune out the ominous crescendo of my parents arguing downstairs. I wouldn't hear the shock of the sharp slap or imagine the burning sting of her cheek. I would be able to turn off the guilt that dripped steadily all night long and stopped me from sleeping.

Their happy reunion had long ago deteriorated into the sullen resentment and flaring irritation they'd felt towards each other in Malaysia. Migration had only exacerbated it. The Patriarch found it difficult to establish his dental practice and make ends meet, so he blamed his wife for forcing him to migrate. She wanted to get a job to help with the family's finances, but this he would not allow. He could support the family, he claimed angrily. She should just do her part and be a good and obedient wife and look after her unruly kids. (We were her children by then, not his.) Little things about her began to annoy him and in his unrelenting quest to make her into the kind of wife that he wanted, he forgot the woman with whom he had actually fallen in love. Even now I can rattle off a list of all the reasons why he hated her, but it's hard to remember why he ever fell in love with her.

Their grudges bubbled like magma just beneath the surface of their lives and it took little friction to cause an eruption. Alone in the inky blackness of my room, with only a crack of light creeping in under the door, I twisted the bedclothes in one fist and swiped the tears from my face with the other. I imagined myself taking dramatic action: throwing myself between them and receiving the blow of his fist on my body, perhaps. Clasping his knees with my arms and imploring him to stop. Snatching up her long-bladed sewing scissors and skewering them into his back. Instead I cried in the dark and did nothing to help her. I was frightened of falling asleep in case, in my sleep, the unthinkable and unmentionable should happen to her and I wouldn't know until it was too late. So I stayed awake and listened. And when I slept, I was terrified of that too, because my body released its anxieties and soaked the bed.

Each morning Sonny shook me awake and I flung off his insistent hand grumpily. As the fog of sleep faded, I sat bolt upright in bed, remembering. Then I scrambled away, pulling the covers with me to check whether I had wet the bed. 'Safe,' Sonny would say, relieved. Or, if I had wet the bed, he'd help me to drag off the bedclothes quickly, furtively, before the Patriarch could discover what I had done. Eventually, I slept on top of a plastic garbage bag so that the sheets would not get wet. The plastic irritated my skin and caused red rashes to appear. When I scratched myself to relieve the itchiness, the skin would break and flake and I'd watch in fascination as tiny beads of blood oozed out like latex from a rubber tree.

Then one night I accidentally discovered the soporific effects of masturbation and a good hard come. I woke up in the morning in a dry bed. *Then felt I like some watcher of the skies when a new planet swims into his ken; or like stout Cortez when with eagle eyes he stared at the Pacific . . . silent, upon a peak in Darien.* It was such a relief. Masturbation replaced Horlicks in my nightly ritual for falling asleep and was far more effective anyway. It blanked the mind and exhausted the body, tuning out the tumult of the arguments downstairs and making me forget for a moment that I was beginning to hate myself and my family.

ELASTICS

'You're a dirty little girl, aren't you?'

The nurse spread a green garbage bag over the foam mattress in the sick bay. I looked down and didn't answer, because she was right. I was a dirty little girl. I couldn't control the boundaries of my body. My anxiety and desperate need to belong leaked and spilled and made a mess.

'Didn't your mum toilet train you? Fancy a big girl like you wetting her pants. Really.' She made me climb onto the mattress and lie down although there was nothing wrong with me. 'Now stay still and behave yourself until the bell goes. Do you want a book to read? No? All right. Call me if you feel sick or need anything.'

She went out of the room and I was left alone.

I'd been playing elastics when it happened.

England, Ireland, Scotland, Wales. Inside, outside, inside, scales . . .

How odd to have been rehearsing in a sunny Sydney schoolyard the names of countries of the United Kingdom thousands of miles away. The girls were playing elastics and I could only watch because Niree had said I wasn't good enough yet. I had to wait until they all got out before I could have my turn. I'd tried hard. I had been practising every night. When the Patriarch was having his shower upstairs, I snuck down to the rumpus room and dragged two chairs away from the scarred wooden desks where Sonny and I did our homework. I borrowed two pairs of Mum's pantyhose and knotted them together. I asked her to buy some elastic and sew the ends together so that I could practise like the other girls, but she thought it was a waste of money. So I had to make do, looping the flapping flags of the control pantyhose waistbands around the legs of the chairs. Ankle height first, then knee height. I hopped and thudded heavily over the tan-coloured skeins of stocking. My tongue lolled out like a dog's when I jumped, Sonny used to tease me. I ignored him and concentrated on scissoring my legs through the bend and give and twanging snap of the hose.

Inside, outside, crisscross, inside, out.

I slid the pantyhose to thigh level, but in a fatalistic kind of way. I knew I couldn't do this because I couldn't jump high enough. When I panted out 'scales!' and my feet thumped down onto the nylon cords, the chairs overbalanced and came toppling down. Once again, I had stretched the pantyhose too tautly over the backs of the chairs and there was not enough 'give' when the loop was at thigh level. The noise of tumbling chairs was muffled by the thick beige shag pile of the carpet, but I still hastily disassembled the pantyhose and put away the chairs neatly in case the Patriarch had heard and was on his way down to investigate the cause of the ruckus.

Each night, after I finished my homework, my spelling lists and my subtractions, I practised elastics doggedly although I hated the game. When you're an eight-year-old girl and you've just moved to Sydney, you simply had to be able to play elastics or there was nothing to do and no-one to play with at lunch.

England, Ireland, Scotland, Wales. Inside, outside, inside, scales . . .

The playground was cracked bitumen with the faded yellow outline of a netball court baked onto it. Around the edges eucalypts and wattle trees sagged over the neat aluminium benches where children sat to eat their lunch. Twigs, cracked gum-nut shells, dirt, birds' droppings and the gold dust of fallen wattle flowers spotted the dull machined metal. However, these benches were still cleaner than the old flaking wooden ones with their curved backs striped red, green and white. Columns of ants crawled along the aluminium grooves and heaved away the bread I'd crumbled. It was rather like looking down at traffic on Parramatta Road. I sat on one of these benches with my lunch on my lap: a bulging brown paper bag with the hieroglyphics of my mother's writing in black texta:

> Grace Tay
> Class 3C
> 1 ham sandwich
> 1 frozen orange Sunny Boy
> 1 banana

When we had arrived in Sydney and I had started school, for the first three weeks she made ham sandwiches for me. She got up early each day, set out the sandwich board and unclipped the blue and white striped plastic bag of sliced bread. She lined up the tub of margarine, then unwrapped and forked apart slices of leg ham. Sometimes she shredded iceberg lettuce and constructed neat sandwiches, triumphantly cutting them into isosceles triangles and wrapping them in plastic film. After a while she just ordered us ham sandwiches from the tuckshop, although I was sick to death of them by then. I took unenthusiastic bites out of my sandwich and it tasted dry and stale. There wasn't enough butter. I pushed a mouthful against my palate. My tongue rubbed against the thin slivers of ham, testing for taste. It was just salty, and perhaps a little off.

When Sonny and I went to school in Malaysia we always came home in time for lunch. One of the servants would cook us egg noodles with a fried egg and slices of sweet barbecued pork. We'd had to start school at seven in the morning, though, and we had to learn Malay. *Ini* Ali, *ini* Siti, *ini ayam*. This is Ali, this is Siti, and this is the chicken. They were all there in the picture books Sonny kept on his shelf, next to our Ladybird and Enid Blyton books. My mother taught me how to read with Ladybird storybooks about Peter and Jane. This is Peter, this is Jane, and this is Pat the Dog. Daddy and Mummy, Peter, Jane, and Pat the Dog go on a picnic. They probably eat ham sandwiches. I simply hated ham.

I slid a glance at my neighbour's lunch. This was Andrew Reynolds. He was the class captain and he had blue eyes—the first blue eyes I'd ever seen—and a head of curly blond hair that reminded me of Little Lord Fauntleroy. I didn't know why he was sitting next to me because he never sat next to girls. Andrew Reynolds usually played with the other boys at the wooden fort or the monkey bars.

He pulled a white buttered bread roll out of his brown paper bag. He ripped open a packet of chicken-flavoured Arnott's chips and scooped out a handful, shovelling them into his mouth. Munching hard, he clenched more chips in his fist and, prising open the bread roll like a clam, he squashed the chips in between the greasy, buttered halves. He jammed the top of the roll down and we both grinned at the satisfying crunch of squashed chips. He glanced at me and did a double take, as though noticing for the first time that I was looking at his lunch.

'I'm on a seafood diet,' he said. Then he shoved his index and middle fingers into the corners of his mouth and stretched them. His jaw yawned wide open, revealing a mangled mess of chewed chips and blots of bread that clung to the crevices and hung from his palate like stalactites. He started to laugh and bits of munched-up lunch spewed out and sprayed my uniform.

'See food, get it?' he said, killing himself laughing.

I looked away from him quickly and fumbled in my pockets for a tissue (my mother didn't believe in hankies; tissues were more hygienic because you used them once and threw them away). Carefully, I wiped away the debris of his lunch, but I wasn't too grossed out by this because I really liked Andrew a lot. In fact, I was half in love with him. He was the first person to speak to me at my new school, and each morning he would prance over to me, unbutton the top two buttons of his grey school shirt, tuck his left palm under his right armpit, and flap his right arm vigorously, making farting noises at me and laughing.

Each Friday afternoon when our class lined up on the bitumen court for square dancing, I tried to manoeuvre it so that I was his partner for a bit, but he would never let me touch his hands or fingers. It wasn't because I was Chinese, I knew that. It was because I was a girl and I had polluting girl germs. In the syrupy heat of a Sydney summer, Andrew Reynolds and some of the other boys would wear their navy school jumpers over their grey school shirts so that they could pull the sleeves right down over their fisted hands, and the girls would then clutch the dangling sleeve ends when we had to clasp each other's hands for the dance. That way we didn't get infected by boy germs either. It's almost chivalrous, really, the thought of all those boys suffering in the baking heat so that we could grasp the ends of their jumpers.

Later on, the teachers put a stop to this silliness and the boys had to take off their jumpers. Then we had to write on the backs of our hands: 'SFAG'. Safe From All Germs. The girls took it a step further and prefixed the charm with an extra 'S': Super Safe From All Germs. The boys retaliated with 'SSFAGEGG': Super Safe From All Germs Especially Girl Germs. Then we ran out of space on the backs of our hands, but we were safe when clammy flesh clasped, gripped and slipped with sweat.

Anyway, there I sat, ignoring Andrew Reynolds after he'd splattered my uniform like birds' droppings. I wouldn't look at him anymore so he got bored. He crammed the rest of his bread roll and chips into his mouth, got up and made one last horrible face at me, his mouth a chasm of churned-up food. Then he ran off to play with the other boys on the wooden fort. I looked after him enviously and wished that I could scrape up the courage to play on the fort too, with its cut-out windows and swaying bridge—but that was clearly the boys' domain. The girls were playing elastics and I could do nothing else but sit there and wait my turn.

I finished my lunch, screwed up the paper bag and got up to put it in the bin.

'Hey, Poo! Come and take my place.' It was Niree speaking. She was the class captain and the prettiest girl in our class. Her hair fascinated me; I always wanted to touch it because it had so many different shades from blonde to dark brown. Her fringe was carefully flicked back with a heat wand each morning and her mother tied her hair up with blue ribbons in two bunches over her ears. On Thursdays she always wore a smart Brownie uniform with a yellow tie. I wanted to join the Brownies too, but I wasn't allowed because the Patriarch said I had to do my homework and practise the piano. Niree was my best friend and I wanted, ached, to be hers too. She knew it, and my neediness made her cruel to me.

'My name isn't Poo. It's Grace,' I said sulkily. On the first day of school, my mother had told the teacher that my name was Pui Fun Tay. Nobody could pronounce it so she said that they could call me Grace. But the boys started chanting 'Poo Fun! Poo Fun! Poo Fun!' They made me hate my Chinese name.

'It's Poo if I say it's Poo. Otherwise I won't be your friend,' she threatened. Then, just as abruptly, her mood shifted and she smiled. 'Come on, don't you want to play?'

Many of the other girls were now 'out' and had lost interest in the game. There were not enough players now.

'You can hold up the elastics,' she said. 'I want my turn now. You can have a go after me.'

I loved her when she smiled at me as though I was her best friend, even though I knew I wasn't. I walked over and changed places with her so that she didn't have to hold up the elastic anymore. I shifted the elastic band until it was at my ankles, the line biting into my white cotton socks. Niree started jumping and skipping and hopping, and I was again filled with envious amazement. How she danced over those lines, dashing her ankles between them, twirling around in a complicated choreography. There was no-one better at elastics and that was why she liked it so much. She was never going to get out and I wouldn't get my turn that lunch time. I hardly knew whether to be disappointed or relieved. The elastic band moved from ankles to calves to knees. At the end of lunch, I would have red welts striping my bare legs.

I shouldn't have drunk so much water at the bubblers, I thought. I could feel the bend and snap of the elastic around my knees and somehow it added pressure to my bladder. I swallowed hard and frowned. I wanted to cross my legs and press my thighs together.

'Further apart,' Niree said tersely. 'It's too narrow.'

She had big feet shod in brown Bata school shoes. She'd gotten a poster of a young blonde girl standing next to a horse when her mother bought those shoes. I wanted those Bata school shoes and the horse poster too, but I got black, square-toed Clarks shoes instead.

'Niree, I have to go,' I said.

'Wait, I'm almost finished. Then you can have your turn.' She was panting hard now. The blue-checked skirt of her uniform flapped and her small-flowered underwear flashed as she scissored her legs skilfully over the thigh-high white lines. The boys had stopped playing at the fort and had come to watch, catcalling and wolf-whistling.

'I see England, I see France. I see Niree's underpants!' they called out.

I flushed with shame for her, but she just smiled and kept on skipping, tangling the lines expertly and slipping out of them easily.

'Niree, please,' I said again. And then I stopped. It was too late. I could feel the wetness snaking down my bare right leg.

'Shit!'

I had interrupted her concentration and she missed a jump, so she was 'out'.

'What's the matter with you, Poo?' she said angrily. Then she looked down at my legs. The floodgates had opened. The trickle had become a torrent and the pool around my black school shoes was spreading darkly over the hot bitumen. The girls looked away, embarrassed, and the boys started to laugh.

'Poo's done a piss!' they hollered. 'Poo's done a piss.'

To my surprise, Niree turned on them angrily. 'Shut up!' she said. She looked at me helplessly, unsure of what to do.

'You'd better go to the loo,' she ordered. 'Kylie or someone will hold the elastic. Go on.'

'No, I'm okay now,' I said. I couldn't bear to stay, couldn't bear to leave. Didn't want to give them a chance to say something behind my back. Wished I was dead.

'Go on, Grace,' Niree said gently. She came over and put her arm around me gingerly. Taking care not to brush my damp skirt, she gave me a quick hug. 'It's okay. You can go.'

It was a dismissal. I changed places with Kylie. We didn't catch each other's eyes. She sniffed involuntarily and I could see her wondering whether the elastic—her elastic—

was now urine soaked. They moved away from the black puddle. I stood there for a moment, not knowing what to do. The girls had started playing elastics again, chanting determinedly as if nothing had happened.

England, Ireland, Scotland, Wales. Inside, outside, inside, scales . . .

It was as if I wasn't there. I walked away to the brick building where the toilets were. It was cool inside and it stank. I leant my forehead against the brick wall and closed my eyes. I didn't go inside any of the cubicles. There was no longer any need to.

Some time later, from a great distance, I heard the bell ring. It was the end of lunch and I had to go back to class. We would listen to some ABC recordings and sing along to 'It's a Small World After All' or 'The Road to Gundagai'. Then Mr Gardiner would open the left drawer of his desk and pull out his wooden recorder, and make us take our bone-coloured plastic recorders out of their red sheaths. We would open our ABC songbooks and he would make us toot mournfully together with him.

Speed bonnie boat like a bird on the wing over the sea to Skye . . .

The bell had stopped ringing and I should have gone to class, but I hadn't moved. Didn't even crack an eyelid open. I wished I could speed like a bird on the wing. Somewhere. Far away. We had come all the way here to Sydney and it wasn't far enough. We shouldn't have stopped. We should have pushed at the boundaries and found salvation in continual flight.

'Grace?'

It was Niree. She was the last person I wanted to see. She said nothing. She took my hands and washed them.

Then she went into one of the cubicles and unrolled some toilet paper, wet it and sponged my legs. She threw the soggy paper into the loo and pulled the chain, flushing it away. She washed her own hands and took one of mine.

'Come on,' she said. 'I'll take you to Sick Bay. Maybe they'll let you go home early, you lucky thing.'

But when the nurse called my house, nobody picked up the phone so I had to wait, lying down on the sticky green garbage bag with the sour smell of my own urine on my clothes.

TWILIGHT TIME

Mum wasn't home when I returned late in the afternoon. I'd waited until all the other kids had left school. I hid in Sick Bay and everyone forgot about me. The offices were closing up when I slipped out and walked home. I didn't really expect Mum to be there because the nurse at school had tried ringing her a number of times to see whether she could come and pick me up. I thought that she must be out shopping, perhaps in Burlington Supermarket in Chinatown, searching desperately for the necessary ingredients—hot chillies, kaffir lime leaves, green peppercorns—that she needed to cook dinner that night; a dinner which would allow her and the Patriarch to pretend for a meal span that they were back home in Singapore. *Nasi lemak. Laksa.* Beef *rendang.* A dinner timed by the clink of bowls and the ticker-ticks of clicking chopsticks. A dinner broken by the Patriarch's barked-out interrogatives: 'Twelve times three? Seven times eight? Nine times eleven? Four times six?' If I didn't return enough correct answers between mouthfuls, after dinner he would take me into the kitchen, pour himself a cup of tepid Chinese tea, pop it into the microwave and set it on 'high' for one minute, then press the start button and make me recite the multiplication table.

'Nine times one is nine. Nine times two's eighteen. Nine three's twenty-seven. Nine four's thirty-six. Nine five's forty-five . . .'

And if I couldn't finish reciting before the microwave dinged, I would be bludgeoned by a frown and his cutting remarks. Then he would reset the microwave and I would recite it again. He was doing it for my own good because I was getting chances in Sydney that neither he nor Mum had had in Singapore or Malaysia.

I expected Mum to come home at any moment. Anytime now, she would erupt through the door, looking hot and harried, two plastic bags full of overpackaged Chinese groceries in each hand, talking nonstop, explaining and exhaling the frustrations of her day.

'*Ai-yo!*' She would look at the luminous green numbers on the microwave clock and give a start of alarm which may not have been exaggerated because we didn't know what time the Patriarch would come home that day. He hadn't said. She would look at me beseechingly because she knew that dinner was going to be late.

'Be a good soul and help me prepare dinner,' she would say, her arms flapping everywhere as she tried to decide on the most efficient way of cooking.

'I have a social studies test tomorrow,' I would say, protesting automatically. 'I have to remember how to spell "Yarralumla".'

But in the end I would give in because if I didn't, the Patriarch would be in a Bad Mood if he got home and dinner wasn't ready on the table. So I would measure out the rice and rinse it three times, then measure out the right amount of water to cook it. The Patriarch didn't like rice which was too dry, but he also didn't like it to be too soggy because he always said that's what Chinese restaurants did to fill up the space in your stomach. They overcooked it with too much water so that the individual grains of rice swelled up and gave the illusion of bulk. That was cheating, he said disapprovingly.

During these preparations the phone might ring and if it was Auntie Percy-phone or Wendy Wu, Mum would tell them how afraid she was to take the train by herself because that necessitated asking for a ticket from the ticket seller, who might not understand her Singaporean accent. I would listen to her telling them about the impossibility of finding a parking space in Chinatown, and how easy it was to get lost around Haymarket. Poor Mum. She would never be able to navigate herself around Sydney. She was afraid of the city because she was always getting lost; she was baffled by construction sites, the temporary concrete barricades and witches' hats that suddenly transformed the contours of the streetscape. She didn't know where to step. But finally, she'd say in a burst of palpable relief, she had made it home, safe at last.

Perhaps she was lost again, because the house remained empty throughout the afternoon. I was glad that nobody was around when I got home from school; I didn't want any witnesses to my disgrace. I went into the bathroom and stripped off my urine-drenched underwear and my blue-checked uniform. I didn't look at my body in the mirror because I was ashamed to catch a glimpse of it.

I was ashamed of its rotundity, ashamed of my lack of control over it. I was angry at my body's betrayal.

I had a quick shower, lathering my body with soap, scrubbing my hair with the baby shampoo we still used. In my fresh underwear, I carried my stinking clothes to the laundry and filled up the sink with hot water and soapsuds. Then I scrubbed and rubbed and drubbed my clothes viciously until my hands were red and raw and wrinkled. I drained the water, rinsed my uniform and panties, rinsed them again, then turned off the tap and wrung them dry. My hands were too small and my fingers too weak. I didn't manage to squeeze out very much water and my clothes were still sodden and heavy when I carried them outside into the backyard to hang them on the Hills Hoist. They dripped over the Patriarch's chilli bushes and lemon grass plants.

By that time I was so tired that I just wanted to sit down in front of the TV and lose myself in 'Bewitched' or 'I Dream of Jeannie'. I went into the living room and jerked in fright.

My mother was sitting on an armchair by the window, staring out onto the street. I realised that she had been home all this time. She must have been home when the nurse tried to ring her. Why hadn't she picked up the phone? Why didn't she say anything or make any sound? I went over to her.

'Mummy?' I said, then remembered that Sonny wanted me to call her Mum, which was what all the other Aussie kids called their mothers. There was something wussy about 'Mummy', he claimed. 'Mum, were you in all day? Did you hear the phone ring after lunch?'

She didn't reply, just stared at the black electricity cables singing out over the railway tracks across the road. She'd been ignoring me for most of my life. I should have been used to it by then.

Pandora was the one who decided that we should live in Sydney. I was conceived in her anxious anticipation, in that limbo space–time when her hopes hovered between two cultures, two lifestyles, two possibilities. When she left Singapore and Malaysia behind in her imagination but had yet to set foot in Sydney. When she temporarily abandoned women's magazines with their sensational stories of Hollywood stars to haunt travel agencies instead, picking up free brochures on package holidays in Australia. When her fingers traced the flat silhouette of Sydney Harbour, the serrated arcs of the Opera House pricking the fluid iron bend of the Bridge.

Engrossed in glossy tourist photographs of Sydney, she barely noticed my weight in her belly. Her body was light with hot hopes. I was born in her distraction. She pushed me out of her body in a fit of absent-mindedness, her attention already engaged elsewhere. Her energy and solicitude were focused fiercely on Jonah, as if she could, by sheer silent will and assiduity, force him to tell his mother nonchalantly, 'Okay, see you, bye!' and migrate to Sydney.

It's funny. She wanted to come, the Patriarch wanted to stay behind. Now that they were here, she wanted to be somewhere else. These days she stayed in the house and wandered in her mind, so that when I found her, she was just gone. Somewhere. Over the rainbow. Into the land of Oz. But at this stage it wasn't too bad. Reclamation was still possible and there were weeks when she was just full of energy and a religious zeal to clean and scrub and launder and wipe and dust and eradicate dirt from the house. To instil order into her uncontrollable life.

Now her silence and stillness were terrifying; I was so afraid for her, and for myself. I went to my room, took a black texta out of my schoolbag and came back to the living room. She hadn't moved at all. It was as though she was paralysed. Or dead. Unscrewing the cap, I took her limp, cool hand and wrote on the back of it: SSFAG. Super Safe From All Germs. (Later on, when she discovered the graffiti, she would twist my ear painfully.) I screwed the cap back on the texta carefully so that it wouldn't make a mark on any of the furniture and upset the Patriarch.

'Mum,' I said again, shaking her shoulder violently. She shuddered into consciousness and looked at me.

'What time is it?' she asked, but didn't wait for an answer. 'I was just thinking about Auntie Wendy Wu, Miss Telecom, you know. How much fun we used to have.'

She lapsed into silence, and I didn't know what to say. Then, finally, she spoke again: 'I suppose I'd better start cooking.'

I followed her to the kitchen where she took out some minced pork and tofu from the fridge. Briskly, competently, she chopped up some garlic and lit the gas burner under the wok.

'How was your day?' she finally remembered to ask as she spooned peanut oil into the hot wok and swirled it around.

I didn't want to tell her that I'd pissed myself at recess. In her distress, her terror of alien life in the inner western suburbs of Sydney, how could there be room for my own tale of shame?

'Fine,' I said, not looking at her.

'True, ah?'

And then I couldn't help it. I burst into tears and told her that I wanted to die, and if I couldn't, I wanted to change schools. I wanted to go to an all-girls' private school. The words poured out in melodramatic style. There was no stoppering them. In my veins, too, flowed the blood of generations of Lim drama queens.

My mother's eyes went helpless with panic. She didn't know how to comfort or soothe. Then she snapped off the gas. Leaving the wok with its sizzling oil and garlic, she went into the living room and put on an LP. The Platters. 'Twilight Time'.

'Wendy Wu used to dance with me, you know,' she said. 'Let's dance.'

'Don't know how to.'

'It's easy. Look.'

She took my hands and pulled me into a dance. We waltzed around the living room, bumping into the bean-bags, and she told me again how much she loved to dance when she was young. She was a beautiful dancer; I was duck-clumsy by comparison. We circled and circled and circled as greyness crept in through the windows. I got tired after a while, and I flung myself down onto a brown beanbag and watched my mother waltzing solo. Grace-fully, she turned and turned and I knew she didn't see me anymore. Alone in her own world. Lost in her own thoughts. Lost to me now.

Dinner would be late that night, the Patriarch's rage unbearable. Even as I write the smell of burnt and black-ened garlic haunts the air.

ADVANCE
AUSTRALIA FAIR

I didn't tell Sonny what had happened at school that day; I knew that he had his own troubles. He was still skinny and small at that stage, and he came home from school sporting ugly bruises every day. He took to wearing the grey long-sleeved winter school shirt even in the baking heat of summer so that his bruises wouldn't show. Even worse than the bruises were the questions that might follow, and the promise of retribution if he dobbed. One of the first Aussie words Sonny learned at school was 'dob'.

'Hey! Ching-chong Chinaman! You'd better not dob, or else,' they told him.

Like me, he tried to hide in the toilets at first, but it wasn't a good hiding place for boys. There were few cubicles and it inspired the bullies to disgusting, horrifying acts of brutality when they found him there. So he simply resigned himself and endured their torments for the first half of lunch, until the library opened and he could find shelter among the shelves of books. He became a library monitor until he started to grow taller and discovered in himself an aptitude for swimming and basketball that gained him entry into the bully boys' circle. But until then, he buried himself in stories about Biggles. Later, in the early 1980s, someone graffitied the wall of a building facing Raw Square, just across from Strathfield Station, where private and public schoolkids gathered at the bus stands each afternoon to eat hot chips and potato scallops, flirt and chat. The profound message that shocked and confronted the public: 'Biggles Flies Sopwith Camels'. I wondered whether it was Sonny's doing, though it seemed so uncharacteristic.

That day when I pissed my pants, I knew better than to try to find Sonny after school. I wanted him to say that it was all right, but at the same time I hoped he hadn't heard about what I'd done or he would be furious. He wanted us to fit in with the Aussie kids. Hated it when we did anything to make ourselves stand out. Tried to correct my accent and my syntax all the time so that I didn't sound like I'd just come straight from Malaysia or Singapore. He was ashamed of me at school, because he was ashamed of himself too. He faded into the brickwork when the school bell rang, became invisible while the hordes of schoolkids— including the bully boys who picked on him—stampeded out the gate and poured down the streets to invade Burwood and Strathfield stations.

It wasn't just that we looked different; our accents and the Singlish we had grown up speaking marked us out as pariahs in the playground. Everyday English was a minefield of mispronunciations for us.

'Hey, Kylie, Poo here has cu-*cum*-ber on her ham sandwich.'

'Cu-*cum*-ber, cu-*cum*-ber, cu-*cum*-ber!' they chanted.

'It's *cu*-cumber, Grace,' Niree informed me kindly.

It's not ca-*land*-er, it's *cal*-ender; it's not sword, it's sord; your orange drink isn't tan-*jee*, it's *tang*-ee; you don't 'on' the TV, you 'turn it on'.

We grew to hate the sound of our voices, and those of our parents. They loved all things British, but they couldn't speak English. Their accents, their syntax and their vocabulary mirrored in language our cultural difference and our social leprosy before the age of multiculturalism. Even when we were right, we were wrong. So, for example, one of the bully boys told Sonny, 'What're youse gonna do, eh? Just youse try dobbin' us in, mate. We'll thump ya good.'

'Well,' Sonny muttered.

'Eh?'

'You'll thump me well, or hard even. But you don't thump me "good",' he said boldly, stupidly.

'Hey, listen a this, guys. Slit-eyes here's tryin' a teach us how to speak English. Hey, Chink?'

One of the boys caught him in a headlock while someone else kicked his bum.

'Go-o-o-o-o-o-al!' hollered the kicker.

Sonny ended up hanging out with the other ethnics at school, mostly Italians and Lebanese then. When more Chinese moved into the area and started coming to school, he scuttled thankfully into their midst, huddled with them near the library at lunch time in what the other kids came to call the Great Wall of China. But he didn't find his place there either. They mostly spoke Cantonese, and we didn't understand it because neither Pandora nor Jonah spoke it at home. Jonah's mother tongue was Hokkien, Pandora's was Teochew. The new Chinese boys and girls dyed their fringes orange and dined in Chinatown. They listened to

Michael Jackson and Cantopop singers such as Alan Tham, Leslie Chung and Teresa Dang. Later, in their late teens and early twenties, they hung out at karaoke bars and Chinese casinos. At a time when teenagers were watching rebellious Tom Cruise and tedious Ally Sheedy movies, they watched Jackie Chan in the *Armour of God*, *Police Story*, *City Hunter* and *Drunken Master*.

Sonny enjoyed the action and loved the kung fu. He wanted to take it up, to practise bisecting inanimate objects with a rushing roar of 'hah!' like Uncle Winston before him. He even learned to enjoy braised chicken's feet at dim sum. But otherwise, Chinese culture was foreign to him. He found himself making gauche mistakes when he went out to dim sum with his Chinese friends. When one of the girls poured tea into his cup, he did not tap the table with his fingers to thank her. They wondered disdainfully why he couldn't speak any Chinese dialect properly, and deliberately spoke in Cantonese when they didn't want him to understand. To them, he was an Aussie; he didn't belong. He drifted out of that group and retreated into the dimly lit, trumpet-dominated world of jazz.

In the late eighties, he abandoned jazz, zeroed in on hip-hop and basketball, and did his best to become black. His jeans grew voluminous—giant denim windsocks— and we occasionally suspected that hair might actually grow under the flipped-back Chicago Bulls baseball cap that he never took off. The LA riots after the Rodney King trial shook the foundations of his world, when he watched the televised images of black Americans looting and beating up Asian shopkeepers. Black was beautiful, black was best. He had only ever associated racism with white Aussies and Chinese.

Yes, the Patriarch was a racist. He was suspicious about budget petrol stations in Dulwich Hill and Lakemba because he was convinced that they were owned by Lebanese who watered down the petrol and ruined your car engine. He grumbled when Hong Kong Chinese and Vietnamese began to move into Burwood and Strathfield. He muttered darkly that Strathfield had been overrun by Koreans. He scowled when he heard people shouting loudly in Cantonese across the aisles of Franklins. He was incensed when a few Chinese patients tried to bargain with him to lower the price of his extractions, root canals and crowns; he was disgusted when they demanded that he add extra dental item numbers to their bills for work he had not done so that they could make larger claims from their health funds and cover the insurance gap. He disliked Indians because he said they smelled of coconut oil. As for the Japanese, who could forget what they'd done during the war?

At the same time, he loved the Tandoori chicken from the local Indian restaurant and was delighted that the Chinese restaurant in Strathfield Plaza now served dim sum every day. He was glad that his wife no longer had to make the drive down to the Burlington Supermarket in Chinatown to buy Chinese vegetables and stock up on Chinese ingredients since she could now buy them in the local Chinese and Vietnamese grocery stores in Burwood. He loved the cappuccinos served in Italian cafes along Burwood Road, spooning up the chocolate-dusted froth and licking it like an ice-cream, crunching happily on his almond biscotti.

He enjoyed the benefits of multiculturalism in the 1980s but clung to a belief in assimilation. He had immersed himself in Australian culture when he first arrived. He watched cricket in the days when Dennis Lillee was a star and the Australian team sported Afro hairstyles. He drank Tooheys beer and could sing along to 'Come on Aussie, come on, come on'. He discovered the salty delights of meat pies and sausage rolls in the milkbar beneath his surgery. He learned how to barbecue and enjoyed it once Mum started marinating steaks in soy sauce, pepper, garlic and red wine, and leaving them in the fridge overnight. He learned to say 'How 'bout a cuppa?' and he became a member of the local RSL although he never went there. He stayed home every Saturday night to watch 'Hey Hey It's Saturday', laughed with Daryl Somers, and admired Jackie MacDonald when she was still around. He thought they were 'nice'. He loved to hate 'Red Faces', was contemptuous of the contestants, but morally outraged when Red Symons gave them insultingly low scores. 'Cod!' he'd say, scowling at Red in palpable irritation, not wanting to take the Lord's name in vain but finding no other suitable exclamation.

And yet perhaps he wasn't so much a racist as a misanthrope; his disapproval seemed to be directed towards the world in general, with no discrimination reserved for any particular race. His politics were conservative and his pleasure lay in complaining; he was the Chinese Bruce Ruxton. Like Bruce, dual citizenship pissed him off; he'd gladly given up his Malaysian citizenship to become an Australian. He reminded us constantly how lucky we were to be in Australia.

'Just remember May 13, 1969,' he told us, 'and be grateful that you're here instead of Kuala Lumpur. We could all have been killed. And if I hadn't sacrificed my career and all the money I could make there in order to bring you kids here for a good education, like all the other Chinese, you'd be suffering discrimination by the Malays in the schools and universities. So just be grateful you're Australian.'

When we started school, he made Sonny and me memorise the words to the first verse of 'Advance Australia Fair'. It was an anthem that puzzled me for a long time because I mixed up the word 'fair' for its homonym in Humphrey B. Bear's signature song in the 1970s and '80s. Whoever wrote Humphrey's lyrics certainly didn't have kids like us in mind.

What a funny old fellow is Humphrey
He gets in all manner of strife
He leads a very exciting life
And honey's his favourite fare . . .

The lyrics were as arcane and incomprehensible to a kid as 'Advance Australia Fair', which was even more remote from my life because when the Patriarch made us learn it, and puzzled over it himself each night, it was still 'Australia's sons' being compelled to rejoice, rather than 'Australians all' doing the same thing. The Patriarch still clings to 'Australia's sons' because, in his attitude towards political correctness, John Howard is his role model. ('I refuse to call a manhole a personhole,' the Patriarch proclaims defiantly. So there.) Anyway, it was a puzzling song then: *In joyful strains then let us sing Advance Australia Fair.*

Fair or fare? And what did it all mean anyway? The fare was the fifteen cents we paid to the bus driver during the school holidays, when we weren't allowed to use our bus passes for a free ride. That was quite straightforward, even though it didn't make sense as far as Humphrey B. Bear's honey was concerned. 'Fair' was much more difficult. Each year we had a school fair where girls sold the hideous cushion covers they'd crocheted and boys hawked wobbly edged, glazed clay ashtrays, bought by proud parents who didn't smoke. Our entry into adolescence was heralded the first time Sonny muttered resentfully, 'It isn't *fair*.' But most disturbing of all, to be 'fair' was to be white-skinned, even though E.M. Forster might have remarked that 'the so-called white races are really pinko-grey'. 'Advance Australia Fair' was pregnant with all sorts of uneasy implications. Was it only white Australians who were supposed to advance? Or did 'Australia Fair' mean that only white people were Australians?

Like the Patriarch, I wanted desperately to assimilate. I wanted to wash myself into clean whiteness; bleach myself into Advanced Australian Fairness. Instead, I pissed my pants and was considered a dirty little Chinese girl.

SOFT-BOILED EGGS

Pandora was always alone in the house. She swung between days of listless loneliness, when dustballs flocculated around the fringes of the Persian carpets on the walls or caught in the crooks of porcelain statuette arms, and staccato bursts of frantic activity when windowpanes were squeegeed, bathroom tiles were scrubbed, clothes were laundered, dried and ironed, and we could smell curries simmering fragrantly all the way down the street like an aromatic finger beckoning us home.

On a good day, she yanked up blinds and jerked aside curtains, threw open windows and exclaimed loudly, happily, as sunshine and gusts of warm air wafted the heavy scent of jasmine and wisteria into the house. She played The Platters as she vacuumed, or wailed along with Aretha Franklin, demanding R.E.S.P.E.C.T. from the empty house. When she felt lonely, she ran up huge phone bills ringing Lida Lim in England, chatting to Wendy Wu, and begging Percy-phone to come and visit us. She went for a walk to Burwood Park and sat on a bench, watching other people strolling through the grounds leisurely, or striding determinedly across it to get to Westfield shopping centre. Then she came home and took out her recipe books and made all the Malaysian food that the Patriarch liked but couldn't get in Sydney. On good days, she ventured out to the supermarket, the post office and the bank, and she wasn't intimidated by other people. She took a train to the city and window-shopped. She stifled her loneliness in constant motion and ceaseless activity.

When we came home, she had a snack ready for us: dumplings, red bean buns, gooey Nonya cakes coloured a lurid slime green and dusted with desiccated coconut. I was happy to sit quietly and eat while she chatted with Sonny about how his day had been. He never told her about the teasing and the bruises that he bore on his skinny body like a pubescent Christ. Instead, he told her that he had heard a Louis Armstrong album and he wanted to learn to play the trumpet. She somehow persuaded the Patriarch to buy Sonny a trumpet and sent him to trumpet lessons after school.

On her functional days, she was clever and competent. She sewed a blue library book bag for me and embroidered my initials on it in chain stitch. She finished off the gaudy tapestry pot holder that we girls had to make for school. She sponsored me for the school's ten-kilometre walkathon and then walked around the neighbourhood with me because I was afraid to ring doorbells or knock on doors to ask complete strangers to sponsor me. Then, after I'd done it, she collected the money with me because I was even more afraid and embarrassed to ask for money. And she paid for all the sponsors who wouldn't cough up the cash. In later years we just went through the White Pages and picked out surnames and initials, then wrote them down as sponsors so that we could save doing the rounds of the neighbourhood. Then she just gave me the money for all the so-called sponsors. It was our little secret, she said. She tested me on my spelling and signed my homework. She was my mother.

But even on a good day, her exuberance began to sag by mid-afternoon and by the early evening, as we heard the Patriarch's car growling up the drive, it had deflated completely. Sonny sprang up from his sprawled position in front of the TV, snapping it off immediately. In a panic, the three of us scurried around the house tidying and cleaning and putting things away before he could come in. She shrank into herself and used us as a barrier.

'That's Daddy now. Go and greet him properly and bring him his slippers,' she told us, as if we were dogs.

'Hi,' she said to him. 'Dinner will be ready in half an hour. You have time for a shower first.'

'Why is there all this water around the sink?' he said, peering closely at the taps. 'You've left the dishcloth sopping wet.'

He yanked open the door of the dishwasher and exclaimed in annoyance.

'*Hi-yah!* Who has been using so many cups and glasses again?'

Sonny and I murmured that we had homework to do and we abandoned her, hurrying away to our bedrooms and hiding behind closed doors until dinner was ready. In the evenings, after dinner, she left the Patriarch sitting alone in the living room, in front of the TV, while she went out the back and did the laundry and ironing. She strolled out into the garden and stared up at the stars.

But on her bad days she curled up into a chair and stared sightlessly out of the window. She could sit immobile for hours, frozen into forgetfulness. As the years passed it became harder and harder to shake her out of it and make her look at you. We came home to a still house that exuded stale air and dejection.

'Come on, *lah*, what's the matter with you?' the Patriarch said in disgust. Fear sharpened his tone and fatigue blunted his sympathy. 'What kind of a wife and mother are you anyway? If I'd known you were going to be like this, I'd never have moved us here. I slave away in my surgery all day long and I come home to this.'

He looked at the rice Sonny had steamed and the tinned frankfurters and baked beans I'd heated up for dinner that night. We hadn't learned how to cook yet, and we hadn't been successful that afternoon in tugging Pandora from the tide of her oblivion.

'You're *slack*,' he said, smacking out the new word he'd picked up from one of his Aussie patients recently. 'All of you. *Slack*.'

Bad-temperedly, he swiped his arm across the table and sent the cheap china dishes with rice, baked beans and frankfurters smashing onto the tiled kitchen floor. Blood drummed in my ears and I pressed my nails into the flesh of my palms until the skin broke. I started to leak uncontrollably into my underwear. In a panic, I looked at Sonny, but I could only see his mop of thick black hair. He hung his head and stared fixedly at his lap.

'Clean that up. I'm going to have a shower.' He stopped at the doorway and looked at his wife. He tried to reach inside for some calm, some compassion, some of that elusive love he felt for her. All he pulled out was frustration.

'You're the one who wanted to immigrate and you just sit there all day long shaking legs. You'd better get your act together or I'm going to get a divorce. I'm sick and tired of this.'

She waited until he was out of the kitchen. 'Get a divorce then. I don't care.'

As soon as we heard him moving about upstairs, we slipped out of our seats silently and began scraping shards of china and scraps of food into a dustpan. My stomach growled and acid churned painfully. I picked up a tomato sauce covered frankfurter and slipped it into my mouth, chewing quickly. It tasted foul.

Pain exploded in my ear as she wrenched it hard.

'Grace, you dirty girl! How can you pick food up from the floor and eat it?' Then something snapped as she realised that Sonny and I were hungry. She knelt in the mush of rice and baked beans, wrapped her arms around me and stroked my back, clinging to me.

'It's all right, it's okay,' she said, and I didn't know whether she was talking about me or about herself. 'I know you're hungry. I'm so sorry. I'll cook something for you. I'll cook . . .'

Her mind blanked out, and she couldn't remember how to cook. She opened the fridge door and stared uncomprehendingly at the eggs, vegetables, cartons, glass jars of sauce, bottles of liquid—they made no sense to her. In that instant nothing looked familiar.

'I'll cook something,' she repeated. Then she sank into a chair and started sobbing jerkily. 'I'm sorry. I'm so sorry.'

While I went upstairs to change my underwear, Sonny cleared away the mess and put the dustpan and broom away tidily. When I came back down, he was hugging her tightly.

They were enclosed in a circle that excluded me and I was jealous. I stood there, waiting to do something, wanting to be useful.

'Never mind,' he whispered. 'Never mind. I'll kill that bastard.'

'Don't talk about your father like that, Sonny,' she said automatically. I brought her a box of Kleenex and she wiped her eyes and honked hard into a tissue. 'And don't use such bad language.'

She made an effort to pull herself together. She opened the fridge door again and took out some eggs. At such times, there was only one thing she could do. She made soft-boiled eggs. Perfectly timed, so that the albumen wasn't too runny or the yolk too hard. Making soft-boiled eggs was an automatic action, below the level of conscious thought. She dribbled soy sauce over them and sprinkled pepper. Then, with the toast Sonny had made and a banana and pieces of orange on the side, she took a tray up to the Patriarch's study. In silence, she offered the tray to him. With both hands.

It was—I don't know what. An apology, certainly; an acknowledgement of culpability. A gesture of submission, perhaps. And a statement of distance between them. A formal change in relationship; not so much the intimacy of husband and wife, but Patriarch and woman. A barrier thrown up between them that he recognised and tried to batter down with sex late that night, after they assumed we'd gone to sleep.

'I love you,' he told her as she lay passively in his arms. 'I'll bring some take-away back tomorrow night for dinner.'

It was his way of making amends. Always, he found it so difficult to apologise to his wife. It was not in his nature, or in his culture for that matter. To him there were no good or bad husbands, only good or bad wives, obedient or disobedient wives. Increasingly, as his irritation and frustration with her compounded, he treated her like an intractable child. He scolded her and mocked her in front of us, using us to twist the knife of guilt he stabbed her with.

'What kind of mother are you to let your own children starve?'

Sonny and I learned to cook shortly after that. We waited until she was having a good day and hung around the kitchen, watching her carefully. We took down simple recipes and begged her to allow us to help with the more difficult dishes. Eventually, between the two of us, we took over the cooking altogether.

To this day I gag reflexively at the smell of soft-boiled eggs.

THE MERRY-GO-ROUND
OF LOVE

Dreams of falling are common in that liminal time–space between waking and sleeping. In his early adolescence Sonny used to dream that he was sliding downwards slowly through thick panels of air. There is nothing graceful about his movement through space. Overgrown and awkward, his limbs splay outwards, knobbly knees and elbows bent at the joints like a cartwheeling swastika. He swims in translucent syrup, so alive, so aware. He feels the air caressing every hair follicle on his supersensitive skin. Overhead the sky arcs electric blue. He's in a state of orgasmic excitement, his muscles taut as twisted piano wire, his cock erect like a fifth limb. Gentle waves of wind wash in and out of his shell-shaped ears. He thinks: not falling, but flying.

And then he looks down. If he'd thought about it at all, he would have said he was planing westward through the air above Parramatta Road and, although unsure of his exact location, he expected to see the red-tiled roofs of inner western Sydney. Perhaps the billboard where, in the early 1990s, giant cut-outs of Elle Macpherson's feet used to spear the sky as she leant forward on her elbows to frame her famous tits. In those days she lounged in behemothic splendour in her white underwear, looking across to McDonald's, looming comfortably over the snarled traffic inching west.

Or perhaps if he twisted his neck sideways he might glimpse the burning vermilion box of the Millers storage building further along Parramatta Road at Petersham. Perhaps rows of tiny terraces with ramshackle weatherboard extensions opening into squares of unkempt garden where rusty Hills Hoists sprouted like vicious weeds from broken concrete yards, and ragged banners of limp laundry lined the shotgun-gleaming railway tracks barrelling towards Blacktown and beyond.

But in his dream he sees none of this. Instead, he looks down and suddenly sees a neatly mown lawn with a black rectangular hole gashed out in the middle of the field. When he notices the mound of dirt beside it, he realises that it's a freshly-dug grave. His grave. At that moment the dark earth rushes up to meet him and he is gripped by terror. He jolts awake. Not flying after all, just falling.

Sonny grew out of this nightmare eventually, but it would recur twice more during his life. The first occasion was when his hero Chet Baker mysteriously tumbled to his death from an Amsterdam hotel window in 1988. Sonny grieved as though he'd lost both best friend and father. The second time was a decade after that, when his mother jumped from the eighteenth floor of an apartment block in Singapore. Each time, he woke up and crawled out of bed, groping in the dark for his trumpet. He ran his fingers over the metal stops and hugged it to himself for comfort.

Sonny wanted nothing more than to be Chet, pouring poetry from the spit-tarnished brass bowl of his trumpet. The weekends of his adolescence were spent burrowed away in the rat's nest of his bedroom, holland blinds drawn down to keep out the glaring afternoon light, the desk lamp throwing his distorted silhouette against the beige walls. He nursed the trumpet like a baby, but in turn he suckled at the mouthpiece; breathed fragile, fluty notes like iridescent bubbles towards the moulded plaster flowers on the ceiling. One bony bare foot rubbing absently on the synthetic pile of the carpet, white Hanes T-shirt drooping baggily over his Levis, stiff black Asian hair brushed and Brylcreemed back into a 1950s pompadour. He perched on the edge of his unmade bed and adopted Chet's brooding, sulky pose from those William Claxton photographs.

But Claxton would never have pinned Sonny down in black and white. Not with those straight, thick black brows, the flat flub of a nose and the awkward angles of his lanky body. Back when he still believed in romance, 'My Funny Valentine' often sighed out of his trumpet, accompanied by the scratchy LP of Chet with the Gerry Mulligan quartet. But perhaps his eyes might have arrested Claxton's attention: benignly cow-like, long-lashed and almond-shaped with the epicanthus fold that Chinese long to possess, they peered disconcertingly at the world, hungry and expectant yet afraid to ask for more because we had always been told as kids that we already had so much. As children we were fed with fear and succoured with guilt.

All the things he wasn't supposed to wish for, all the desires that would have been interpreted as ingratitude by our parents—what thanks for this trauma and sacrifice of immigration to Australia!—were spun out into the four corners of the ceiling. Sonny didn't merely play the trumpet; he prayed with it. Eventually, prayers changed to paeans of adolescent disillusion: snatches of simple-note melodies and murmured jazz phrases that congealed the clichéd but heartfelt sentiments of alienation and misunderstanding adolescents believe unique to themselves.

Absorbed in the effort of exhaling music, head bowed hopelessly over his trumpet, he started with a yelp of surprise as Mum exploded like a Star Wars Stormtrooper through the door, snapping off the lamp and yanking up the blinds.

'Do you have any white clothes?' she demanded. Colour segregation was religiously observed where her laundry was concerned. Whites would have nothing to do with blacks or other colours. 'I'm doing a load of white laundry now.'

Her nose twitched and she sniff, sniff, sniffed the air like a hound. 'Your room stinks. You forgot to change the odour eaters in your school shoes, didn't you? Hah!'

She pounced on two shrivelled grey socks poking out from scuffed black shoes the size of small boats. 'You're such a dirty boy, Sonny. Why didn't you put these socks in the laundry?'

A cursory glance around the room revealed dog-eared manila folders stuffed with notes for history, a rain-wrinkled book of Bruce Dawe poems which had lost its cover, and the smudged and scribbled hieroglyphics of trigonometry. Crammed into his bookcases, where his textbooks should have been, were boxes of Arnott's Shapes biscuits, Smiths salt and vinegar crisps and plastic wrappers of mini Mars Bars. Over his desk and strewn across his bed were NBA T-shirts, shorts, a sports towel and the school uniform he'd forgotten to put in the laundry. Old, smelly underwear hid like criminals under his bed.

All this she absorbed with a single X-ray glance. Sonny cringed as her right hand snaked out automatically towards his head, thumb and index finger assuming mechanical pincer motions as they gripped his left ear and twisted hard. The cartilage of his ears cracked as they were yanked out of shape. Sonny always maintained mournfully that his ears resembled Prince Charles's because of this favourite punitive act of our mother's.

On her rampage through the minefield of his room she tripped over a camouflaged barbell. Pain detonated instantly.

'Ssssss!' she inhaled in a hiss of agony. 'Your room's a disgrace. You'd better clean it up before your father sees it.'

(It was always 'your father', never 'my husband'.)

But Sonny was never in time to avoid the furious telling-off, the roars and bellows that thundered through the two-storeyed house and that made me scurry to my room, desperately cramming clothes and books into my own cupboards.

'You kids don't appreciate anything. When I was growing up I never had a bedroom of my own. We didn't even have beds of our own until I was eight. We slept three to a bed and had to put up with each other's smells and kicks. You'd better learn to appreciate how fortunate you are and clean up your room. I didn't sacrifice a great career and migrate here to live in a messy house.'

The door slammed and angry footsteps thumped through the silent rooms. For the next few hours anger and outrage seeped through the house and permeated its cracks and corners. Mum would be sorry that she had got Sonny into trouble. Yet again. She spent the rest of the afternoon cooking his favourite dish for dinner, only to be unspeak-ably hurt when he refused seconds.

'Eat some more,' she urged as she piled globs of mild beef *rendang* and *choy sum* stir-fried in garlic and brandy onto his cooled rice.

'Don't want any more.'

'Stop sulking and eat it,' the Patriarch ordered. 'In my day most people only had meat once a week unless they were very rich. And then it was mostly gristle and tendon.'

Sonny hung his head and did his best to eat it, spoon-ing *rendang* into his mouth until it not only looked like shit, it tasted like it too. Where she'd got the idea that he liked beef *rendang* was completely beyond him. He had never liked spicy food and at that age, his idea of a good meal was an all-you-can-eat buffet at some American-style steakhouse.

Rebellion was an art at which we were particularly untalented, though we gave it our best shot. But how could we compete against the furnace roar and the searing gusts of the Patriarch's anger? Or the guilt induced by our mother's sorrowful sigh: 'If I'd known this was going to happen we wouldn't have migrated.' Immigration is an act of sacrifice on the part of your parents that you can never atone for. So we sought refuge in resentful silence and built stony walls of unspoken hate. We brooded, we sulked. Sonny avoided everyone's eyes all night, especially Mum's, and she grew more frantic and agitated as her ten-tative overtures of friendliness went unseen, unheard and unreturned.

'What fruit do you want?' she demanded after dinner, bringing to the table a plastic tray of custard apples, ban-anas, Californian Sunkist oranges, Batlow apples, Japanese nashi pears, flushed persimmons and waxy sultanas. The variety of fruit available in Sydney never ceased to thrill her. How often had she told us that when she was growing up in Singapore after the war, she'd had to share one apple with all her siblings. She never got over the marvel of having a whole piece of fruit to herself. The vegetable crispers in the fridge were constantly overburdened with new and exotic fruits that she had just discovered in the local Italian fruit market. ('Mr Iacono showed me how to choose juicy water-melons today,' she would say proudly. 'Next week he's keeping a box of first-grade Bowen mangoes for me. Top quality!') Much of the fruit rotted away before anyone ever got to it, and the reproachful headlamps of her gaze would light upon her family then.

'I'm too full for any fruit,' Sonny muttered. Casting a sidelong glance at the Patriarch falling asleep on the peach leather lounge in front of the '7.30 Report', he picked up his plate and shuffled to the sink to rinse away the remains of uneaten *rendang* into the insinkerator. Mum trailed after him with her tray of peace offerings, bleating unhappily.

'Too full for any fruit?' she repeated, a look of dazed incomprehension glazing her eyes. 'What about roughage? Don't forget your bowel movements, Sonny.'

'We had *choy sum* tonight.'

'Still, you don't want to get constipation. Very painful, you know.'

'Don't have it.'

'Your father and I do,' she reminded him, as if consti-pation were hereditary. Sonny didn't answer, determined not to take any interest in his parents' internal plumbing. She tried again. 'Take some grapes at least. Are you shitting properly anyway?'

For her, love was expressed through the provision of clean clothes and fresh fruit, and the supervision of regular bowel movements.

Sonny shot her a look of disgust and turned away. At the doorway, between the kitchen and the living room where the Patriarch snored in his white singlet and tracksuit pants on the couch, toothpick dangling from the corner of his mouth, Sonny paused and looked from one parent to the other. He shook his head.

'I hate being Chinese. Chinese are so gross,' he said as he walked away to lock himself in his room, brooding to the sound of Chet Baker.

I tried to get Mum's attention.

'My bowel movements are fine,' I said as I grabbed a banana, snapped off the black top and peeled it. 'Traffic on the Harbour Bridge is regular as clockwork with no delays at the tollbooths.'

But she hardly heard me. She was busy cutting a Batlow apple into six precise pieces and arranging them on a brown glass plate.

'Take these out to your father.'

Later that night, after she had done the dishes, she retreated to her domain at the back of the house to do the laundry. Her eyes were glassy with unshed tears and the soft lines around her mouth curved slackly downwards as she turned shirts inside out and spritzed pre-wash on the collars.

Hoping for some attention at last, I perched on a bamboo stool in the laundry and read out my school essay to her. But her ear was not attuned to Gavrilo Princip or Germany's Blank Cheque to Austria–Hungary. She craved Sonny's forgiveness and friendship, but it wouldn't be forthcoming for the next few days. Not until the Patriarch's

Black Mood had evaporated and Sonny was no longer the recipient of those contemptuous glances and bludgeoning remarks. Only then would he deign to talk to her.

When he was much younger, Sonny had graciously allowed Mum to lavish attention on him. And if he was feeling generous he doled some out to me, so that a peculiar friendship sprang up between us. On the weekends he'd allow me to enter the sanctuary of his room and riffle through his LP and cassette collection. As he struggled with his maths, I sat in a patch of sunshine and squinted at Miles Davis, Dizzy Gillespie, Wynton Marsalis, Charlie Parker, Bob Barnard, James Morrison and Vince Jones. Trumpet tunes and snatches of Gershwin melodies formed the soundtrack to my childhood.

But as the years went by those patches of forgiveness and friendship became few and far between. Pique and misunderstanding became a matter of habit; we knitted our separate resentments together strand by strand, and wrapped them like blankets around our shoulders, gripping them tightly so that they would not fall away and leave us exposed to love, hurt and the whole damn pain of living.

As a family, we were doomed to the humiliation of begging pathetically for love and attention from the one member who refused it to us. Mum wanted Sonny's, Sonny wanted the Patriarch's, the Patriarch wanted his wife's, and I wanted my mother's. All my life we rode that merry-go-round, chasing love in front of us and never catching up, never looking behind to see who might be offering it until it was too late.

THE SPITE OF LIFE

Madam Tay was coming to visit us. She had been threatening to do so for years and now she was actually going to come—for a long visit, too. She hadn't seen her son for five years so she applied for a three-month visa. She arrived on my birthday, at the start of the summer holidays. The Patriarch ordered Mum to make sure that we were neatly dressed and ready to go to the airport by seven-thirty on that Sunday morning. She jerked us out of bed at six-thirty.

'Happy birthday, Grace. *Nah.*' She thrust a small un-wrapped box into my hand. I already knew what was inside: the gold watch with the Roman numeral face and brown leather strap that she had bought for me two weeks before from one of the cheap jewellery stores in the local shopping centre. 'Hurry up and get ready or Daddy will get angry.'

Sleepy and sulky, we waited at the airport for an hour and a half. The flight was due to land at seven-fifty but it was late. It arrived at eight-fifteen and we waited for another three-quarters of an hour before Madam Tay toddled out of the arrival gate, a fat old woman with grey frizzy hair like steel wool and huge pink glasses tilting on her flat snub of a nose, dressed in a bilious green *samfoo* and a white cardigan with pearl buttons.

'*Ai-yah*,' she groaned as the Patriarch hurried forward to kiss her cheek and take her trolley. She gripped his arm and leant heavily on him before turning to inspect us. She started speaking but we couldn't understand what she was saying because she spoke in her Hokkien dialect. Then she tottered forward and wrapped her flabby arms around Sonny. There was a strong whiff of Tiger Balm and mothballs. An old Chinese lady smell. A Madam Tay smell.

'Ah Sonny, ah,' she said, stroking his face and arms. 'Good, good.'

It didn't take us long to realise that her English vocabulary was restricted to 'good', 'coffee' (or 'kopi', as she pronounced it) and 'TV'.

Hanging on to Sonny's arm and pawing him all the while, she turned her head and said something to the Patriarch, then we began to move off to the car park. Madam Tay walked between the Patriarch and Sonny, chubby fingers pinching their arms in a lover's deadly grip. Mum and I walked behind and sat silently in the back of the car as we drove home.

Changes were made immediately. She didn't like the guest room at the back of the house so she moved into my room, which was next to the master bedroom at the front end of the house. I dragged my clothes from the closet and hauled them downstairs to the guest room next to the laundry, emptied my desk drawers and stacked the contents on the floor. Sonny and Dad would move the desk down later.

'Can't I take my bed as well?' I asked Mum. 'Or at least my mattress. It'll smell forever if she sleeps on it for three months. I'll need a new mattress.'

'Shh,' Mum cautioned in a whisper, looking furtively towards the living room where Madam Tay sat with the Patriarch, still clutching his hand tightly and speaking in a breathy whine. 'Sonny,' we heard her bleat. 'Sonny, ah.' Mum nudged him and, rolling his eyes at me, he shuffled into the living room and allowed her to paw him again.

Mum cooked rice porridge for lunch and I helped her to make the meatballs, rolling together a gooey paste of minced pork, garlic, ginger, shallots and chopped bits of Shiitake mushrooms. We set the table and Mum called them in for lunch.

'Don't forget what I taught you,' she hissed at me in an undertone. 'Call your grandmother to eat.'

Madam Tay waddled in and sat next to the Patriarch. She patted the seat next to her. 'Sonny, good, good.'

Sonny came in and I saw that he was now wearing a thick gold necklace with a rectangular gold pendant like a dog tag. She'd brought over lots of gold jewellery and some money for him. She was determined to love him because he was the only son of her eldest son.

'Amah, *chiak*,' I said obediently.

With her index finger she pushed her slipping glasses up her nose and stared at me as if seeing me for the first time. A slow, wide grin spread across her face, splitting it like a slice of melon. She flashed pink gums at me. She began to speak in Hokkien, the guttural words tumbling forth as she spooned hot porridge into her mouth, making clucking noises and spitting it back into her bowl when she found it too hot. Finally, she stopped and looked at me expectantly. I tried to remember what Mum had told me to reply.

'*Wah bay heow tiah*,' I said with my Aussie accent. I don't understand.

She was outraged. She looked at my mother and began scolding. In silence we sat and ate our porridge, letting the incomprehensible stream of words eddy around us. The tone was plain enough. Despite the fact that Mum spoke a different dialect and didn't know much Hokkien, Madam Tay blamed Mum for not teaching us her language. She accused our mother of trying to drive a wedge between us and herself. Finally, she turned her attention back to me.

'No good,' she said. 'No good.'

She got up from the table and left her lunch cooling in the thick porcelain bowl. She tugged Sonny up from his seat and made him help her to her room so that she could lie down. Even tucked out of sight, her displeasure resonated through the muted house. We didn't see her again until dinner that night. Mum had made roast chicken with potatoes, pumpkin and green beans because it was my favourite meal then. Madam Tay came in and stared incredulously at her meal, adjusting her spectacles fussily in order to see better.

'No good,' she said. 'No good.'

The Patriarch tried to explain to her that it was my birthday so Mum had cooked me a special birthday meal. Grumbling, she lowered herself to her seat and we were then allowed to sit down. She looked around her.

'Sonny?' she demanded.

'*Hi-yah*. Where's that boy?' the Patriarch said, exasperated. 'Never on time, *one lah*. Sonny, where are you?'

The answer came hooting through the door. Sonny had brought down his trumpet and he now started to play the opening bars of 'Happy Birthday'.

'Sonny, how nice,' Mum said. She started singing along with the trumpet: 'Happy birthday dear Gra-ace, happy birthday to you.'

It was a solo effort. Nobody else sang; Sonny because he was trumpeting, Madam Tay because she didn't know how to; the Patriarch just squirmed uncomfortably in his seat.

Finally he said, 'Happy birthday, Grace. Come, let's eat.'

'Amah, *chiak*,' I tried again. This time she ignored me. She waited for my mother to carve the chicken and place the food on her plate, then we ate in tense silence.

Whenever I think about Madam Tay, a clear image of her dentures flashes into my mind. I woke up every morning and stumbled into the bathroom to be greeted by the wide grin of her acrylic dentures floating in a glass. During the day her ill-fitting dentures clicked when she talked, occasionally troubling her. She took them out and left them lying on tables, benchtops and windowsills. Sometimes she would fall asleep in front of the TV. Her mouth dropped open, saliva dribbled down the groove of her cheek, and once her upper denture fell out and reposed on her left shoulder like a general's epaulette. Her whole face changed its shape when she didn't have her dentures artificially propping up her mouth and giving her a semblance of bone structure. Her upper lip collapsed and her thick cheeks sagged like a bulldog's, beginning the cascade of liver-spotted flesh that continued with her dewlap and disappeared into the neckline of her *samfoo* top.

Sonny later lost her favour and all the cash and jewellery she'd brought with her from Malaysia when she caught him shambling around the house, smacking his lips loosely and pretending that he'd lost his dentures. He had an elaborate Marcel Marceau routine in which he groped the surfaces of coffee tables and benchtops blindly, sighing a long drawn-out '*Aieee-yah*'. Then he'd pretend to find the dentures and polish them in the hollow of his armpit. He grimaced hideously, contorting his mouth into weird shapes that resembled Munch's *Scream* as he carefully inserted the invisible dentures and mumbled them into place. He often did this behind Madam Tay's back, especially when she'd been scolding Mum for being extravagant, lazy, a bad wife or a hopeless daughter-in-law. Impotence fed our petty acts of spite.

'Sonny, you're so naughty,' Mum would say, but she couldn't help laughing. Perhaps she was even gratified that her son took her side and stood up for her when her own husband would not. 'You shouldn't show such disrespect to your grandmother, you know.'

Madam Tay caught him mimicking her one day.

'*Ai-yah, pi-see!*' she exclaimed. That was one of the few Hokkien words we learned from her. Naughty. We were the *pi-see* kids. She waddled off furiously to tell the Patriarch. She burst into tears and screamed that she was cutting Sonny out of her will and, furthermore, she wanted him to return the gold necklace and pendant she'd given him.

'Fine,' Sonny said as he took off the necklace and gave it to her. 'Now I don't look like an extra from *Saturday Night Fever*.'

'Come on, *lah!* What do you think you're doing?' the Patriarch raged. 'Do you think I sacrificed everything and came here to Australia to put up with this kind of behaviour from my kids? I'm fed up with you all. You deserve two tight slaps.'

And that's what Sonny got, and I got the same as well because I'd laughed at Sonny's performance. Then Sonny was grounded for two weeks and he had his pocket money suspended for that period. It only fuelled his resentment against the Patriarch and his hatred of Madam Tay.

From the start Madam Tay was in a vicious contest with Mum, Sonny and me for control in the house. At first it looked as if she would win hands down. The Patriarch was on her side and she fawned on him. After his wife's blank passivity and his children's sullen and fearful avoidance, it must have been gratifying to receive undivided attention from his mother once again. Meal times were changed because of her. The rice my mother cooked each night was now waterlogged and swollen because, Madam Tay claimed, it was easier for those dentures, although nothing stopped her from tearing into the biggest pieces of roast duck or braised pork. We could no longer watch TV even when she wasn't watching anything because she told the Patriarch that television rotted our brains and we ought to be studying anyway. One day we came home to find that she had gone into the garden and brutally hacked away all the jasmine and wisteria because they were decorative and useless. In their place she'd planted tomato seedlings. My old bedroom stank of the urine which she collected in two-litre plastic ice-cream buckets to fertilise her tomato plants. More likely kill them, Sonny said.

'If she ever goes I'll need my room fumigated and sterilised,' I grumbled. The Patriarch overheard me and cuffed my ear.

But slowly, insidiously, the tables were turned. It began with the silent treatment we dealt her. Whenever she came into the room, Mum, Sonny and I got up and left immediately. If we were cooking in the kitchen and couldn't leave, we pointedly ignored her. If Mum wasn't around and Madam Tay started complaining to us, Sonny deliberately turned up his stereo so that Jimmy Barnes screeched deafeningly that all the flame trees went by the weary driver, drowning out her scolding until she was forced to walk away because she couldn't stand the sound of Cold Chisel.

Patriarch-meted punishments flew fast and thick. Undeterred, we engaged in acts of retribution. If she grumbled to the Patriarch about us, then suddenly, mysteriously, her dentures disappeared and were found hours later half-ground into the dirt of the tomato patch. We captured huntsman spiders and released them into her room. The hot water system in our house was unreliable so when she took a shower, we ran into the kitchen and laundry and turned on the hot water taps at full blast so that she would suddenly be flooded with cold water. She complained to the Patriarch about all these things but she couldn't prove that we had actually done anything, and even he began to think that she might be a bit paranoid. She stopped picking on us but continued trying to bully Mum, as she had all those years ago in her house in Singapore.

Our malevolent spite was becoming a knee-jerk reaction to Madam Tay, and it infected Pandora. Gradually she realised that the power relationship had changed. In Sydney, she was on her home turf and Madam Tay was the alien.

All the advantage was on her side. She silently condoned and encouraged our campaign against Madam Tay. After a telling-off by Jonah one night, she decided that she'd had enough. On the following day, after Jonah had left for work, she bundled Madam Tay into the car under the pretence of going to Westfield shopping centre. Instead of the three-minute drive down Shaftesbury Avenue, however, she took a long, circuitous, disorientating route through Strathfield, Homebush, Flemington, past Rookwood Cemetery, through Chullora and back towards Burwood. Half an hour later, she left the car at the far side of Burwood Park and dragged Madam Tay through it. When they reached the middle, Pandora turned around and jogged away. She ran back to the car and drove away, leaving Madam Tay stranded.

Pandora drove across to Westfield, parked inside the carpark, and slowly walked back towards the park. She sat in a cafe opposite the arched entrance and watched the old woman wandering around in terrified confusion, unable to ask for directions or help because she couldn't speak any English. When Madam Tay crossed the street and drifted into the shopping centre, Pandora slipped behind her and followed her at a distance. She felt a sour pleasure as she saw the domineering, fault-finding old woman lost and helpless. She reached out for passing arms, babbling in Hokkien. Young kids shrugged her off impatiently and laughed at her. Older women stopped and tried to help.

'Sorry, love. Can't understand you. You'd better go see security or someone. Go into Grace Bros. They'll point you to the right people.'

'No good,' bleated Madam Tay. 'No good.'

Eventually two security guards came and escorted Madam Tay away. Pandora was now in a quandary. She didn't feel she was ready to rescue her mother-in-law yet, but she also needed to keep an eye on the old woman to make sure she was all right. She stood browsing in a shop, frowning and debating what to do. Then, to her relief, she saw police officers entering the centre management office. A few moments later they brought Madam Tay out. She was crying and pleading with them in Hokkien, but they just kept shaking their heads uncomprehendingly.

No good,' she said. '*Pi-see*. No good.'

Pandora went to the supermarket and bought vegetables and a tray of chicken thighs for dinner that night. She drove home and put everything away in the fridge. Only then did she pick up the phone and ring Burwood Police Station to report that her mother-in-law had wandered out of the house that morning and was now missing. An hour later, Madam Tay was returned to the house by a female police officer. Pandora thanked her effusively, gave her a freshly baked green Pandan cake to take back to the station, and shut the door. She turned and looked at the exhausted, weepy old woman. Where was her power now? Her scornful taunts and spiteful belittlements?

'If you tell Jonah what happened today,' Pandora told her in broken Hokkien, 'I shall take you somewhere even further and leave you there next time. Or I shall have you arrested by the police again. They will throw you in jail and nobody will rescue you because nobody will understand you. Do you understand me?'

Why could we not be content with disarming Madam Tay? All three of us knew what it was like to be victimised, but we couldn't stem the sadistic pleasure of humiliating her. Our vindictive campaign against her did not end after that day, although she had been abruptly silenced. Sonny openly mimicked her, and I joined his vicious, childish taunts. Even Pandora participated. She knew that Madam Tay didn't know how to lock the toilet door. She waited until Madam Tay was on the toilet, then she crept upstairs and wrenched open the door while the old woman was squatting on the dunny.

'God, you don't even know how to use a commode properly,' Pandora exclaimed in disgust. Later, after Madam Tay left, Pandora would be aghast at her own capacity for cruelty. For now, however, she enjoyed the heady pleasure of power and revenge.

Between us, we broke her. She was afraid to leave the house and terrified of staying in it. She didn't dare to tell Jonah that she wanted to cut short her visit and return to Malaysia, for he would ask her why and she didn't dare to dob us in. So absorbed were we in our victory over her that we didn't really notice until the end of her stay how much the old woman had deteriorated. She habitually stayed in her room, with the curtains drawn and the door shut. Out in the garden, the tomatoes ripened and dropped to the earth with fat splats, and the patch became overgrown with weeds. When she ventured out of her room to go to the toilet or to come downstairs for a meal, she often forgot her dentures, and she wandered around the house with the buttons of her blouse undone. We shrieked 'yuck!', 'gross!' at the sight of the flabby flaps of her wrinkled breasts. She just stared at us blankly and moaned, 'Ai-yah.'

When she flew out of Sydney, I opened the windows of my old room, vacuumed and shampooed the carpet, and scrubbed down the walls with antiseptic detergent. I persuaded Mum to throw out the old mattress and buy me a new one. I aired the closet until the reek of Tiger Balm and mothballs had disappeared, then I transferred my clothes back into it.

The phone rang late one night and the Patriarch learned that Madam Tay had died of a heart attack shortly after returning to Malaysia. Neither Mum, Sonny nor I doubted that we had killed her. The holidays were over and we slunk back to school quietly. In my English class we read through and acted out the bush ballads of Henry Lawson and Banjo Paterson. Niree and I were given 'The Man from Ironbark'. I was astonished at the guilt and grief that rose like a flash flood inside me. We stood at the front of the classroom reciting the ballad, and my voice began to quaver and my eyes watered.

> *And all the while his throat he held to save his vital spark,*
> *And 'Murder! Bloody Murder!' yelled the man from*
> *   Ironbark*

I could tamp it down no longer; I burst into tears and sobbed uncontrollably as Niree cast an uncertain look at me and doggedly continued reciting.

> *And when at last the barber spoke, and said "Twas all in*
> *fun—*
> *'Twas just a little harmless joke, a trifle overdone.'*
> *'A joke!' he cried, 'By George, that's fine; a lively sort of*
> *   lark;*
> *I'd like to catch that murdering swine some night in*
> *   Ironbark.*

'It's only a poem, Grace,' Mrs Dillon said impatiently as I wiped my eyes with the back of my hand.

Jonah flew back for Madam Tay's funeral. Pandora refused to go, saying that someone needed to stay home to look after us and to drive us to our various school and extracurricular activities. Guilt and self-pity flooded her and she spent days crying for herself and her bewilderment at who she was, how she had reached this point in life. Once upon a time she had wanted to escape the vulgar meanness of the Lim family. Now she looked in the mirror each morning and saw her brother Winston staring back at her.

GLOSSOLALIA

All my life I've had to compete against men for my mother's attention. First it was the Patriarch and, of course, Sonny, whom I really liked so I didn't mind that much. But then I had to compete against God, and that really topped it. I was fourteen when Mum discovered God and started speaking in tongues.

After Madam Tay's death Mum took to wandering down to Burwood Park every morning. There she sat, alone in the sunshine, entertaining dark thoughts. She returned from the park one afternoon with a lurid-covered Good News Bible and excitedly announced that she had found God and was Born Again. God had forgiven her her secret sin of murdering Madam Tay. Suddenly, her bad days were a thing of the past. She spent her time singing Christian choruses and humming hymns as she did the laundry and gradually took over the cooking again. The phone was constantly ringing and she was talking to people whose voices and names I grew to recognise but whose faces I had never seen. She was actually happy.

She tried to force us all to go along to church with her. I refused at first. Sunday mornings were for sleeping in and watching Bill Collins present a Shirley Temple or Andy Hardy film festival on midday television. How many people of my age, I wondered, had actually seen Mickey Rooney in *A Yank in Eton*, and was that perhaps something to be deeply embarrassed about? Sonny went along with her instead.

They both got sucked in to the whole church thing. Sonny played the trumpet for the band. I don't know whether he did it for religious reasons, or whether he just wanted a band to play in. Whatever their motives, they left me alone with the Patriarch on Sunday mornings. We sat at the breakfast table with toast, tea and the two Sunday newspapers between us. We pretended to be absorbed in the news. Occasionally we might reach for the same piece of toast or catch each other's glance, and then we'd quickly look away, both feeling awkward. Eventually, tense and unnerved at having breakfast with his daughter, the Patriarch would get up abruptly.

'I'm going to do some gardening,' he informed me. 'You should do some laundry if you've got time.'

I did the laundry, then cooked noodles for lunch. They nestled in a large porcelain dish on the table, waiting for Mum and Sonny to come home.

'Where's your mother and your brother?' the Patriarch demanded irritably. 'Give them the opportunity and they gallivant all over the place, running wild.'

Together, we ate lunch in silence. Waves of disapproval radiated from the Patriarch and hummed in the air, alerting Mum and Sonny to the Bad Mood when they came in.

'*Ai-yah*, sorry *lah*!' Mum said. 'The service went over-time and then we all went out to lunch.'

'Come on, *lah*. Can't you even show some consideration and call home? Grace went to all the trouble to make lunch for you and now you tell me you've eaten.'

'Oh dear. Grace, so sorry *lah*. Maybe you better not make lunch next time. Sonny and I can always eat some toast or something.'

The Patriarch understood that she didn't want to be tied down to coming home at a regular time after church on Sundays. He bristled at the idea of his wife socialising with strangers. 'Who are these people you had lunch with?'

'Oh, just friends from church,' she said evasively. 'You don't know them anyway.'

The Patriarch scowled. He could see his wife entering an entirely different sphere of life. He hadn't said anything at first because she was happy for once, and she didn't slip into depression as easily these days. But he hated the fact that she was developing a social circle that he was not a part of. The faceless strangers who absorbed her attention provoked his curiosity and his jealousy.

'Maybe Grace and I will go to your church with you next week,' he said.

'Dad,' I protested. 'You go if you want to.'

'Jonah, are you sure? You might not like it.'

'We'll both go,' he said.

Sometimes she was just so easy to read. On the one hand, she had been nagging us to come along to her church since she started going. She was on a mission to save her family and convert them to Christ. She would be an evangelist for the Lord in the mission field of her own home. On the other hand, she visibly enjoyed the freedom from home and husband that church gave her. She loved having her own friends; a time and space where she had no need to pander to his moods and whims.

'Great,' she said. She pasted a bright, cheery, Christian smile onto her lips. 'I'm sure you'll really love it.'

And that was how I came to be sitting in a plastic chair in a converted warehouse building in Surry Hills on a Sunday morning, stifling yawns while clean, bright, Omo-white people stood and sang and clapped and chanted happily. They were actually *white*; my mother, so afraid and intimidated by the *ang moh*s all her life, was actually mixing with white people. I could hardly believe it. Who would have thought she'd find her place in Sydney in a mostly white Pentecostal church?

This was like no church I'd ever been to in my life. Where were the wooden pews, the altar, the stained glass windows, the organ, the hymns, the hushed awe, the *dignity*, for Christ's sake? Instead, the band played, coloured lights dazzled like a disco, backup singers bellowed, guitars wailed and drums thundered while Christian choruses flashed up on an overhead screen. There was a temporary lull.

'Why don't you take some time to turn to your neighbour and greet them with Christ's love,' the chorus leader suggested.

Suddenly, alarmingly, a hug-fest broke out. Complete strangers turned around and started hugging and kissing the Patriarch and me. Poor Chinaman Patriarch, he suffered even more than me. I could see him visibly shrinking inside his skin at such sudden and unexpected physical contact with *people*. There were so many scents: talcum powder, Brut 33, Old Spice, Yardley floral perfumes, Australis, Chanel, sweat. I was pressed into fleshy shoulders and armpits as friendly Christ-loving Christians grabbed me and hugged me tightly as if I was their long-lost relative.

'God bless you, love,' someone told me. 'I love you in the name of the Lord.'

'Thank you. That's very kind of you.' My mother had raised me to be polite to strangers.

'Where do you come from?' This from a thirty-something woman with a yard of brunette hair and big 1980s two-for-the-price-of-one budget glasses.

'Burwood,' I said.

'No, I mean, where do you *really* come from? Originally?'

'Helsinki,' I said.

'Oh, really? How interesting. Is that in Japan?'

I looked around for my mother and saw her hugging another teenage girl just slightly older than me, kissing her on the cheek. Jealousy and misery simply swamped me. How could she give herself so completely, so intimately, to these people?

'Hey, Grace.' Sonny had come down from the stage, his trumpet clutched in his hand like an extension of himself. 'How do you like it so far?'

'Who's that girl Mum's talking to?'

He looked to where I was pointing. 'That's Susan. She's Mum's prayer partner and spiritual daughter. Her own mum's a junkie in rehab, I think. Something like that. She rings Mum up each week to pray and chat. Come and meet her if you like.'

'Hey, Susan!' he called out. He left me and walked over to Mum and Susan, who hugged him tightly. They made a neat little triangle that excluded me.

The chorus leader clapped his hands. 'All right, guys. We're gonna praise the Lord some more and whip the

Devil, right? Because we're engaged in a spiritual warfare against the forces of darkness, but my bible says that the gates of hell shall not prevail against the army of the Lord! Thank you, Jesus! Are you with me, church?'

They whooped and cheered loudly and the band swung into another song. Crashing chords from the synthesiser and jarring riffs from the guitars. Voices raised in shouting song and palms which stung from clapping time with the heartbeat of the drum. I looked in amazement at my mother and saw her arms upraised like the Village People doing 'YMCA'. Many other arms stuck out vertically from the congregation too. Then, incredulously, I watched as people started hopping up and down, jumping and kicking out their legs as if they were in aerobics class. Yes, all over the auditorium bright blobs of colour were bopping up and down like those balls in the Lotto machine.

'Mum, what do you think you're doing?' I hissed in an agony of embarrassment as my mother hopped awkwardly from one foot onto the other, like a duck with cold feet.

'I'm dancing in the spirit,' she huffed between jerky, uncoordinated lurches. What had happened to my mother, the waltz queen and cha-cha champion? Her arms were still upraised, her stiff fingers spearing and stabbing the air.

'I don't believe this.'

Then the mood switched abruptly. The lights dimmed and the band softened, sweetened by the chimes on the synthesiser. Lulled into quiescence, I closed my eyes and heard people around me humming and murmuring love words to God and singing melodies of their own in a sort of baby language of 'ga-gas' and 'goo-goos'. It should have been chaotic; a cacophony of clashing sounds. Instead it was unspeakably erotic, that tangling of strange tongues and twining of individual melodies. Waves and waves of it, flowing and ebbing, flowing and ebbing. The synth grew louder and the drumbeat stronger. It pulsated now, those hummed chords of melody intermingled with ecstatic cries of 'Oh God! Oh Jesus! Sweet Jesus! Oh God, I *love* you!'. Louder and louder it grew. I felt my flesh tingle and my palms grow moist. The sound was pushing at the ceiling, pounding it with cries of 'Hallelujah, Lord! Yes, sweet Jesus, yes!'. And then a tidal swell of music and voices, keen, sharp, edged with agonised rapture. Building, building, building up, up, up to a long crescendo and then—oh! Orgasmic. Simply orgasmic.

The music died away, the voices drifted into a murmur and then silence; the lights overhead slowly brightened and the chorus leader melted away from the front of the stage. The minister of the church, Pastor Rodney Philippe, stepped up to the microphone, adjusted it and began to speak. I hardly heard a word he said. My body was quivering with arousal and my mind was like putty. I'd come to *church*, for Christ's sake. The house of God and happy Christians. How could my underwear be damp? My face was burning with shame and guilt; I was sure everybody could see it. Throughout the sermon I gripped the edge of my seat and wondered whether God would strike me dead. And then, finally, something expected.

'Church, let us pray.'

I didn't care about praying; I just wanted the service to end so that I could go home. But it didn't end. They had this thing called an 'altar call' at the end of the service; sinners were invited to come up to the front of the stage to repent and be Born Again.

'If anybody would like to give their life to God, please come up here right now. I know some of you may be scared,'

Pastor Rodney Philippe told us earnestly, 'but don't let that fear stop you. Some of you may think that you've got plenty of time to get your life right with God. Well, let me tell you this, guys: you simply can't tell when God will call you home. I know a young man—we'll call him Charles—who came to my meeting one night many years ago. Charles felt the call of God in his life. But, brothers and sisters, Charles was weak. "Let me have a few more years," Charles told me, "then I'll get my life right with God."'

'But, brothers and sisters, Charles didn't have a few more years. No. That night, when Charles left our meeting and headed down to Kings Cross, he was run over by a bus. Ladies and gentlemen, brothers and sisters, you cannot tell when your time will come. I am pleading with you, I am begging you to give your life to Christ now. If you want to do this, please stand up. Don't be frightened. We all support you. Brothers and sisters, if you've brought a friend or a loved one along today, give them the support they need and stand up with them. Stand up for God.'

'Ow!' My arm was jerked and I was hauled upright to my feet. I looked about in alarm at the mosaic of bent heads around me.

'Mum, what are you doing?'

'Don't you want to give your life to God, Grace? I'll support you, you know.'

'Mum, you're embarrassing me.'

'Grace, look at me. Let me do this one thing for you.' Her eyes were pleading, eloquent with some kind of need I didn't understand. 'I want you to know the love of God, Grace. God never fails; he will never disappoint you, you know.'

Everybody in the surrounding rows was looking at me now. What was that word I'd read just recently in *Pride and Prejudice*? Mortified. Like Elizabeth Bennett, I was mortified.

'All right, Mum. All right.'

She hugged me tightly. She was so pleased.

'Grace,' she said, 'I am so proud of you.'

She took my hand and led me down to the front of the altar where a dozen people were already thronged. Mum and I joined the holy huddle and let Pastor Philippe pray over us. We repeated the Sinner's Prayer after him, and then I thought it was over. But no. Not yet. Like a Demtel two-for-the-price-of-one TV ad, there was more.

'After this morning, the Devil is going to find ways of attacking you because you now belong to God. Well, let me tell you this. God loves you and he wouldn't leave you without help. The Holy Spirit can help you in your walk with God. Do you want the gift of the Holy Spirit, brothers and sisters?'

'Take it, Grace,' my mother whispered in my ear, as if it was a shopping bargain and the salesman had just thrown in a free packet of steak knives.

'Yeah, why not. Whatever.'

'Brothers and sisters, the presence of the Holy Spirit will manifest himself to you. Some of you may be Slain in the Spirit. You'll feel a warm, tingling glow all over you and you'll fall irresistibly. But God won't let you be hurt when you're Slain in the Spirit. Others of you may receive the gift of tongues. Don't resist it; it's a very precious gift.'

He started to pray over individuals, starting from the left side of the stage. I was on the right. He put his hands on them and cataracts of tears poured down their faces. People began to drop like flies around me. On the ground, a carnage of Christians. Others burst out into an awful caterwauling. My heart pounded and I felt sick. I wasn't going to be able to manifest the Holy Spirit and Mum would know that I was just a fake. She wouldn't love me anymore; not like she loved Sonny, or that girl Susan. I simply had to manifest the gift of the Holy Spirit. Maybe I could just slip away. But then it was too late. Pastor Rodney Philippe was standing in front of me and his toffee eyes bored into my skull.

'Don't be afraid, Grace,' he said gently as he put his large, slightly sweaty palms on my head and began to pray for me. It was simply dreadful. I was the last one left. Everyone else who had gone up to give their lives to God now lay comatose on the carpet or blabbing in teary voices.

'Allallallallallallallallallalla . . .'

'Shooshooshooshooshoosh . . .'

'Ticketyticketyticketyticketytickety . . .'

What should I do? Fall back and risk concussion when I hit my head on the carpet because I wasn't really Slain in the Spirit so God wouldn't protect me from being hurt? Or babble? Babbling was easier, but what should I babble? And then, a lifetime of watching Saturday morning cartoons paid off in that urgent instant. Inspiration struck. I raised my hands stiffly in the 'YMCA' position and opened my mouth.

'*Scooooo*by-dooby-dooby-dooby-dooby-dooooo! Scooby-dooby-dooby-dooby-dooo . . .'

'Hallelujah! Thank you, Lord!' cried my mother.

DELIVERING US
FROM EVIL

In the autumn of my fifteenth year Mum pleaded with
Pastor Rodney Philippe and his wife, Josie, to come and
cleanse our house spiritually. The Patriarch had decided to
continue going to the bargain-basement warehouse Pentecostal church on Sundays. God had saved our souls but
he couldn't salvage our fraying family ties. We might be
one in Christ, but we were pulling further and further
apart. Mum was worried about Sonny; she feared that he
was *backsliding*. He was seventeen, sullen and withdrawn.
He was hardly ever home, choosing to spend most of his
leisure time with his girlfriend. When he was home he hid
in his room and played the trumpet all weekend. Chet
Baker tunes crept out mournfully from under his closed
door. He made snide remarks when the Patriarch quoted
bible verses at us.

'Don't forget that your lives here are a preparation for
the afterlife,' the Patriarch nagged. 'How do you expect to
face God with such a smelly, untidy room, Sonny? You live

in a pigsty. How can God welcome you to heaven? "In my Father's house are many mansions . . . "'

'And a good thing too. I bags the one furthest away from you,' Sonny said.

'Honour thy father and mother!' thundered the Patriarch.

'Fathers, do not provoke your children to wrath!' retorted Sonny.

'They bleed on both sides,' I said. They both glared at me. Whoops. Wrong text and wrong timing.

'Stop it,' Mum begged. 'Just stop it.'

She decided that we all needed deliverance. She had been reading a book given to her by Pastor Philippe called *Pigs in the Parlor*, written by two Texan Baptists, Frank and Ida Mae Hammond. The simple thesis of the book was that the world was teeming with demons who, like bacteria, invaded our bodies and homes and stirred up contention and sinful thoughts and practices. The devil needed to be driven out of our lives. Deliverance would set us all free and turn us into one soppy, sentimental, huggy American sitcom family. 'Does everyone need deliverance?' demanded Frank and Ida Mae. Personally, they had never met anybody who didn't. In the age of quick cash at the ATM, microwave meals and instant coffee, deliverance was a quick fix to family problems created through the sediment of different times, histories and cultures.

Sonny and I awaited the arrival of Pastor Rodney and Josie Philippe with mixed feelings of awe, anticipation and dread; awe and anticipation because it was widely known among our Pentecostal circle that they specialised in spiritual warfare and the deliverance ministry; dread because we knew ourselves to be sinners tainted with the stain of sexual sin. We feared the supernatural revelation of our unnatural desires.

Sonny was still plagued by horny thoughts about his non-Christian girlfriend Hwee Mei, who he'd met at a jazz nightclub. I know this because the Patriarch was renovating the upper section of the house and I had moved back downstairs into the guest room temporarily, which meant that Sonny's room was now set back to back with mine. There was a musty, blackened, disused chimney in between. Late at night I could hear his groans of despair echoing eerily through the blocked-up flue of the chimney as he wrestled with his recalcitrant cock.

'Oh Lord, Lord, I beseech you,' he moaned in an access of abject remorse. I imagined his knobbly kneecaps scrubbing the synthetic pile of the carpet in front of the fireplace, his bum stuck into the air and his torso perpendicularly prostrate to the rusty grate as he sent prayers like wishes up the chimney to Father Christmas or Father God. Apologies rolled off his tongue.

'Have mercy on me, a sinner. I'm sorry that I put my hand under Hwee Mei's jumper last night and squeezed her boobs and stroked her nipples. I'm sorry I put my hands in her panties and was excited by her wetness. I'm so sorry! I repent of daydreaming that I was fucking her hard when I should have been concentrating on my trigonometry. And I'm sorry for saying "fuck" to you. Have mercy on me and forgive me. Remove my evil thoughts and wash my black heart white as snow. And please help me to remember the sine and cosine rules for my maths test on Thursday.'

I lay in bed, still as a corpse, scarcely daring to breathe lest the expulsion of stale air should whisper up the flue and alert him to my wakefulness. Tension pulled my tendons taut as violin strings. The delicious thrill of the eavesdropper, the vicarious pleasure of second-hand sex, plucked my body like a bow and set it trembling. I listened as he groaned and fell into bed, tossed restlessly, then gave in to temptation and began to jerk off on his fantasies of fucking his girlfriend.

I considered my own sexual fantasies at the time inferior to Sonny's because they were based on fiction rather than fact. True, I'd been an accomplished masturbator for years now, ever since the Patriarch halted the Horlicks ritual. But that was automatic, more like thumb-sucking in many ways, really. I was still squeamish enough about sex to wish to cloak it in romance. Biology lessons had not helped either. Wanting to get ahead in science class to placate the Patriarch, I had thumbed through Gray's *Anatomy* and had been horrified by the intricate interlacing of formaldehyde-brown muscles and white ligaments that formed the basin of the female perineum. I had seen cross-sections of wrinkled, withered, disembodied penises. Sliced and diced. These pictures, coupled with my knowledge of sweaty, slightly gawky private school boys who were always in need of a sock change, repulsed me from the idea of sex with some guy I actually knew. So I lay in the dark and listened to Sonny wanking instead.

A frenzy of washing, scrubbing, dusting and general house-cleaning had preceded the Philippes' arrival, but less than half an hour after they stepped into the house, we learned that our efforts had not gone far enough. Josie sniffed the air and felt troubled and oppressed in spirit. After a heavy dinner of my mother's famous fried rice noodles washed down with Chinese tea, Josie communed with God as she absently shelled lychees and popped the eyeballs of fruit into her mouth, sitting back and listening to the stutter of stilted conversation.

Finally, she placed the teacup down and leant forward.

'There's something really wrong here,' she said abruptly. 'My heart is really burdened for this family. I feel a sort of . . . oppression in this household, and I believe it is affecting the family. The Lord has told me that, somehow, Satan has managed to get a foothold in this house.'

My mother promptly burst into tears. Her face crumpled into soft folds which formed shallow channels for the rivulets that ran down her sodden cheeks.

'It's true, I know,' she sobbed. 'I opened the door for Satan to come in with my besetting sin. The Holy Spirit has convicted me of this many times, but although I always repent, I always revert back to my extravagant ways. I can't seem to stop spending money on clothes. I just love shopping.'

Her voice cracked and quivered as the confession exploded from her. She disintegrated into a rambling litany of Dior scarves, Zampatti suits, Trent Nathan blazers, Country Road cotton shirts, cashmere cardigans and Oroton handbags.

Josie eased herself out of her wooden chair and crouched beside Mum, slipping a plump, comforting arm around the shivering shoulders and discreetly moving a tissue box across the table so that it was within Mum's reach. Slowly, the tormented sobs receded into hiccupping breaths, succeeded by a vigorous foghorn blowing of the nose.

Meanwhile, I sat rigidly on my wooden chair, my gaze fixed on the shrapnel of fruit shells on the table. I was mortified and a little angered by my mother's excessive and uncontrollable emotionalism. I had heard her confession of her besetting sins many times before and, although a very real and deep source of remorse to her, they had become vaguely reminiscent of corporeal embarrassments—like inadvertent farting, they were best not mentioned. They were not in good taste. Then I looked up and my heart plummeted further.

Oh, for God's sake, I thought. Sonny was hovering shyly by the doorway, hopping from one foot to the other, hoping that a small scrap of attention would be thrown his way. Too absorbed in his own besetting sin of lust of the flesh to be aware of our mother's lust for clothes, he was completely startled by the sudden, staccato revelations of her private vice. That he was unhappy about this was perfectly clear to me. He obviously felt torn between sympathy for my mother's plight—the empathy and secret relief of one fellow sinner for another—and annoyance that our mother believed her own trivial offences had opened the door to the Devil.

I saw the shallow rise and fall of his thin chest and the reddening tips of his ears, and, aghast, I realised that he was psyching himself up to Confess. I was appalled by his stupidity, for there was no doubt in my mind whose besetting sin would draw down more wrath upon the sinner's unfortunate head. Between profligacy of the purse and the stench of illicit sex, there could be no comparison. If he threw his cards down on the table and spread out his fantasies for us to see, the consequences would be of truly apocalyptic proportions, not only for him but for me as well, for his shame would also stain me in the Patriarch's eyes.

'All of you,' the Patriarch always said. The ties of consanguinity were strengthened through collective condemnation by the Patriarch during our childhood. All of you need to clean up your rooms. They're a disgrace. Who's taken the scissors? All of you never put things back where they belong. Why didn't you let me know you wouldn't be home for dinner? All of you treat this house like a hotel. All of you deserve two tight slaps. All of you are good for nothing. All of you.

In fact the only thing holding Sonny back was the Patriarch's austere presence. Sonny's eyes darted desperately from the Patriarch to Josie and back again. I willed him to look at me so that I could warn him with an urgent shake of my head. But it was no use. The urge to confess, to glory in the guilt of letting the Devil into the house, to abase himself in public, express his contrition and be absolved from his sins, comforted and assured that Father God still loved him and accepted him, even if the Patriarch didn't—all this outweighed the inevitable scolding and punishment by the Patriarch. I could see him physically scraping up his courage to speak and, in my agony of fear, I could hear his thoughts racing frantically like mice in a maze.

'Er, er, er, Josie.' Sonny was stammering so badly that nobody paid any attention to him. Josie continued to stroke my mother's bowed shoulders and murmur soothingly while my father looked at Rodney in helpless male discomfort at female tears. Then Josie spoke and Sonny's moment was lost, swept away unremembered in the small eddies of excitement her next words conjured.

'Be comforted, Pandora. The Lord has told me that the oppression doesn't come from this family, but from the house itself. There is spiritual bondage in this house caused by the actions of the previous owners,' Josie said gravely. She raised her eyes and looked each of us in the face.

'The Lord knows that this is a godly household that fears and loves him. That is why he has sent Rodney and me to help you. Rodney?'

Pastor Rodney Philippe closed his eyes and pinched the bridge of his nose between thumb and index finger as if he were repressing a sneeze. We waited in silence until he opened his eyes and peered myopically at us.

'The Lord has confirmed to me what Josie is saying,' he told us at last. 'We need to go through this house, room by room, and cleanse them all in the blood of the Lamb. We need to break the hold of Satan and his minions in this household.'

Collectively, we left the kitchen and trooped solemnly around our house. We started in the laundry, where Josie sensed the spirits of Mischief and Discontent.

'Talk to them,' she insisted. 'Tell them that your lives and your minds are under Jesus' protection and they can't do their dirty work on you. Go take authority over them in Jesus' mighty name. Don't laugh, Grace. Resist the Devil.'

So we held hands and claimed authority in Jesus' name and exorcised the demons of Mischief and Discontent. From there we proceeded to the living room, where we booted out the spirits of Anger, Insolence and Dissension.

'If any of you feel the urge to cough or throw up, don't try to repress it,' Josie told us. She was so excited. 'Sometimes indwelling demons get blown out through your nostrils or they come out through your mouth.'

We went from room to room identifying demons, gearing ourselves up for battle, pleading with God for his mercy and authority, shouting in strident triumph as we drove them wailing from the house. And then we entered Sonny's bedroom.

I could feel palpable waves of anxiety emanating from his tall, lanky frame. It wasn't too hard to divine his dilemma. He both yearned for and dreaded the revelation of his lust-filled fantasies and semen-soaked sheets. To confess in front of the family, to voluntarily demonstrate to the world that he was a depraved and unworthy sinner come to true repentance, was one thing. To have those sordid secrets ferreted out and flung back as an accusation was another altogether.

I, too, waited in gut-wrenching apprehension. For if Sonny had sinned, so had I sinned vicariously via the chimney flue. If by some remote chance God could actually reveal to Josie and Rodney Philippe Sonny's vice, would not my own be similarly exposed? I had betrayed Sonny in eavesdropping on his agonies. Now I feared to lose his casual friendship. And again, I also feared the Patriarch's reaction. Now I see that, to me, the Patriarch has always been god. He doled out the commandments in our household and I followed them dutifully most of the time and flouted them whenever I could. When I was caught out, if his anger could not be averted or sufficient propitiation made, I waited in resentful resignation for his wrath to fall upon my head.

Rodney Philippe's heavy brows slashed down in a deep V-shaped frown over his nose as he entered Sonny's bedroom. His nose twitched slightly and, alarmed, I shot Sonny a quick glance. His face was drawn and white with terror and his mouth opened and shut uncertainly. He scarcely knew whether to pre-empt accusation by blurting out his confession, or to hope that God had not spoken to Rodney.

Please God, please God, I gabbled in silent prayer.

'There's a heavy atmosphere in this room,' Rodney began ponderously. 'I smell something foul . . .'

'Your shoes!' the Patriarch roared. 'I keep telling you to air your room and keep it tidy, Sonny, but you never listen to me. Now you see. Pastor Rodney can smell your stinking shoes.'

And he was right. There they were, crowding the far side of Sonny's room, eight pairs of shoes with their toes pointed to the corner of the wall in malodorous shame: black school shoes, Converse basketball boots, Nike running shoes, tennis sneakers, brown tooled-leather Windsor Smith lace-ups, black Doc Martens, hiking boots, and a battered pair of R.M. Williams riding boots. Stuffed into the school shoes and the Nikes were soiled sports socks. Despite the glimpses of stained and greying insoles, an unpleasant odour similar to Chinese salted fish permeated the untidy room.

Mum was simply appalled. Her hand shot out automatically and her fingers reached for Sonny's ear to twist and yank at it in a purely reflexive action. 'How many times have I told you to change your school socks every day and put your dirty clothes in the laundry basket?' she demanded, mortified at this evidence of her son's lack of good hygiene practice, which might reflect on her mothering. 'Pick them up right now and put them in the laundry. Go on.'

Humiliated yet vastly relieved, Sonny did as he was told and we trooped out of his room. If there is a God, perhaps he sometimes looks down with compassionate eyes and intervenes.

FALLING

The Devil hadn't been driven out of the home. Religion had failed to deliver. Despite Josie and Rodney Philippe's best efforts, deliverance hadn't worked. My family was falling apart. The Patriarch and Sonny could not talk without shouting at each other. Their conflicts were weighted with the bitter histories of arguments past. We sniffed the air and smelled their hatred; it leaked and polluted the house like toxic fumes, choking us with misery and numbing us into despair.

The Patriarch wielded his frustration like a hammer to pound his family verbally. Church had not softened him; it only toughened his tendencies towards arrogance and domestic tyranny. His was a religion of rigid rules, constant condemnation and instant retribution. He lived a disciplined, morally upright life, practising dentistry in the daytime and pondering over doctrine in the evenings. His bible was always open, passages underscored, notes scribbled in the margins.

233

He memorised bible verses and hurled them like javelins at our perceived failings. In the end he always fell back on: 'Children, obey your parents in the Lord, for this is right.' In this command western platitudes overlapped with eastern certainties in a way he found reassuring.

But we were not the filial, obedient, slipper-fetching children the Patriarch had expected. When he compared our attitude towards him with his own respect towards his parents, he was simply bewildered. He remembered those backbreaking days of planting rubber seedlings, of whippings when he didn't do well in his exams, of having to accompany his mother everywhere and cater to her every whim. And he wondered why we couldn't see how lucky we were. Instead, we openly ridiculed his petty idiosyncracies and slapped him in the face with our perpetual sullenness. He was appalled at our cold rudeness, the way we turned and walked away from him when he was telling us off.

'Don't walk away while I'm talking to you,' he said, his voice trembling from outrage laced with hurt. 'That's the rudest thing you could ever do to a Chinese father. If I knew you all would turn out like this I would never have given up my practice in Malaysia and immigrated to Australia. My old partner is now a millionaire.'

'Your choice,' Sonny said.

'You're ungrateful, good for nothing. If I spoke to my father like that I'd get two tight slaps.'

'Big fucking deal. Go ahead. It's not like you've never done it before.'

'You've broken my heart. My eldest child and a son at that, turning out to be such a disappointment. After everything I've done for you, all the sacrifices I've made—'

'Bullshit. You did it for yourself. I didn't ask to be born and I sure as hell didn't ask for you to be my father. I may be a lousy son, but you're a fucking loser of a father.'

'Get out of my house until you can treat your father with some respect.'

Sonny dropped out of school just before his Higher School Certificate examinations. He and his girlfriend Hwee Mei moved into a small 1960s red brick unit in Enmore. He joined a jazz band and worked three nights a week playing in various pubs. During the day he unpacked boxes at the local supermarket while Hwee Mei finished her secretarial course at TAFE. He never came home and rarely called. I was desperately afraid of losing touch with him. Losing him.

Each day after I finished school I caught a train from Burwood to Newtown and walked up Enmore Road until I reached the turn-off to their apartment block. I spent the afternoons hanging around that tiny one-bedroom flat. I vacuumed the dingy carpet and scrubbed out the bathroom. I piled dirty clothes into a large garbage bag and hauled them to the laundromat at the end of the street. I did my homework to the monotonous rattle and whirr of washers and dryers spinning clothes clean. I lugged the garbage bag home and sorted out the laundry, neatly pairing stiff cotton socks into rolled balls and carefully folding T-shirts and jeans as if I was a sales assistant at a shop. If Hwee Mei had started cooking dinner by then, I hung around to help and chat to her. Like Pandora before me, I tried to make myself necessary, to worm my way into Sonny's and Hwee Mei's affection—or tolerance, at least—through my assid- uous attention to their needs. I made myself their servant but I would rather have been their slave, for then I'd never have to leave that cramped and dreary flat to return to my parents' house.

'Don't you have anything else you'd rather do, Grace?' Hwee Mei sometimes asked me. 'You're just sixteen. Haven't you got other friends from school you'd rather spend time with?'

'Sure, I've got lots of friends,' I said, trying for convincing nonchalance. 'But I'd rather hang out with you guys.'

Sometimes, when they were both in a good mood, they let me tag along with them to the pub. I'd sit at a corner table and keep Hwee Mei company while Sonny played. Brightly, chattily, I asked her questions about herself and pretended to have a deep interest in the database and spreadsheet programs she was currently learning. When I got home that night, I would write down everything she said and memorise the details of her life and her interests so that I wouldn't forget. I found out which were her favourite movies and I hired the videos so that I could discuss them with her. She was a sucker for Hong Kong soaps and Hollywood teen movies starring Molly Ringwald as the class reject who got the vapid, clean-cut American preppie guy at the end even though she wasn't the wealthy, beautiful prom queen bitch.

'You like *Pretty in Pink* too? Hey, I love that movie!' I exclaimed overenthusiastically, having fast-forwarded my way to the end. Surely she had to see how much we had in common, how we should be best friends.

But there were some nights when she and Sonny didn't want me around. They packed me off with the excuse that I should be doing my homework or spending more time with people my own age. On those nights, I hung around outside the flat and waited to see whether they would go out. If they did, I trailed after them, just as Winston had followed Donald Duck so many years ago, and crept into the cinema so that I could see the same film and pretend to myself that I was really with them. If they caught a bus and I lost them, I went to the pub, nodded to the bartender who knew I was Sonny's sister and wriggled into my usual corner. I felt comforted by the familiar raucous din of conversation and the stale smell of beer.

'Where have you been?' the Patriarch barked out each night when I came into the house.

'At Mitchell Library. Studying.'

'Why can't you study here? All of you run wild nowadays.' But he left me alone after that. As long as I brought home decent grades, he didn't much care what I was doing. 'Have you had dinner? *Nah*.' He shoved some money at me and told me to buy dinner for myself next time I was working late at the library. He always made sure I never went hungry.

Mum would sometimes warm dinner for me in the microwave. She set it down on the kitchen table and drew up a chair, as if she wanted to talk. But she only ever wanted to know about Sonny. Had I seen Sonny, how was he, was he eating properly, did Hwee Mei know how to take care of him and keep their flat tidy, was everything all right with his job, when was he going to come home to visit her? She was starving for the intimate details of his everyday life.

Whenever Mum phoned Sonny, Hwee Mei was the one who picked up the phone. Sonny was never available. He was always sleeping, in the shower, at band practice or at work. On the few occasions he answered the phone, he just emitted a few surly grunts at her until, buffeted by his silence, she was forced to hang up. He was angry with her and she didn't know why. Perhaps he felt that she should have protected us from the Patriarch; perhaps he despised her for not having the courage to leave. She didn't dare to ask him what she'd done wrong. Instead, she accepted his guilty verdict and drifted around the house in an impenetrable bubble of hurt and loneliness, hardly ever seeing me or hearing my voice.

She could not forgive the Patriarch for throwing Sonny out of the house. She could not accept that Sonny no longer needed or wanted contact with her, that Hwee Mei was now the most important woman in his life. Where was her Sonny who had once hugged her and whispered to her, 'Never mind. It's all right. I'll kill that bastard for you'? She wanted to punish the Patriarch. She left the laundry until late at night, just before he was ready for bed.

'Come upstairs now,' the Patriarch said. He started to switch off the lights.

'Don't do that,' she said, turning them back on. 'You know I can't see.'

By this time she had developed night blindness, just like Lida Lim. Each afternoon, as dusk fell, the house blazed with lights for she was afraid of being in the dark. She stumbled into furniture, kicked unknown objects and once broke her toe.

'I have to finish this load of laundry and hang out the clothes to dry,' she said. 'You go ahead first. I haven't even had my shower yet.'

'What kind of a wife are you? If you didn't spend so much time gallivanting all over the place with your church friends you'd have more time to clean the house properly and see to your family's needs,' he said. He meant his own sexual needs, of course. In the end, he waited up for her and forced her to have sex with him.

'I'm tired,' she said, hunching her shoulder defensively against him.

'Come on, Pan. It's been weeks. You're always tired.'

'I can't help it if there's so much work around the house.'

'If you can't handle the housework as well as church, then I'll ban you from going to all your church activities,' he threatened.

'Oh, all right, *lah*. Go ahead then,' she said resentfully as he pulled at her pyjamas and pawed at her flesh. He was angry to find her dry.

'I have a right,' he insisted with the vehemence of the guilty. 'Ephesians 5:22. "Wives, submit to your own husbands, as to the Lord. For the husband is head of the wife, as also Christ is head of the church."'

She closed her eyes and thought of the story she'd heard about her own mother straining away from the shopkeeper, leaping off the bed, crawling into the corner, darting around the room like an animal in a trap. She resented her husband's familiarity with her body; the way he knew how to arouse her. She was determined not to be aroused. She wanted the punishment of pain for them both. She shut her eyes tightly and began to chant out loud. 'Our Father, who art in heaven, hallowed be thy name. Thy kingdom come, thy will be done on earth as it is in heaven . . .'

'Stop it.' Jonah grasped her arms and shook her as he heaved and panted uncontrollably above her. 'Stop saying that.'

'Give us this day our daily bread, and forgive us our trespasses as we forgive those who trespass against us . . .'

'Damn you.' Infuriated, he slapped her. He hated her
at that moment, and hated himself for wanting her, but he
couldn't stop himself from pummelling her with his need.
He cursed her with each vicious, breathless thrust. 'Aahh!
Damn you, damn you, damn you!'

'For thine is the kingdom, the power and the glory
forever and ever. Amen.'

He rolled off her. Wearily, he turned his face towards
his wife. She was lying completely still. A rivulet of water
wandered down her cheek, following the grooves that
cupped her silent mouth like parentheses.

'Have it your way then,' he growled, too late. He got
out of bed and scratched his crotch, grabbed his pyjama
trousers and climbed into them.

'Martyr,' he accused as he stalked out of their bedroom.
He stopped short when he saw me huddled in the hallway,
my arms wrapped around my knees. 'What are you looking at?'

'Rapist,' I said, crying. He snarled and raised his hand
to slap me. I quickly squeezed my eyes shut and looked
away, bracing myself for the blow. Then he dropped his
hand and shoved me away. He stomped downstairs into the
guest room and slammed the door shut. When I pressed
my ear against the door I could hear the uneven rasp of
harsh sobs. I didn't know who he was crying for: himself,
his wife, maybe for all of us. 'Pan, I love you,' I heard him
cry. 'Oh God, God.'

I drew back from the door and made myself hate him.
I cursed him with vile epithets in my mind as I went upstairs
into the master bedroom. How apt the name seemed
then. The room where my mother had been mastered.

'Mum?' I said. I drew the quilt over her rumpled naked-ness and climbed onto the bed. 'Mum? Are you all right?'

'Go away, Grace,' she said, turning her face away from me.

Still I hesitated. 'Do you want me to help you to the bathroom? Shall I turn on the light?'

'Just go away and leave me alone.'

The next day I went over to Sonny and Hwee Mei's place. I wanted to let Sonny know what had happened so that he could visit Mum, or at least give her a phone call. She needed him, not me.

Hwee Mei opened the door. 'Oh, it's you again. Sonny's still sleeping. He didn't get in till late last night.'

'It's okay.' I followed her into the kitchen and saw the pillar of dishes in the sink. 'I'll do the dishes while I wait, shall I?'

'No, don't. Just sit down.'

Slightly surprised, I did as she said. She made me a mug of coffee, as usual, but she didn't make one for herself. She rummaged around for some Tim Tams, arranged them neatly on a plate and brought them over to the table.

'Look, Grace.' She hadn't sat down and her knuckles were white and tense on the back of the orange vinyl chair. 'I don't know how to say this. I know you're very close to Sonny and all that. Look, I'm pregnant, okay?'

'You are? Hey, that's great! When did you find out? Do you know if it's a boy or girl?'

'Look, we haven't much money,' she said, ignoring my questions. 'I'm going to have to stop work when the baby comes, and Sonny still hasn't established himself prop-erly yet. It's really hard for me to say this, but do you ever stop to think that every time you come around here, you're costing us money?'

'What do you mean?' I couldn't believe I was hearing this, yet was I really that surprised? I had pretended all this time that Hwee Mei was my best friend and closest confidante, that I loved her almost as much as I loved Sonny and that she felt the same way about me. Who was I kidding?

'I mean, look at that.' She gestured to the mug of cooling coffee and the plate of Tim Tams. 'Coffee and bikkies don't drop free from the sky, you know. We have to pay for it.'

'But I didn't ask for any coffee or any Tim Tams. I'm sorry if I haven't been more considerate, but I don't have to eat and drink something whenever I come to visit. In fact, I can help out. I can bring stuff over, especially now that the kid's on its way. I don't do much else with my pocket money anyway. I'm not really into clothes and all that, you know.'

'Look, Grace, we really like you, but you shouldn't come around so often. It's time you built your own life. You don't go out with your friends and Sonny says you've dropped out of church. I know you only went because Sonny went, but that's exactly what I mean. You live your life through Sonny. It's not healthy. You have got to get your own life.' She crossed her arms defensively over her body, as if protecting her child, Sonny's child, from me. 'We're a family now. Me, Sonny and the kid.'

How is it possible for someone to be kicked in the guts over and over again and not develop some sort of warning signal, some sense of self-preservation? How is it possible to keep on falling and never hit the ground? How is it possible to still keep on hurting when all emotion should be dead?

'Yeah. When you're right, you're right. Guess I'll see you around, huh?' I got up and walked out of the flat.

LOVE IN A HOTEL ROOM

Pandora had always depended on someone else to rescue her; she was incapable of saving herself. A dutiful Chinese daughter and then a submissive Chinese wife, she had never learned to fight for anything she wanted, to take up arms against a sea of troubles and, by opposing, end them. Perhaps she never really knew what she wanted anyway, since she did not know herself. She could never understand herself because she only ever slid furtive, side-long glances at life. She was comfortable, if unhappy, with her oblique but familiar vision of the world.

When she felt that she could not bear her marriage any longer, she looked to Josie Philippe for help. Unfortunately for her, Josie was out of the country. Rodney Philippe answered the phone and told her that Josie was leading a three-month mission trip to Bangladesh. He launched into a monologue about the great things the mission team would do and it was with some surprise, mingled with irritation, that he finally noticed the harsh rasp of sobs on the other end of the line.

'Pandora, what's wrong?' he demanded. But he knew her only as a pastor, not as a human being. Over the years she had been in his church he'd had 'fellowship' with her, but neither he nor Josie had ever developed anything as simple and strong as friendship. He sighed internally and did his duty now. 'Pandora, I'm coming over, all right? I want you to go into the kitchen and make yourself a cup of hot tea. All right? Hang up the phone now.'

He spoke to her as if she were an idiot-child, but she did as she was told. She waited in the kitchen for him to tell her what to do next. She could think of only one thing: was she going to get a divorce? It would be such a scandal in the Lim family, even rivalling Lida Lim's adventures over thirty-five years ago.

Lida Lim. Dead for so many years now, run over by a reversing milk truck one chilly grey English winter's morning as she tap-tapped her way across the street with her white cane. Had she been happy before she died? Nobody knew. Tom the English Sailor did not marry her in the end. His mother forbade it, so he left Lida and settled down instead with a nice English girl named Emily who worked as a secretary in a real estate office and read Barbara Cartland novels in her spare time. Lida Lim went on to her next man, whose name we had long since forgotten. He worked as a bouncer in a nightclub and pored over the footy pools during the week. He, too, left her when he discovered that her night blindness was deteriorating and she could no longer venture out of the house after dark. Despite the flashing strobe lights and silver disco ball, she was as blind as a mole inside his nightclub and easily disorientated by the throbbing music. If he'd wanted a missus who just stayed home and nagged, he'd have gotten bloody married, wouldn't he, he said when he walked out. At the time of her death, she had been living with a Pakistani called Ashis who ran a High Street take-away and looked after her when her retinitis pigmentosa degenerated into full blindness. None of the Lims went over for her funeral except for Winston. Then he tried to sue the milk company for compensation but the case was thrown out of court.

Lida Lim might never have been married, but at least that meant she'd never had to consider divorce. Pandora was miserable with Jonah, yet she was terrified of getting a divorce. True, there was no need to consider the children; they were old enough to take care of themselves now. But there were all sorts of other factors to consider: the self-righteous anger of Winston and Daphne, who were not divorced despite their unhappy marriages. Chinese women didn't divorce, Daphne told her. That kind of thing was for westerners. Chinese women just put up with their husbands and were grateful for their children. And the condemnation of her church friends. Marriage was a sacrament, the church insisted. Whom God had joined let no-one put asunder and so forth. If they rejected her because she got divorced, who else did she have in Sydney? And after years of enduring Jonah's presence, could she accustom herself to his absence? Where would she go? The house did not belong to her. She had never worked in her life, hadn't even finished her arts degree because she'd become pregnant. How was she to survive without Jonah?

As usual, she needed a man to rescue her. Rodney Philippe came and threw her a lifeline. He sat in the kitchen with her as she cried and crumpled her way through a box of Kleenex. He listened as she spoke haltingly, painfully embarrassed, of divorcing Jonah. Perhaps. He probed and prodded her family history out of her. He prayed with her and showed her scripture verses, and they talked some more. Divorce was not the answer, he told her sadly. Didn't he himself know that marriage was not an ideal institution, and that married couples weren't always happy or compatible? Take himself and Josie, for example. They had gotten married when they were so young, straight out of university. Over the years they had both changed and grown in different directions. They were such different people now, and they didn't rub along smoothly very often, but although they didn't have children, they were still together, weren't they?

'But you always look so happy together,' Pandora said.

He smiled ruefully. That was faith, he said. Act loving and God will give you the loving feelings. So had the feelings come, she asked? They would come, he assured her. He had faith in that, and she should have faith in God as well. God could save her marriage if she was willing to stop being a victim and take victory in Jesus' name. Their God was a God of miracles. He healed the sick and made the lame walk and leap with joy. He opened the eyes of the blind and raised the dead and, if she wanted it badly enough, if she was willing to believe, he could heal her marriage too. Yes, she wanted it. She would trust God and have faith in him. They made a pact to meet regularly, to study the scriptures and pray together that God would heal both their marriages.

Rodney Philippe came over during the weekdays, when Jonah was at work. He drank coffee and ate the little sandwiches she made, then they got down to business. They studied the biblical role of husband and wife. They looked at God's plan for relationships. And they prayed that God would give them the desires of their hearts. She began to trust him; she told him that Jonah had sex with her whether she wanted it or not, and she submitted because it was her wifely duty to submit to her husband in everything. Rodney was surprised at the quick surge of fury he felt. He was deeply upset by the bred-in-the-bone chauvinism of these Oriental men.

'That's not submission, that's rape,' he said angrily. Then he inhaled deeply. 'Listen, Pandora, Jonah's misquoting scripture, twisting it for his own ends. Just tell Jonah "No" next time.'

It was easy for him to say that. He finished his luke-warm coffee then drove off back home, leaving her alone. She didn't dare to refuse Jonah. She was afraid of his anger and, even more than that, she was just so tired. So she lay under Jonah and closed her eyes, pretending that it was Rodney Philippe making love to her. A man who would lay down his life for his wife, so he claimed, just like Christ. She wished she was his wife.

'I love you, Pan,' Jonah said. He wrapped his arms around her possessively. 'Do you love me still?'

'Mmm.' She hated him for asking the question.

Pandora waited by the front window until Rodney came over again. She loved the way the dark green door of his Holden Commodore swung open quickly and he sprang out, full of life and energy. The driver's door slammed and he jogged round to the front passenger's side and pulled the door open. He stuck his head inside and she briefly admired the tight curve of his bum. Then he withdrew his head like a turtle and straightened up, closing the door, bible in hand. He wheeled around and the car alarm beeped as he strode towards the front door.

'So have you heard from Josie?' she asked as she poured boiling water from the kettle onto the granules of instant coffee in his mug.

'No.' He shrugged. 'I guess she's pretty busy. The Lord must be blessing her work. How are you and Jonah going?'

She put the kettle down carefully and stirred the coffee, pouring in the precise amount of milk that he liked. With both hands, she set the mug in front of him. Then she sat down and arranged herself into the familiar posture of submission, her hands folded and her eyes lowered to her lap.

'Not good. Don't know how much longer I can keep going. Look, it's not him I want inside me.'

She glanced up at him. He sprang up from the kitchen table with that quick, nervous energy that she admired and knocked over the cup of coffee she had so carefully prepared. It spilled over the table and dripped onto the floor. The cup rolled, tipped and smashed on the tiles. He ignored it. He came around the table and took her into his arms to kiss her. His hands streaked down and around to her bottom and he grabbed fistfuls of it through the thin wool of her grey skirt. Then, impatiently, he scrunched up her skirt and his fingers burrowed under her panties to cup her flesh. For an instant, she was totally shocked. Where was the wooing and the romance? she wondered. Where were the words of love and tenderness?

'Pandora, we can't do this here.' He untangled his hands from her clothes and stepped back. 'I've got to think about this.'

'You're right,' she said dully. He was picking up his coat and shrugging it on.

'I'll call you,' he said on his way out.

Sure you will, she thought. But he called the next day, and she felt that maybe she could trust him after all. 'Do you want to meet today?'

'Sure.'

'I've booked us a room at the Hilton,' he said. 'We can meet there and talk or whatever. You can take the train from Burwood to Town Hall.'

'Sure.'

'I've never done this before,' he said as he let her into the room. He was nervous. He took her hand and his palm was sweaty. 'I just want you to know that.'

'I haven't either.'

'We don't have to do anything you don't want. I don't want to hurt you or anybody else.'

'I don't want to hurt you or anyone else either,' she said in return, and she wondered whether the whole scene would take place according to some B-grade film script, with both of them helpless to do or say anything but mouth off clichés.

'It's important that we don't hurt anybody,' he insisted, and she understood that he wasn't just talking about Josie and Jonah, but also about the church. Nobody could find out or his career would be sunk. She agreed. She sat down on the couch. He knelt by her and eased off her pretty high-heeled shoes before seating himself. Then he swung her legs onto the couch and placed her feet on his lap. He began to massage her feet like the tender lover he wanted to be.

'You've got cold feet,' he observed as his fingers stretched the skin of her arches.

'They're always cold.' She was always cold.

'Your bones are so fine, so delicate.'

His hands left her feet and worked their way up her shins, then calves, loosening up the bunched muscles there. He pushed her skirt up slowly and stroked the dimpled flesh of her thighs. 'Lift your hips up,' he whispered. She obeyed, and he tugged at the elastic waistband of her underpants and slid them down her legs. He stared at the coarse nest of black curls at the top of her thighs. 'Will you open up for me, Pandora? Please?' Jonah never asked, she thought, spreading her thighs wide, and he never did this for her. She closed her eyes and tangled her fingers in Rodney's thick brown hair as he bent his head and gave her the gift of tongues.

He undressed her slowly and kissed her all over. He licked at the stretchmarks across her belly and lapped at the cellulite of her thighs. 'I love all the different textures of your skin,' he said as he pulled her off the couch and led her to the bed, turning down the covers so that she could slip inside. The sheets were cold so she snuggled against his warmth and allowed him to part her thighs. 'Pandora, I adore you,' he said as he entered her to piston in and out. 'I've wanted to make love to you for so long now.'

He said he adored her. That was all right. That was safe, wasn't it? She knew where she stood with that. Adoration was intense, momentary, physical. It was what men said when they couldn't say 'I love you' because they couldn't fulfil the impossible demands and responsibilities of love. Adoration was realistic; it didn't make and break the same promises as love.

'I adore you,' Rodney said again. 'You're so quiet and serene and gentle. You make me feel so peaceful.'

She turned her face towards his and he saw himself mirrored in the stillness of her dark brown eyes.

'Tell me about yourself.'

'What do you want to know?'

'Everything. I want to know every single thing about you.' With his index finger he smoothed away the slight frown that dipped between her brows. 'Start with your child-hood. What were you like as a kid? I bet you were such a cute little kid.'

She opened herself up to him and told him things that she had never told Jonah. She told him about being born under the sword of death, about being unwanted by the Lims and Tans, about singing for her special treat with Donald Duck in hawker centres, about everything that she had ever wanted and dreamt of being. She wanted him to understand her, to know who she really was. Look at me and see, really see me.

But he couldn't; like so many western men, he was blinded by his own fantasies of Oriental women. Quiet, gentle, passive femininity that transformed into voracious, insatiable sexuality in bed. Lady and whore in one. He stroked the soft, smooth skin of her back, squeezed her small bird-like bones, kissed the passive oval of her face, and failed to feel the bitter passion and disappointed dreams that bubbled deep inside her; the rage she didn't know how to express, that she could only escape from by shutting down her consciousness and sinking into mind-numbing depression.

'I want to lose myself in your tranquillity,' he mumbled into her neck. 'You've got such an aura of calm.'

'Yes, I'm practically inscrutable,' she said sadly. Then she sighed, because all her life she had tossed up bright dreams to the gods, and always they came shattering back down, so when would she ever learn to stop needing so much and be happy with what she had? She *would* be happy.

He romanced her in a way that Jonah had never been able to, and she made herself content with that. She loved the short little phone calls throughout each day, the bunches of flowers that he brought her, the little gifts, the short, hand-written notes with little verses of love from the Song of Solomon—*You have ravished my heart with one look of your eyes. How much better than wine is your love, and the scent of your perfume than all spices*—and the longer, erotic letters. Like a lovestruck teenager, she pressed some of his flowers and folded his notes carefully and put them into a carved wooden jewellery box that she buried in the vegetable patch.

(Years later Jonah dug up the box accidentally when he was turning over the vegetable patch to plant roses. In his old age, he wanted to be surrounded by the scent of roses. He took it out, shook off the earth and maggots, and opened it. The notes and letters were all unsigned. Even at the height of his infatuation, Rodney Philippe was careful in his love. With trembling fingers, Jonah unfolded a note, smoothed the page and read. He took the box inside and called for me. Is this yours? he asked. I looked at the box, brimful of letters and pressed flowers, and scanned the note that he held out. Yes, I said, they're mine. He looked me in the eye. Here you are then—I didn't read them, only that one you're holding. He gave me the box and went back out to the garden to turn over the soil.)

Pandora became acquainted with the world of daytime hotel rooms. She and Rodney combed through the Yellow Pages looking for suitable hotels, careful never to return to the same one or to establish a routine that might be traced.

At first she was charmed by the thrill of cheating, the titillation of wickedness and the decadent romance of lying naked in her lover's arms, sipping champagne at two in the afternoon.

Then Josie Philippe returned triumphantly from her mission trip to Bangladesh, where they'd saved souls, seen God performing miracles, and established two new churches.

'I don't want to stop seeing you, Pandora,' Rodney said as he burrowed between her thighs. 'I can't.'

'I don't want to hurt Josie,' Pandora said, as she knew she must. 'I've got nothing against her.'

But she lied. She did want to hurt Josie because she wanted to take away what Josie had. She began to hate Josie and she felt a tight-lipped triumph every time she saw her because she and Rodney shared a secret that made Josie an outsider. At the same time, though, she wanted to destroy Josie with the truth, fling it in her face like acid.

'We won't let her find out then. Pandora, I have to have you. I simply adore you. I'm in love with you.'

'Then do something about it.'

He stopped his thrusting, shocked into stillness.

'Do something about it?' he echoed. 'What?'

'What do you think?'

'You mean divorce Josie?' She just looked at him. 'I thought you didn't want to divorce Jonah.'

'I'm willing to now. I love you too, Rodney.'

'Let me think about it.'

Love made a mess of everything. The hotel rooms began to depress her. Rodney was running short of cash and he looked for cheaper, tackier motels now. They were no longer glamorous and decadent; they were sordid. Worst of all, she felt like a cliché stuck in a timeworn and unoriginal groove. She saw Rodney less frequently now that his wife was back. He had to be more careful so his schedule was irregular. He no longer rang her at home or sent her little presents, and he asked her to stop sending him letters and gifts as well.

'We've got to be careful,' he said. 'People might talk.'

Deep inside her, she began to despise him then. If he had been evil she could still have loved him and hung her hopes of escape on him. But he wasn't evil, just human and weak. She despised the pusillanimous morality he still paid lip-service to, and his inability to act. She despised herself as well, for she knew that she, too, was incapable of taking drastic action without his support. Pandora began to despair.

'Don't worry. I'll ask her for a divorce,' he assured Pandora. 'It's just that the timing is really tricky. She's just come back from such a great trip and she's in really high spirits at the moment. I don't want to spoil her mood.'

'What about *my* mood?' Pandora demanded. 'You say that you love me, but you won't do anything about it.'

It was on the tip of her tongue then. *If you loved me, you would* . . . But she swallowed the words and crushed them down into her diaphragm, for she understood instinctively that, once uttered, the words would suffocate his love in resentment.

'Look, you're a lot stronger emotionally than Josie. Whatever happens to you, you always cope. Right throughout your childhood and throughout your marriage. Chinese women always cope. Isn't that what you said? Josie's different. She might look strong and confident, but she's very insecure emotionally. I've got to ease her into the subject. I don't want her to lose her faith in God as well as in me.'

So she gave him time. He already had her love, so she gave him the only things she could give him now: her loyalty, her support, and lots of time for him to ease Josie into the idea of divorce. She listened to him as he complained about the huge arguments he had with Josie, about her temper tantrums that made his life a living hell. Things were going to be so different when they together, he assured her. He couldn't wait. Pandora made herself believe him. She hung on to his love and convinced herself that she would not become yet another statistic. *When my love swears that he is made of truth, I do believe him, though I know he lies*. She made love with him in a small motel room on Parramatta Road, their moans and shudders masked by the heavy traffic passing outside, and she believed him when he whispered that it was all right; they were going to end up together. Everything would work out. Meanwhile, Josie went away on a mission trip to Nigeria at Christmas and they had more time together. Then Josie came back again. Still Pandora waited.

Josie rang her at home one day.

'Hi Pandora. We haven't seen you for a while.' Her voice was bright and chirpy. 'Rodney and I have been pretty busy since I've been back, but we keep saying we ought to get you and Jonah over for dinner.'

'I'll have to ask Jonah when he's free,' Pandora said.

'You do that. I hear you've been taking care of Rodney while I've been away, so we want to thank you guys. Give us a call back when you've talked to Jonah, okay?'

Pandora rang Rodney at his office. 'Josie just called. She invited Jonah and me over for dinner at your place.'

'Oh my God! Does she suspect anything?'

'I don't know. Maybe. Have you told her that you want a divorce?'

'Yes, I brought it up the other night. We agreed to think about a separation while she makes a life for herself. She's got a great ministry going now.'

'Rodney, don't lie to me. Don't lie to me the way you lie to her.'

'I'm not. Christ, what am I going to do now?'

He sounded so agitated. She waited for him to tell her that he would pack a suitcase and move out of the house he shared with Josie. That he would file for divorce. She had waited for him for so long.

'What else did she say?' Rodney asked. 'Was she upset or in a temper? Did she sound all right?'

'I don't know. Maybe you should ring her and find out.'

Pandora hung up. She pressed her face against the wall and wrapped her arms around herself, hugging herself for comfort. She was beginning to see that however much Rodney claimed to adore her, even to love her, Josie was always going to be his first priority; Josie's feelings, insecurities and needs. And maybe Rodney really got off on being needed that desperately. Maybe it fed his ego, made him feel important and powerful. Gutless, Pandora thought fiercely. He was such a gutless man. He said that he was unhappy with Josie, but he was too gutless to make a clean break and let them both start over. Instead, he continued with their war of attrition, hoping that Josie would be the one to call off the marriage finally and absolve him of responsibility.

On the following day, after Jonah had gone to work, Pandora spent the morning cooking pork stew for Jonah's dinner. She packed a suitcase and scribbled a letter to him.

She put it in an envelope, sealed it and placed it on the kitchen table, leaning against the pot of pork stew. Then she rang Rodney at work.

'What is it?' He sounded harassed and impatient. 'You shouldn't be ringing me here, Pandora. You've no idea what's happening at the moment. This place is a hotbed of suspicion. It's all gonna blow.'

'I'm leaving Jonah,' Pandora told him.

'What? Are you crazy?'

'I'm going to take a bus to the park at the end of Glebe Point Road now. The one by Blackwattle Bay. If you love me as much as you say you do, you'll come and get me. I'll wait for you there.'

'Pandora, don't do anything stupid.' His voice was panicky now, then angry. 'Listen, I don't deal well with ultimatums, okay? I've got back-to-back meetings this afternoon.'

'That's okay. I'll wait for you.' She hung up. She switched off all the lights and power points in the house and checked the windows and doors to make sure that everything was secure. Then she let herself out of the front door and locked it, slipping the key under the money plant on the verandah. She picked up her suitcase and walked to Burwood Station.

It was such a beautiful day, the sky so blue over Blackwattle Bay and the sunshine so sharp that the shadows could cut you. Pandora walked over to a shaded bench under a tree and sat down to wait. She watched mothers playing with their kids in the sun, lunch-time joggers passing, an old man who spent the afternoon throwing a stick for his dog, kids rollerblading after school. She kept an eye out for a dark green Holden Commodore. Sometimes she thought she caught sight of the back of a head, or the cut of a coat that looked familiar and she started up, her heart pounding, but it was always someone else. Buses came and went. Shadows lengthened. The sun set slowly, throwing out burning streamers of pink and orange over the bay. The sky darkened gradually and Pandora couldn't distinguish anything in the grey light. Too late, she realised that she had completely forgotten about her night blindness. Time passed and she couldn't see anything. All she could do was sit there on the park bench, in the dark, clenching the handle of her suitcase and waiting for Rodney Philippe to come.

THE COMPULSION
TO CLEAN

I had sex for the first time on the night that Hwee Mei
threw me out of her home and out of her life, and it
was pretty unspectacular. I'd gone to Sonny's pub with the
adolescent idea of drinking myself into a stupor, like in
the movies. How would we respond to the climaxes and
crises of life if it weren't for the movies? They were a manual
for growing up. They taught me everything I knew about
how to behave as a western adolescent, how to mouth
the clichés and arrange my body into the appropriate
postures and attitudes of various emotional states. I interna-
lised their soundtracks and replayed them in my head.
They amplified the meaning of my mundane existence and
added poignancy and significance to otherwise bitter but
banal events.

Cut off from contact with Sonny, unable to live vicariously through him, I clung to the tatters of badly written
scripts. I tried to get plastered but the barman knew I was
Sonny's sister and had just clambered over the legal age, so
he stopped me after I'd gulped down two beers like cough

medicine because I didn't like the taste. However, he let me hang around and that was when Hēmi came over and sat beside me. A handsome Maori who spent much of his days surfing and most of his nights playing the guitar and singing, Hēmi was a member of Sonny's band. I didn't know much about him except that Hwee Mei thought he might be gay without knowing it since his main ambition in life was to become an opera singer. 'It's not impossible. Look at Kiri Te Kanawa,' he insisted. After a few drinks his favourite party trick was to launch into the aria 'E lucevan le stelle' from Puccini's *Tosca*: *My dream of love has vanished forever, the moment is fled. I die in despair and never have I loved life so much*. He completed his performance with the requisite heart-rending sobs at the end, covering his face with his long brown hands as his shoulders shuddered.

I can't even remember how it happened now; I guess I'm a one-drink wonder and even two schooners go straight to my head. One moment we were in the pub and the next thing I knew I was in Hēmi's room in a tumbledown terrace house near the Newtown flour mills. I still had my T-shirt on but not my underpants, and Hēmi was heaving and panting on top of me, his dark body a dead weight pinning me to a mattress which had a rather peculiar odour of sweat and baby powder. Sex wasn't particularly painful, but neither was it comfortable. I think I felt as if my body didn't belong to me. After the whole thing was over I turned to look at him.

'Now are you going to tell me that you love me?' I said cynically.

'Get real, Gracie-girl. It's just sex,' he said. 'I hardly know you except that you're Sonny's sister. Shit, don't tell Sonny about this. I need my job.'

'Don't think he'd care one way or the other.'

'You're a funny one, Gracie-girl,' he said as he rolled on top of me again. 'All that need and no-one to hang it on. Well, don't go falling in love with me and all that shit. I'm out of here soon as I get my break.'

Still, he was rather sweet to me while it lasted and I didn't get VD, and maybe that's all you can expect these days. If I stayed overnight he'd raid the fridge in the morning, sniff the sour milk and jog out to get some more so he could fix me cereal for breakfast. He wouldn't let me clean for him or do anything for him. 'This is not your home, Grace,' he said, drawing the boundaries clearly. On warm afternoons he'd jam a baseball cap over my head and one over his—'All that black hair attracts a lot of heat,' he'd say—and we'd sit on the back steps munching chips while I read and he played the guitar, singing anything from 'Dock of the Bay' to 'Nessum Dorma'.

'This is nice,' I said once.

'Yeah, it is. Just don't get used to it.' But he put his arm around me and gave me a hug.

'Don't worry. No expectations at all.'

And it was just as well. He auditioned for some music college in Canberra and was accepted, so off he went to follow in Kiri Te Kanawa's footsteps.

'Good luck. See you round,' I said, just before he left for Central Station. My generation cannot say 'goodbye'. We have lost the formal rituals of leave-taking.

'Yeah. I'll call you,' he said awkwardly, fidgeting with the battered handle of his guitar case.

'Will you?'

'Nah, not really.' He grinned then, honest to the last, and I realised how much I liked him—really just *liked* him—at that moment. 'Take care of yourself, Gracie-girl.' And then, because he didn't know how to leave without saying it although he didn't mean it either: 'See ya later.'

There was not much else for me to do so I just studied and finished school. After the HSC I moved out to Newtown. I circled job ads in the newspapers and went for interviews, but in the end I just started cleaning houses. My fingers were raw and red because I kept forgetting to wear gloves, and my knuckles swelled up painfully. I mopped, dusted, vacuumed, laundered clothes and ironed them and there was such satisfaction in mindless work. I brought order into other people's homes. I removed trash from their lives.

At home I'd read until the early hours of the morning, but I still had trouble sleeping. My flatmates and I sometimes trolled King Street to pick up convenient cocks, back in the days before King Street started to look like Oxford Street, Paddington, with hip cafes and trendsetting clothes stores; back when dingy shops sold African beads, belts, bells and beanies. My flatmates were looking for a good fuck; I was just looking for a cure for insomnia. In the morning, if I didn't have a cleaning job to go to, I fixed breakfast for the stomachs attached to those cocks: freshly ground Italian coffee, cereal and toast, sometimes even bacon and eggs. I accepted their groans of appreciation—'You're amazing, Grace,' they always said, ha ha—and put them out of the house as soon as I could. Then I stripped the bed, laundered the sheets and effaced all signs of human intrusion into my home. I showered, scrubbed myself vigorously and cleaned my teeth carefully with a soft-bristled toothbrush. Gentle circular motions, round and round.

And, of course, I flossed. Habits of hygiene are harder to break than family ties.

I hardly saw Sonny anymore. I didn't know what he was doing for a living. Occasionally I saw his name on cheap posters pasted onto lampposts, advertising the dates and places where his band was playing. Otherwise, I assumed he was wrapped up in Hwee Mei and his baby. I was afraid of intruding on their domesticity. If they were actually happy, I thought, then they should be given a chance. That baby should be given a chance to break the pattern, to grow up quarantined from the inevitable hurt and disappointment of failed relationships in the Tay family. Perhaps Hwee Mei felt the same way. She didn't like Sonny contacting us, neither did she like us to visit. When Mum went around to play with little Mary Tay, she hovered protectively, as though the baby might catch some germs from Mum. As for the Patriarch, we'd never had much to say to each other and he stopped speaking to me after I became a cleaner.

'You've got a good brain, Grace,' he insisted. 'It comes from the Tay side of the family. All the Tays have good brains and they put them to good use. Look at your cousins. All doctors and engineers. How can you not want to go to university?'

'Just don't, that's all.'

'And cleaning. What kind of a career is that?'

'I don't want a career,' I explained to him. 'I like to clean and I just want a mindless job that will leave me lots of time to read and watch movies. You know, like Otis.'

'Otis?'

'Redding. "Dock Of The Bay". Watching ships roll in and out and all over the place. Wasting time. That sort of thing.'

'You're making a big mistake,' he warned. 'I'm so disappointed in you. After everything I gave up in Malaysia, all the sacrifices I made, this is how you and Sonny repay me. Both of you drop out of church and don't go to uni, and what do you end up doing? Cleaning and unpacking boxes! Wasting your lives away. You all are useless. Good for nothing.'

It was more difficult to sever ties with Mum. She needed me although she didn't realise it. I covered up for her. When I was free I went over to the Burwood house and made sure that the place was cleaned. As I vacuumed and dusted, I looked for any telltale signs that she was having an affair and destroyed them. I cooked curries and stews and stored them in the freezer so that if she was running late after one of her afternoon assignations, she could just take something out and defrost it for the Patriarch's dinner. I didn't want her to get into trouble.

On the day that she decided to leave the Patriarch, one of my clients postponed a cleaning job until later in the week so I had the afternoon free. I went over to my parents' house to do the laundry and ironing, and I saw the envelope that she had left on the kitchen table. I ripped it open and read it, then I tore it into tiny pieces, dumped it in the trash can and took the plastic bag out to the big green bin at the side of the house. I went back inside and rang Rodney Philippe's office but there was no answer. Maybe I was wrong, I thought. Maybe he really had gone to get her. Maybe he wasn't just screwing around with her. Maybe he did care for her and love her.

But I knew that he didn't. He couldn't. If he had really cared for her, he wouldn't have kept her in limbo-land for the last couple of years. What did she see when she looked at him? All I could see was a selfish and gutless man who didn't have the courage to make a choice and take what he really wanted, to live with the consequences of his actions. Instead he made two women unhappy. Did he really think that his wife would not suspect he was having an affair? The rumours had been rumbling in the church for years, he just didn't know it. Pandora had become yet another statistic, just an 'other woman'.

I tried ringing his office again but the line was engaged. I had no idea where my mother was and Rodney Philippe was the only one who could tell me. I had no choice; I found my mother's car keys and drove over to the church. His secretary said that he had gone home as he wasn't feeling well, so I walked over to his house, taking the chance that Josie wouldn't be there having one of her numerous women's groups or mission meetings. The screen door was unlocked. I pulled it open and stepped into the house. I could hear the sound of someone sobbing. I followed the noise to the study and found Rodney Philippe kneeling on the floor, the bible open on a chair in front of him. His face was blotchy with tears, mucus dripped from his nose and he was reading from Psalm 51.

> Have mercy upon me, O God, according to your loving kindness . . . Wash me thoroughly from my iniquity, and cleanse me from my sin. For I acknowledge my transgressions, and my sin is always before me. Against you, you only, have I sinned and done this evil in your sight . . .

'You fucking bastard!' From his desk I grabbed an ugly cut-glass crystal vase that some grateful member of his congregation had probably given to him, and I hit him and hit him and hit him with it until the skin broke on his head and blood oozed angrily through the scalp. I could have killed him. I wanted to. His blood would cleanse my mother's shame, his pain would ease hers.

'Grace, stop that! Have you gone mad?' He struggled to his feet, light-headed with tears and dazed by the attack. 'Give me that.'

He reached over and wrestled me for the vase, wrenching it out of my hands. 'What's the matter with you?'

'You didn't just sin against God, you fucking gutless prick. You sinned against my mother.'

He stood there staring at me, this man who had laid his hands on me so many years ago, promising to lead me into salvation and the love of God.

'You know?'

'Of course I know. Who do you think's been covering your fat arse all this time? You with your wussy notes and lying love letters.'

'I loved your mother,' he said. How easily he put her behind him. 'But we were wrong. We sinned against God and we've got to repent.'

I looked at him and saw such a pathetic man. 'Oh, never mind. Where's Mum? I know she's waiting for you somewhere. She left a note behind for my father.'

'Does Jonah know—'

'I just want to know where my mum is,' I interrupted. 'C'mon. Please.'

'She's in the park at the end of Glebe Point Road.'

It was very dark when I arrived. She sat so still under the tree that I didn't make her out at first. I didn't know how long she had been sitting there, waiting. I wanted to cry, but I walked over to her instead.

She heard the sound of footsteps and turned her face towards them. 'Rodney, is that you?'

'No, Mum. It's me,' I said. 'Rodney's not going to come.'

'I can't see,' she said. 'I think my retinitis pigmentosa is getting worse.'

'It's okay. We'll take care of it.'

'You should go to the eye doctor and get your eyes checked too,' she said. 'It's hereditary, you know. Your Auntie Lida Lim had it. Your father says the Lims have bad genes.'

'Let's go home, Mum.'

In the end I had to move back home to take care of her. To become a mother to her. She just let herself go. Stopped caring for her appearance, lost interest in clothes, couldn't care less about the house or her husband or me. She lost her eyesight over the next few years but it didn't matter much by then anyway. She was already used to spending her days sitting at the window, staring sightlessly out into the garden to where the jasmine and wisteria once grew. Now there is only a tangled mess of tomato vines and ferocious weeds that nobody tends.

THE INSUPERABLE
LONGING TO FALL

After my mother's wake and funeral the relatives returned to their normal lives. The doctor uncles went back to their hospitals and GP surgeries in Singapore, Sydney, San Francisco and Sussex to heal and play golf. Death had made little impact on their lives because they saw it, or traces of it, every day. They were not hardened, merely resigned and accepting. Pandora's death would soon have ceased to be a topic of conversation, would have been a taboo subject at subsequent clan gatherings, had it not been for the horrific and unspeakable sin of suicide and, of course, Sonny's dramatic slaying of the Cod God.

Sonny's obscene action had actually redeemed my mother's memory in their minds. The secret condemnation they exhaled to each other behind a raised, half-cupped hand was instantly transferred from my mother to Sonny. The scandalous circumstances of her death were far out-weighed by the unspeakably unfilial behaviour displayed by Sonny.

Uncle Winston and Auntie Shufen could have explained, but they never did. Certainly they felt guilty enough not to demand compensation for the ruined rosewood furniture and the fish, although when the Patriarch insisted on replacing everything (excluding the pagan Cod God), their refusals were half-hearted and not sustained for long. Uncle Winston and Auntie Shufen exited abruptly from our lives. A few months after the funeral, Uncle Winston started shitting blood and discovered that he had bowel cancer. The Patriarch wanted to fly to Singapore to see him, but he refused all contact with our family. Sonny's sin had tainted all the Tays and made us pariahs.

Auntie Percy-phone told us that Winston was firmly convinced that the messy deterioration of his body was caused by the loss of the Cod God. He dedicated the rest of his life to trying to replace the Cod God and squandered what remained of his illegal lottery winnings in extortionately priced anti-cancer programs involving organic food, coffee enemas and Ohira Mountain Extract pills. We never spoke to him again and when he died, the wake and funeral were held without us. In fact, apart from Auntie Percy-phone, we never saw the Lim relatives again. Not even Wendy Wu.

For an instant, we found ourselves in the same economy-class carriage on a train of grief. But the major terminus had been passed long ago and people had begun to get off at their suburban stops, until I alone was left on that train. The older cousins disappeared into their glittering towers of financial success. The Singaporean aunties went back to buying Dior lipstick, quilted Chanel handbags, Gucci shoes, Armani evening gowns and Versace suits that were too hot for the climate. They planned package trips to Disneyland for their kids and tours to London and Paris for themselves. They even planned to come to Sydney, although I knew they wouldn't contact us.

Their kids were armoured with the iconoclastic irreverence of childhood and they turned my mother's death into a joke. They flung themselves off the top of their bunk beds in six-foot suicide attempts and re-enacted Sonny's slaying of the Cod God, wrestling with their bolsters and giggling. The wake and funeral were barely hiccups in the competitive round of their rigidly disciplined lives, centred on school, after-school tutoring in mathematics, science, English and Mandarin, followed by piano or violin lessons, swimming or ballet lessons, and furtive late-night games on computers or Sony play-stations.

As for me, well, I cannot return to normality.

In the days after the wake I take to wandering the streets of Singapore. Each night I come home to Auntie Percy-phone's flat. Each morning I wake up just before dawn and watch fluorescent kitchen lights flickering on in the HDB apartments a few metres from my barred window. I lie awake and listen to people scrubbing off the sediment of sleep. I hear the sounds of flushing and the loud gurglings of the pipes that pass through the bathroom next to my bedroom, and I try not to imagine the sewage swirling around in them. I can't get back to sleep. I drag myself out of bed and shower in the darkness. Then I make myself a cup of coffee with the ground beans and the Bodum I've brought from Sydney, and I sit in the dark kitchen, staring out the window, spying on the strangers preparing for life.

By six-thirty the hawker stalls in the market below the apartments are setting up for the day, while in the new shopping centre near the MRT station, Delifrance prepares to compete with sticky croissants, *pain-au-chocolats* and pastries. It is in these quiet hours of the morning, I suppose, that I feel most at home in Singapore, and I can begin to accept that part of me which is embedded here and refuses to wither away no matter how many times I chop and sear those roots. I let myself out of the flat and walk in the early morning coolness. In the distance the electronic tones of the MRT station sound as a train pulls up to the platform. Buses rattle along the estate feeder roads, picking up schoolkids and people on their way to work. Cars whine on the Pan Island Expressway and pedestrians impatient for the lights to change step out onto the pristine roads, dodging traffic and irate police officers issuing fines for jaywalking.

Breakfast is ready by the time I've taken my morning stroll. I turn into the hawker centre and wander from stall to stall, debating between a bowl of fish porridge, *nasi lemak* or a couple of spicy, smelly, vermilion-coloured *otak otak* wrapped and roasted in banana leaves. When my mother was alive she used to crave such things for breakfast. Spooning soggy Weetbix into my mouth or scraping Vegemite onto my toast, I exaggerated my incredulity that anyone could eat anything so pungent and spicy that early in the morning. How is it that my dead mother's tastebuds now coat my tongue and nudge my cravings?

I sit on a red stool at a rickety table, sip coconut juice from a plastic bag expertly sealed with a tight twist of pink string, and watch old men shuffle in for breakfast, their white singlets tucked into dark dress pants, brown slippers on their feet. They order, sit down at other tables, unfold closely printed Chinese newspapers and slip into a world that is foreign to me. Out here, away from the city centre, it could almost be a scene from the stories my mother used to tell me.

After breakfast I pass the local school and look through the chain-link fence to where neat, black-haired kids in crisp white shirts, navy skirts or shorts and white sandshoes parade in geometric shapes around the playground, standing to attention while they sing the Singaporean national anthem in a language that I cannot understand. The kids fascinate me. Did my mother stand to attention like this in the dripping heat as she sang 'God Save the King' and her principal read out letters from Queen Mary's secretary? Did she march like this when she was in her school? How would I have coped? I try to see my own legs pumping up and down in unison with others in those intricate drills. I simply cannot imagine what I would have been like, who I would have been, if the Patriarch had not cannibalised his fear and migrated to Sydney. I go back to Auntie Percy-phone's flat to do the laundry—separating whites from colours and darks from lights, of course—and to sweep and mop the cool white tiles of the flat. Cleaning is such a calming, satisfying activity.

Later in the morning I walk over to the MRT station to catch the train that departs Pasir Ris to slither west into the city. One day I get off at City Hall and change for the Dhoby Ghaut, Somerset and Orchard line. In the viscid heat, my T-shirt sticking to my back and arms, I wander down Orchard Road from shopping centre to shopping centre, hotel to hotel, until I stop in Fort Canning Park and look across to St Andrew's Cathedral, where Por-Por had come to pray with Percy-phone and Pandora so many years ago, only to be thrown out instead; where the Patriarch had married my mother. On another day I stop at

Raffles City to look at Raffles Hotel. My mother had always talked about staying there. The next time I go to Singapore, she used to tell us, I'm going to book myself into a grand red room in Raffles Hotel, take high tea, stroll along the verandahs and corridors and pretend I'm someone in a Somerset Maugham novel. But the next time she came to Singapore, she threw herself off an HDB apartment block.

On another day I venture further westward and wander through the tangled streets of Chinatown. The skyline is splashed with giant calligraphy. From the cinema posters, beautiful Hong Kong actresses toss their hair and flash their eyes at daring heroes who split the air, hovering in mid-Taekwondo kicks. It's exactly as she described it, all those years ago. Just cleaner, more sanitised. I peer into dark and obscure doorways where wizened Chinese herbalists guard their boxes and jars of gnarled ginseng roots, ground pearls, Tiger Balm and various jellies, pastes and powders behind green-tinged, scratched glass counters. From the black and white photos that form my mother's memories of the cityscape, I look for the ghosts of buildings that are no longer there. I feel self-conscious and inadequate because passers-by and hawkers of 'genuine' Rolex watches for only twenty-five dollars call out to me in Hokkien, Mandarin and Cantonese and, of course, I can neither understand nor respond. I realise how completely I had depended on Mum whenever we went somewhere Chinese. I had been culturally lazy, content to smile and nod and let her order the dim sum dishes and demand more tea and the bill.

Finally I get off at Lavender one day. ('It's not la-*ven*-der; it's *lav*-ender,' I still hear Niree say.) I walk up Lavender Street and turn left into the Indian district along Serangoon Road. I sniff the aroma of grilling *roti prata*, simmering curry, oil and incense as I zone through temple-land, passing the Temple of a Thousand Lights, the Sri Sreenivasa Perumal Temple, the Angullia Mosque and the Kali Amman Temple. I know that on the day before she died, Mum had been found wandering along Serangoon Road. This was why she had come back to Singapore. She wanted to come back to where it had all begun. To trace the moment when she could have made another choice and life would have been completely different.

She had been looking for her childhood home—the terrace shophouse with the cracked cement courtyard—but had given the taxi driver the wrong street address. Actually, there was no right address. The entire terraced neighbourhood in which she had grown up had been bought by the government in the early 1980s and bull-dozed. This was before the days when colonial shophouses were preserved to attract tourist dollars. Whole streets and narrow lanes were eradicated to make way for brightly lit, air-conditioned, neon-signed shopping centres. Exasperated by her increasing incoherence and distress, the taxi driver had eventually dumped her near Dhoby Ghaut. Lost in the city she'd always considered her 'real' home, her white walking stick tapping wildly in front of her, she must have wandered up Selegie Road and crossed over into Serangoon Road.

Did she, at that point, sniff the same pungent air as me and become aware of her utter foreignness in her home-land? On that last afternoon, did she suddenly wish that she was back in Sydney, where she could at least orien-tate herself with ease? The city where she had crisscrossed George Street and cut through the Grace Bros building or the Strand Arcade to get from the QVB to Pitt Street Mall a hundred times. Had she missed the mechanical ticking of the pedestrian lights in Burwood which signalled to the blind when they could cross in safety? Did she finally realise that, whatever she might now be, she was no longer Singaporean? Perhaps she had longed for a familiar voice, even if it was only that of the guy in the car park ticket booth at Strathfield Plaza asking her how she was doing that day. Perhaps she had yearned for the breeze on her face and the gentle slap of water against the wharf at Mortlake Bay where Sonny and I sometimes drove her on Sunday afternoons. She had sat in the sun, shaded by her unfurled umbrella, while we took turns reading the newspapers out to her. Perhaps—horror of horrors—she had even missed Brian Henderson intoning at six-twenty-eight on weeknights: 'And that's the way it was . . . I'm Brian Henderson . . . Good night.' She'd then quickly switched channels to the SBS news and Mary Kostakidis before the theme to 'A Current Affair' could sound.

Nobody ever found out what had happened on that last afternoon in Singapore. Eventually she was brought back to Uncle Winston's apartment, distraught and barely intelligible, her speech reduced to a stuttering patois in which English, Malay and Teochew nouns had been erased from her vocabulary to be replaced by the word 'thing'. Lost and disorientated, unable to see and frustrated by her inability to communicate, she found herself suddenly surrounded by an alarming world of unnameable Things. She phoned the Patriarch in Sydney that night and irritated him with her incoherence, hurt him when she forgot his name.

'I wanted to find that thing where I used to live and I told the thing to turn left at the thing, but he went past the other thing and couldn't do a . . . this thing. Then we went round and round until he got lost. And then finally he said he was at this thing and I had to get out, so I paid him and got out. I asked this one to show me what to do with that thing but nobody stopped until finally a young man stopped and helped me across. I knew I was at the wrong thing, but I thought that if I walked to the other end of the thing I would find the station and get on the thing. But even though I had my stick I kept walking into things and turning at the wrong thing until I got completely lost.'

The Patriarch had been characteristically terse with her. Her incompetence annoyed him as much as it worried him, and as usual he showed his concern in a hot blast of scolding. Upset and shaken, Auntie Shufen told us, Pandora went to feed the six guppy fish that she had acquired during her first week in Singapore, when she was striving to recapture and relive her childhood memories. Long ago, Donald Duck had given her six guppies that he'd caught from the river for her tenth birthday. She could never remember what happened to them, but she suspected that one of the boys had mischievously poured them into the stormwater drain outside the terrace house. It was Auntie Percy-phone who bought the guppies this time. Using the leverage of guilt and the last vestiges of pity for the disabled, Auntie Percy-phone finagled a small fish tank out of Uncle Winston.

It was one of Pandora's greatest pleasures, during those last weeks, to sit by the fish tank each day and slowly dip her fingers into the cool bubbling water. She said she could feel the tiny currents running over her fingertips and, occasionally, the feathering of a fin brushing her skin.

On that last day, however, when she dipped her fingers into the water to calm herself, it was still. No tiny tidal ripples, no bubbling, no sense of sleek miniature bodies slicing through the fluid. In a panic, her fingers groped and grasped, inched from one corner of the tank to the next, one hand soon joined by the other, until she was up to her elbows in water which slopped out of the tank onto the opulent Chinese carpet. Uncle Winston was furious that she'd soaked the carpet. He sounded just like the Patriarch. She ignored him.

'Where are my guppies?' she called out, over and over again, her distress crescendoing along with the volume of her litany. Her sodden fingers fluttered helplessly in the whirling eddies of water she created in the tank.

Finally Auntie Shufen told her. '*Hi-yah*, don't make such a fuss, *lah*. Winston fed them to the Amazonian Cod. He got no more fish food and was too lazy to go down to the NTUC supermarket and buy some more. Sorry, *lah*. I go and get you some more guppies tomorrow, okay?'

But it was not okay. As the shops began to open the following morning, Pandora stepped out onto the balcony of Winston's apartment. She leant over and felt the sucking space below her. Slowly, she took off her red Ferragamo pumps and climbed over the edge until she sat on the railing. Nobody was there to see her except God. She looked up and out, and saw nothing but white light.

'God,' she said. 'Oh, God.'

She flung herself off the balcony and fell into the void of his love.

'Pan!' Auntie Shufen rushed to the spot where a pair of red Ferragamo pumps pointed towards the balcony. She looked over the edge and saw the mash of organs and shattered bone, shuddered, and quickly turned away. Then she picked up the red Ferragamo shoes and took them back inside the flat where she rang the police. In the end, Auntie Percy-phone identified the body. She stared at the pulped flesh and crumpled material of the shirt and trousers, at the spreading tide of blood that thickened and darkened in the growing heat until Pandora lay in her own black hole. All my life my mother smelt of soap and talcum powder—clean and child-like. In death she reeked of bitter violence and disappointed dreams.

This story was what Auntie Shufen had whispered to Sonny on the night of the wake, when I dozed off and woke up to his madness.

'And that's it?' I asked him incredulously when he finally told me. 'You think she killed herself because Uncle Winston fed her guppies to the Cod God?'

How ridiculous are our last straws, then.

For Sonny, it is quite straightforward. The burden of her blindness, coupled with years of insecurity in relationships—with her parents, siblings, husband, friends and, finally, even with us, her children—had literally pushed my mother over the edge. Sonny has found his answers and Uncle Winston was largely to blame; he had somehow provided the flint sparking the conflagration of despair that enticed her into taking that wild step into space. Sonny will look no further beyond that. He has his own life now; a partner, a child. His family. He needs to put all this behind him in order to salvage his future.

But there are no clear answers for me. Not then, not now. The more I peer into the pond of her life, the less I am certain of anything. Currents move under the surface, strong and tidal, pulling and pushing until I can no longer pinpoint that originary moment of her decision, the one incident that broke the dam of her resistance and swept her into death. I can't locate it, but still I sift through the public fragments of her private life. Looking for answers, looking for reasons that will never satisfy. Searching for the real person behind my mother.

Finally, there are no more excuses for me to hang around in Singapore. Nothing more will be gained and my presence is an alien intrusion on the cityscape. A glimpse of me on the streets causes an awkward stumble in the steps of my relatives; a sudden wrenching of the neck, faces carefully turned away; a hurried, furtive crossing of the street. Cousin Adrian gets fined for jaywalking and I have to admit it gives me a sour pleasure. I should return home. Auntie Percy-phone says as much.

'You should go back to Sydney, Grace. You've mopped my kitchen floor and scrubbed my bathroom tiles for long enough. You've got to get back to work. Or better still, go and clean up your own home.'

'Come back with me,' I beg Auntie Percy-phone. 'I can't go back alone.'

'I won't stand between you and your father, Grace,' she says sadly.

'We need you.'

'I can't try to be Pandora.'

'But you love him. You said you've always loved him.'

'Love is not enough.'

And really, who am I to argue otherwise?

So I leave Singapore behind. Although at last I've learned to love my mother's homeland, this time I won't be coming back.

THE HUNGRY GHOSTS

When I return to Sydney I don't recognise the Patriarch anymore. His hair has been bleached white and he looks cadaverous. His skin is like yellowed parchment, brittle and dry, spotted with age. He is getting old, I suddenly realise.

'Are you going to stay here or will you move out?' Oh, how he hates the fact that he has to ask. He's not used to it, and he can't tell me what he wants either. 'You can stay here if you like. I don't mind. It will save you paying rent.'

When I was a child I was as frightened by the Patriarch's stony silences as I was by his lashing anger. Now I hurl that silence back at him. I press my lips together and turn away from his unspoken plea. I will not weave a lifeline with words and toss it to him. We don't talk to each other much these days. Silence screams the things we cannot say.

'Well,' he says hesitantly, 'I have to go to work.'

For the Patriarch, the narcotic mundanity of scaling, drilling and filling teeth, of extractions and root canals, crowns and bridges, will see him through his grief during the day. But in the evening he comes home to a noiseless darkness. He doesn't eat, he just sits in the kitchen in a daze, unable to recover from the concussion that life has given him. He is so alone.

In the end I decide to stay. The blood of generations of dutiful Chinese daughters flows in my veins too. He is not fit to take care of himself although he anxiously tries to assure me otherwise.

'I'm all right, really,' the Patriarch says. 'I'll be retiring soon anyway. You don't have to do this, you know.'

'It's okay. I want to.'

But he feels the resentment in my care.

'Well. Thank you,' he says awkwardly.

He needs me now. I tell him brusquely what to do and he obeys meekly, like a fearful little child. The desire for revenge still throbs like a toothache in me. Sometimes I bait him with barbed words and I see him clenching his temper, forcing his anger back down into his body. He has inherited my mother's dyspepsia; hurt and unhappiness rumble in his bowels and rack his body. He turns away and disengages from conflict, no longer a tyrant, not even a competent opponent. I am almost ashamed of the power that I have over him now, a power I must try to control because now I can actually hurt him. And maybe I had that power all along, maybe my mother did too, but we just never recognised it.

My twenty-sixth year is a year of regression. I'm back to my old cleaning job, back in my father's house in Burwood, back in my old room looking out to the railway track. At nights I find that, as in my adolescence, I cannot sleep. The Patriarch chases dreams in his sleep, is chased by nightmares in return. I lie awake and watch a spider crawl across the ceiling. Horlicks no longer works, I know. Two-thirty creeps towards three o'clock and then to four. I have such a long day ahead of me. In growing rage I burrow my fingers under my nightshirt and underpants, close my eyes and begin to stroke myself. Urgent, violent strokes that seem intent on ripping flesh from bone. Eventually, at last, I manage to jerk myself off. No pleasure, no satisfaction. Only release and exhaustion.

'Fuck. Fuck it all,' I say as I begin to doze off into hideous dreams.

Mother, dearest mother, how I hate you. If your body were lying before me now I would snatch up a knife and stab you, stab you, stab you until you opened your eyes and cried out in anguished pain. I would rip open your heart and bathe my frozen hands in your warm blood. I would make you look at me and see me. I would make you feel the hunger in my eyes—the eyes of your ghost child returned. But you have disappeared into your black hole. And in doing so, you have shattered my own crystalline darkness; the jagged edges of the void inside shred me until I haemorrhage my longing, my desire, my very self into the woman that you might have been.

For how do I know who you really were? You kept yourself whole and secret, hidden away from the greedy hands and lips of your husband, the neediness of your son and daughter. How was it that you could pour yourself into the careless hands of strangers so that everything I have learned about you since was gleaned from the reminiscences of people I hardly know? I banged and battered at the steel grille of your heart but you kept it resolutely locked. In my frustration I mocked you and belittled you, and you retreated even further behind your bars.

'What kind of mother are you anyway?' I said in anger, and the hurt in your eyes fed my viciousness. 'You're a fucking hopeless mother.'

But you were the only mother I had. You slipped away from me. Like my father, I loved you so much but I never understood you. You bewildered me. Death has short-circuited our relationship and now I can't reach you; we will never connect. I stitch down words to the page but your life unravels as soon as I grasp the fraying threads.

These days I dream the Patriarch's dreams. His night-mares seep into my sleep. I see you watching me from the other side of the red wooden bridge you crossed to reach the other world. In my dreams I step onto the bridge and run towards you but the span lengthens as I run. My feet pound the red slats, but the faster I run, the more slats appear like railway sleepers barrelling endlessly before me.

'Mum, talk to me,' I cry out. 'Don't leave me like this.'

What do you want me to say, you ask me, as you asked my father so many years ago. And, like him, I can't resist the question that I'm not supposed to ask. Did you ever love me, I demand, and because I asked—because you didn't volunteer it, because you never volunteered it—I will never know. Mum, do you love me, I ask over and over again in my dreams each night. Each time you answer yes, yet I'm right back where I started. I run onto the red bridge and the span yawns wider than ever before. Love is the answer, but my question is wrong. If you loved me, why have I never felt loved?

When I was a little girl, before you abandoned the lore of your Chinese childhood for the lure of Anglo-Christian acceptance, you used to tell me about the Hungry Ghosts, the spirits of the restless dead who rampage the earth seeking to satisfy their ravenous appetites. They are outsiders, searching hopelessly for food, fulfilment, acceptance, peace. Do you remember how, each year, on the night of the Feast of the Hungry Ghosts, we sneaked out in the evening when the Patriarch had fallen asleep in front of 'Sale of the Century'? You made Sonny and me bring a small red bowl of rice, the leftovers of our dinner, pieces of fruit and glossy photographs of clothes that you had cut out of women's magazines. In the dim indigo light we walked along the embankment above the railway tracks running from Burwood to Croydon.

You stopped halfway along the road at a T-junction and, when there were no cars whizzing by on Railway Parade, no curious eyes to watch us, you knelt down and built a makeshift altar. You burnt a fat red candle and stuck joss sticks into a clean peanut butter jar. Reverently, with a quick, fearful glance over our shoulders in case the spirits were watching, hovering over us, we offered the food and burnt the paper gifts. Then Sonny and I ran home, our sandals slapping the asphalt and the wind tearing through our hair like fingers, screaming with terrified excitement in case the Hungry Ghosts descended and devoured us too. It was just a game to us; we made our offerings to placate ill-tempered, discontented, vengeful sprites who were caught between one world and the next. Whereas you—an outsider in a foreign land—made yours out of empathy with the dislocated dead.

These days I imagine that you have joined the ranks of the unearthly exiles. A Hungry Ghost, phantasmal vagabond, you wander around trying still to fill that bleak black hole inside you. In death, as in life, you remain displaced. This year, during the Feast of the Hungry Ghosts, I leave a plate of your favourite food and a cup of Tikuanyin tea for you in our garden. I tear out the fashion pages from *Vogue* and *Harper's Bazaar*, I cut out advertisements for beautiful handbags and glamorous gowns, and I burn them all for you. In death you shall have nothing but the best. I rip out pictures of comfortable living rooms, renovated country kitchens and elegant bedroom suites, consigning them to the fire. I want you to have a home.

As flames curl the paper and it crumples to ash, out of the corner of my eye I catch the curve of your cheek and the flash of your smile. When I turn to look full-on, I can no longer see you for I do not have the *yin* eyes that can gaze upon the dead. But I know that you have understood my best intentions. I look down at the conflagration of my love and then I walk away, back to the house.

The Patriarch sits in the darkness of the living room, the phone cradled in his hands. I switch the light on because he shouldn't be alone in the dark.

'There were some phone calls for you while you were out. Here, I wrote down the messages.' He indicates the notepad by the telephone with names and numbers written neatly.

'Thanks. They're probably just cleaning jobs.' I scan them quickly and I am surprised to see Sonny's name and number there. I will call him back, but not too soon and not too eagerly. I have learned not to lasso him with my love.

'Grace, you don't go anywhere but work,' the Patriarch says tentatively, astoundingly. We make it a policy these days not to comment on each other's lives. 'Perhaps you should get out more. You should get a life of your own.'

He is right, of course. I should, and I will. Eventually. Still, I can't resist a spiteful jab at him. 'Like you let Mum have a life of her own?'

His eyes leak unexpectedly, his nose bleeds with painful sobs, and immediately I regret my malice. He turns away, groping for the Kleenex.

'Dad, are you all right?' I ask helplessly. He takes my shoulders and I can't prevent the wince because I'm so shocked. We have always been careful not to touch. He thinks I am revolted by this unexpected contact, his touch. I'm not sure how I feel. His hands drop away.

'Grace,' he says. 'Are you ever going to forgive me? Am I always going to be the villain in your story? I didn't mean to be a bad father or husband, you know. I should have done things differently. I wish I could go back and change it all.'

I say nothing because I understand the futility, the absolute pointlessness, of 'I should have' and 'I wish'. I glance up at him and suddenly I see him looking at me with my mother's bleak, blank eyes. Hungry Ghost eyes which fill me with guilt. Why are grudges so difficult to let go of? Why is it so hard to love?

'There's nothing to forgive,' I say, and at this moment I am amazed to find that I actually mean it. Maybe I won't mean it tomorrow, but it will do for tonight and it will get easier as time passes.

Questions still remain unanswered; there will never be a reconciliation with those we have lost. But maybe this is all I can do, maybe this is all we can ever do: to make up to the living our debt to the dead.